BRAIDED LOVES

About the author

Ger Burke is a novelist and short story writer. She has had many literary successes in print and in radio since becoming a full-time writer. These include being short-listed for the Frank McManus Short Story Award and long-listed for both The Fish Short Histories Prize and the 2012 Fish Flash Fiction Competition. Her short stories have been published in magazines and anthologies. *Braided Loves* is her second novel.

She lives with her husband on the shores of Galway Bay.

Praise for *My Father's Lands*, Ger Burke's first novel, set in 16th century Ireland.

"… *a novel that compels you to anger, ferocious passion and what it truly means to be Irish … the art and craft of story-telling at its absolute best.*" Ken Bruen, author of *The Guard*.

"*The historical facts are absorbed almost imperceptibly as we live with the characters in their growth from young adulthood to middle age … And indeed they live with us long after we have finished reading about them.*" Aistir.

"*Burke manages to bring in the elements of the history of this period … the choices offered to the Gaelic nobility, the attempts to secure Spanish aid and the disaster at Kinsale, while not losing sight of her characters.*" Books Ireland.

" … *successfully draws us back in time to one of the most defining moments of Irish History … themes are contemporary: love, loyalty and the quest to find where one belongs.*" The Irish World, London.

BRAIDED LOVES

Ger Burke

First published in 2013 by
Wordsonthestreet
Six San Antonio Park,
Salthill,
Galway, Ireland.
web: www.wordsonthestreet.com
email: publisher@wordsonthestreet.com

© Copyright Ger Burke

The moral right of the author has been asserted.
A catalogue record for this book is available from the British
Library.

ISBN   978-1-907017-21-6

Cover design, layout and typesetting: Wordsonthestreet
Printed and bound in the UK

Acknowledgements

My thanks to all those writer colleagues who provided their critical input in the writing of this novel.

A special thanks to my editor, Tony O'Dwyer.

Thanks also to close friends and family who supported and encouraged me along the way.

To
my mother and father

I heard my voice crackle as it mentioned sex. I awoke confused. It took me a few seconds to realise that I was lying in my bed and that the discussion I was hearing was coming from the radio. The reception was poor, but I kept it because David had given it to me for our third wedding anniversary.

I reached out and tapped it on the side, annoyed with myself for having dozed off when my interview was being broadcast.

As the tone became clearer, my voice emerged sounding serious, convincing and full-bodied like the red wine from the hospitality suite I'd been drinking prior to the interview. I was saying that teenagers should be encouraged to know about their bodies. Odd, my voice in the bedroom talking not only to me but also to everybody tuned to this station.

"Enjoy your trip to the States." Cue that my time was up.

As I listened to my voice saying 'goodbye', I felt disconcerted. I was there and yet I was here, lying on the firm hardness, conscious of being alone. When I stroked David's side of the bed, the sheet felt cold. The futon downstairs would be still warm from him.

My head thudded with a hangover pain. The air coming through the open window was moist and cold, October weather. The peach-coloured curtains lifted in the breeze.

I peered at my watch. It was eight-thirty. David had left an hour ago. He got up at six, did his exercises and showered. The percolator went on at seven.

He would have eaten apple strudel with his coffee, his habit when worried. I wanted to go downstairs and join him for breakfast but, of course, I was too stubborn. I wondered if he remembered to listen to the radio.

"Pee-you. Yuck. What's that smell?" My intrepid eleven-year-old daughter. Her voice floated in to me but I ignored it. She would let me know soon enough that Rachael was wetting the bed again.

Thinking back to last night failed to bring consolation. David had nagged about my drinking. He drank very little himself, an Irish Cream on the odd occasion, so he expected me to do the same. We argued about whether I should have a third gin. I persevered, and for good measure made it a double. He kissed me chastely on the forehead and informed me he was going to bed.

Later, when I swayed up the stairs and found the bed empty, I tottered down again and found him asleep in the spare room. We planned that guests would sleep in the futon, never David.

Last night was the first time he left our bed. He had already detached himself during the day and now he was doing it at night. I felt discarded, like last week's newspapers. We would be apart for six days, while I was on my book tour in America, and yet he had slept in the spare room.

"You stink." Esther's voice intruded again. "You pong like a skunk."

Rachael's response was teary. "Leave me alone. Get out of my room."

"I know what the smell is. You've wet the bed. Again. Or worse. Is it poo?"

I dragged myself into a sitting position and clambered out onto the floor. Then sheathed in a dressing gown, I went to calm my daughters.

Rachael stood beside the bed, head lowered, shivering in her wet pyjamas.

Esther yanked at the duvet and exposed a stain, large and wet, in the middle of the sheet. "See, you can see the damp patch plainly."

I looked, instead, at the poster of *101 Dalmatians*. For an absurd moment, I wished that one of the dogs would leap out and bite Esther on the ass. "Go downstairs."

"Mom. I was only telling her that she ..."

"Go downstairs, Esther."

"It's not fair. I didn't do anything."

I sprang towards her.

"Alright. Alright. I'm going. I'm going."

While Esther and I had been talking, Rachael had drawn her head into her shoulders like a turtle. My nose tingled as it always did when I was about to cry. I reached for her but she recoiled. Undeterred, I wound my arms tightly around her. Her face was wet against my nightdress.

"I didn't mean to, Mom. I never felt it coming. Honest," she said when we drew apart.

"I know, sweetheart. You've been so good. It's not your fault. It could happen to anyone."

"I heard shouting after I went to sleep last night."

"If you were asleep, you were dreaming."

"Mom! You know what I mean." She looked at me in wide-eyed indignation. "I wasn't dreaming. You and Dad were arguing."

I coaxed her hair back from her eyes with my fingertips, pretending not to notice that they were full of tears. I felt vulnerable enough myself. The last time David challenged me about my drinking, Rachael had 'an accident'. Our slanging match then had been as loud as last night's. The coincidence was too much.

"Are you going to split?"

I tweaked Rachael's nose. "Split! Where did you hear that kind of language?"

"She means separate." Esther's voice startled us both. "I understand what she's saying. There's a way to *split* things between people who don't live together anymore. Teacher told us about it. She said it's the mother who's poor when the father leaves."

My older daughter as usual had clarified matters. "I thought I told you to ..."

"I came back for my book." Esther waved a copy of *Summer of My German Soldier*. "The mother and father are the pits in this too. They make Patty's life hell."

Ignore the implication, Teresa, I told myself. "Esther, when you get downstairs feed Roamy."

"Fine. He smells better than Rach anyway."

Rachael's voice was pleading. "Sure you're not, Mom. Getting ... whatever it is Esther was on about."

Hoping to divert her, I said, "Let's get you out of those wet pyjays and we'll put on your Goldilocks sheets and pillowcase. Then we'll make some hot porridge."

"Or we could put on my Popeye ones and have spinach," Rachael said, making a feeble attempt at a joke.

I scrunched up my nose. "Spinach and porridge. At this hour of the morning. Your taste buds are as weird as your father's."

"Throw on her Winnie the Pooh sheets and have honey." Esther was at her worst. "Get it? Poo. Winnie the P ..."

"Esther!" My severe tone propelled her down the stairs at top speed.

Rachael pulled off her pants and pyjamas and threw them in the laundry basket. The sheets followed. As she rummaged in the press for clean ones, she said, "Mom. Don't tell Dad that ... that it happened again. He hasn't read to me for ages." She hesitated. "He wouldn't read to anybody else. Would he?" Her voice was small.

I hugged her again. "No. We're his family. Who else would he read to?"

"But Esther said ..."

"Tommy, Dad reads to Tommy Canny." Esther had blundered back upstairs. "Tommy told me, the last time we were at Rita's." She paused. "And there's no dog food left so I can't feed Roamy."

I said nothing. An image of a laughing David, resting on a recliner beside the fire in Rita's kitchen, appeared in my imagination. On the table was her freshly baked brown bread flanked by a selection of homegrown vegetables. Wearing a gold décolleté, she fed him luscious purple grapes.

14

The reason he's spending so much time in someone else's house is because he's fed up of the hassle your drinking causes. The thought irritated for a second before I rejected it as nonsensical. I focused on the immediate problem of finding food for Roamy. "Give him some bread and milk," I suggested.

"Mom. He's a dog, not a baby."

"Yeah, Mom," Rachael said, "he's not a baby." Anxious to make up with her sister, she added, "Essie, remember when Nana used to give us that. She called it goody."

"One day you blew your nose into it," Esther said. She looked at the wet sheet. "And it's grosser and grosser you're getting."

"Yes, but do *you* remember the time when a crow shi... went on your hair ...?"

They romped down the stairs laughing, their crisis over, mine beginning.

My jealous reaction to Esther's news that David read to Rita's son Tommy surprised me. This was Rita Canny she was talking about; Rita, an old friend and long-time colleague, who was going out of her way to drop me off at the airport tomorrow; Rita, whose husband Noel was slaving in Scotland. David liked to help people when they needed it. Goddamn it! There was something wrong with me if I was unable to banish childhood resentments. I was an adult now. Rita was not a rival.

David, Rachael and Esther were my life. They defined me. I loved being part of a family. Being a teacher and writer also made me proud. I was looking forward to my Halloween book tour to the States but I never felt whole until I returned to them.

"Approval and dependency are similar," Rita, her lips pouting, and waving her nail-varnished hands in the air, told me once. "You need David's approval, so you are dependent. You're a strong woman Teresa yet you act like a pussy cat, happy only when David strokes you." Rita was a cat lover. There were times when I thought she even scratched like her Tiddles although, to be fair, mostly she purred.

That was the nearest Rita and I had ever come to a

disagreement. We often spoke with frankness about each other's lives. Neither of us took umbrage or at least that was the pretence. I attributed Rita's cattiness to Noel having to work on North Sea oil rigs to support them.

And there was some truth in what she said. I was Teresa Goldstein and incapable of being anybody else. When David came home, changed his clothes, showered and spent time with Esther and Rachael, I often found myself trailing from room to room after him, trying to keep him talking. How sad is that!

"Press it harder."

Still sluggish and hung-over following the previous night's gin, I had dressed and gone downstairs to find Rachael in the utility room, banging at the door of the washing machine.

"The button I mean, silly, *not* the door," Esther sighed in exasperation.

"What are you doing?" I asked.

Rachael smiled. "I've put the sheets on." She looked towards her sister. "It was Essie's idea."

"I bet it was." My heart beat faster as the drum turned and the washing machine hummed.

Rachael, picking up the cold tone, shrugged.

"The ones she peed on," Esther said. "I put them in with the other dirty clothes."

A tension headache crept up the back of my neck as I peered into the washing machine. All I could see were the clothes spinning around, no sign of the naggin of gin I had hidden there. "Let's go into the kitchen and make the porridge I promised you."

"We thought you'd be glad we put on the sheets," Esther said. "There's no pleasing you."

"Let's go into the kitchen," I said again, in a tone that brooked no debate.

"Oh, okay," Esther said.

"Fine," Rachael added, in an equally sullen tone.

I put some quick-cook oats into the microwave and hurried back to the utility room where I sat on a stool and prayed for the wash cycle to end.

Then Esther's voice. "Mom, porridge is ready."

"I'm not really hungry," I said, trying to sound calm. Once I had spoken, my mind careered into overdrive. On this morning's broadcast, I had sounded self-assured and knowledgeable about adolescents and their raging hormones. The interviewer, I told myself, was impressed by what I had to say. Despite my attempt to boost my confidence, I believed I was a fraud. There was an appalling absence of physical love, spontaneous and enjoyable, at the core of my life, yet I had the arrogance to counsel others. *Do not be afraid to respond to sexual stimuli; relax into it; go with the flow; enjoy committed passion.* Extracts from my book. How lovely it all sounded; how untrue of my experience.

Memories of my mother's conviction that as a child, I was in constant danger from lustful men and her bizarre behaviour, prayerful and well intentioned, towards me surfaced. I shut them out quickly.

In my turmoil, I imagined that the bottle of gin had smashed and splattered against the washing-machine porthole. My shriek of alarm brought Roamy to the door of the utility room, sniffing for danger. Jumping off the stool, I strode up and down the small space. A dog smell wafted from Roamy's bed. I almost tripped over him twice as I paced. I bent and buried my face in his coat, wanting him at least to still love me.

Craving a drink, I went into the kitchen where Rachael and Esther were eating and from there I sidled into the front room.

There was a gap in the drinks cabinet. It was where the gin bottle, that recently caused the trouble between David and me, used to stand. It was unlocked only because I'd given my word that I wouldn't touch any more of the spirits there.

A bottle of brandy tantalised from the shelf. I needed a drink so that I would feel more in control if the bottle shattered or my mind started playing memory games again. My hand shook with anticipation as I reached up, grabbed a brandy glass and poured. *Brandy makes you randy. Gin makes you sin. Rum makes you come.* The old rugby song echoed in my head, reminding me of

David's favourite sport. Thoughts of him fanned the guilt about breaking my promise. I gulped the brandy and followed it with another.

I began to unwind. The bottle in the washing machine was well cushioned. The tension in my neck eased. I screwed the lid onto the brandy bottle. If I were to wash the glass, it would mean going out to the sink in the kitchen and arousing Esther and Rachael's suspicions. I took a tissue from my pocket and wiped it as best I could before putting it on the shelf. Everything appeared the same except for the volume in the bottle. I hoped David wouldn't notice if he checked to see if I had kept my promise.

Luckily, I had completed the cover-up when Rachael's dry hand touched my sweaty one. A dollop of ice cream, mingled with porridge, garnished her sweatshirt. "For you." She handed me a slightly burned piece of toast.

I moved to caress her dark hair but drew back. She looked so much like her father. Nibbling at the bread, I strolled with her through the hall back into the kitchen.

Feeling her eyes, David's eyes, fixed upon me questioningly, I resolved that when I got back from my visit to the States nothing like this would happen again. I'd discover a good hiding place for the booze and make amends to David. There would be no more rows.

Then, intent on retrieving the gin safely, I left the kitchen and resumed my vigil by the washing machine.

Sunlight shone through our sitting-room window onto the wooden floor. I stood, my head thumping, and observed a skeletal tree standing on a bed of autumn leaves outside as I waited for Rita to arrive to bring me to the airport. My book tour to the States was about to begin. We'd planned to have a cup of tea, and then set off at our leisure. I moved away from the window and, in an attempt to curb my impatience at her lateness, I re-checked the flight details: date, 26th October 1987; time of departure, 14.00 hrs; flight number, *EI* 135. I was still impatient.

"If she doesn't show up soon, you'll miss your flight." David was unusually tetchy also. He paced back and forth as if he were going instead of me.

"Dad, all the witches costumes will be gone in Mulligan's if *we* don't go soon as well. They only ever have a few."

"Oh, don't have a vampire, Esther," Rachael quipped. "I've left the front door open for her. Bet she'll be here in a minute."

David's face relaxed. "You're right, Rachael. We're panicking for nothing. I've never known Rita to let anyone down."

She breezed into the sitting room at a quarter past nine, an hour later than she'd promised. "Hello all. Sorry. Got held up."

We waited for her to elaborate. She didn't. David, his bad humour forgotten, turned to me. "I'll talk to Rita while you get your coat. Kids, get ready and we can all leave together."

Roamy shuffled into the room, lay on the mat by the hearth and turned over on his back at Rita's feet, ready to be tickled. She stooped to rub his belly and he squirmed with pleasure. I thought Roamy only did that for us.

"We thought you weren't coming," Esther said.

Rita glanced up from Roamy and smiled. "Well, I'm here now so go and get ready. Come on. Chop, chop."

Her clothes, I noted, were even more glamorous than those she wore to school. Leather trousers and knee-high boots, a silk emerald scarf knotted around her throat. Designer fitted jacket, long hair crimped, perfect make-up. "You look well in leather," I said as I turned to leave. I meant it sarcastically. Her bum looked huge.

"Thank you," she answered, mistaking my statement for a genuine compliment.

"It's getting late," David said to me.

"I know."

Rachael was rummaging through coats on the hallstand. "I can't find my warm woolly one," she said.

I had to remove several and dump them on the stairs banister before I found it for her. Then I had to put them all back in some kind of order.

Esther said, "I can't close this bloody zip." I spent another while helping her before I put on my own coat and said goodbye to them both.

"Don't forget to bring us something back," they chorused as I hugged them.

Esther asked, "Mom, are you crying?"

I hastily wiped away tears with the back of my hand.

"Mom, you'll be back in a week," Rachael said.

"With presents," Esther added.

David and Rita were still talking animatedly in the room. Probably discussing what story David would read for Tommy while I was away.

"Ready for off," I called.

David had his hand on the small of Rita's back as they came from the sitting room.

It should have been perfect. A fine October morning. Two beautiful daughters. A lovely husband. A sleek well-cared-for dog, me rushing to the airport to travel to America on a prestigious book tour, my lawyer husband bringing our children on a Halloween shopping spree, Rita, a devoted friend. That's what made it so sad. I was ruining it with petty jealousy.

Rita said goodbye to everyone. "I'll put your case in the boot, Teresa."

David hugged me. "I'll miss you, Tess."

"Will you?"

"Of course I will."

I felt small, torn apart by needless suspicion. The drinks I'd consumed the previous night had fanned my paranoia, made me unreasonable. Nevertheless, I noticed David's demeanour before I closed the door. Cool, tranquil, different to the morning's harassed David.

"You alright, Teresa?" Rita asked, when I sat into the car.

My head was about to burst. "Fine," I answered, "never better. Let's go."

An afternoon light of atypical brightness poured into Granny Goldstein's Boston apartment. Through the window sunlight, reflecting from the snow, reminded me of the morning I had left Claremorris. This kind of weather seldom came to Boston in late October. I pulled my tracksuit top closely around me and shivered. The clothes I had packed for the trip were too light for the extreme cold.

It was five days since I had boarded the plane at Shannon bound for Boston. I found it hard to forget the way David had been when I'd left. Calm, self-possessed, as if he were relieved to be rid of me. Esther and Rachael were their usual selves, wondering what I was going to bring them back.

Never mind, I'd be home soon. It was hard to believe that my trip was coming to an end. I was pleased that my schedule had allowed me to spend two nights with Granny Goldstein, David's mother. But despite the restful time I'd spent with her, I felt wrecked. My three days of rushing through Chicago, New York and Boston doing interviews were exhausting. In each of the three cities I talked about my sex education manual.

It seemed an age since I had last seen David and the girls; by now, I was longing to make contact with them. When I last rang, Vera, his assistant, answered. "Oh, Mrs. Goldstein. How are you?" Then I heard a conspiratorial whisper. "David! It's your wife." I imagined her body language, a questioning glance, the helpless shrug as she spoke to my husband trying to find out whether he wished to speak to me.

"Tell her I'll call her back," he'd said.

A few minutes ago I was cold. Now sweat was seeping through my palm as I clutched my AT&T card. I wondered if David had deliberately avoided talking to me. Or the unthinkable. Was he about to abscond? He hurt me when, before I'd left for the States, he'd abandoned our bed for the first time since our marriage. But that didn't mean he was going to run off. *Get a grip*, I told myself.

Now my hand trembled as I picked up the receiver. Yearning for the reassurance of his voice, I dialled the number for Ireland and was starting on the 94 for Mayo when Granny Goldstein hollered, "Concierge is at the door. Cab for Express is here." I didn't know whether I was disappointed or relieved that I hadn't time to get through to him.

I pulled on my raincoat, grabbed my hand luggage and followed Granny Goldstein out of the apartment and through to the reception area where I'd left a suitcase earlier. The concierge, a hunk from Cuba, undressed me with smouldering eyes as he offered to carry the case to the cab. "No need, hon. It's quite light," Granny Goldstein assured him. She picked up the case and carried it across the expanse of marble flooring to open the front door, stepping back as fluffy snow fell over the threshold.

Outside the air was still. The cab driver stacked my luggage in the trunk while I kissed Granny Goldstein.

"Safe journey, hon. Hope you're feeling okay. You look a bit peaky."

She was alluding to the cocktails I had consumed at lunch. I smiled, opened the door of the cab, turned towards her, blew her a kiss and said, "Maybe I did eat too much of your lovely macaroni and cheese but it was so delicious how could I resist?"

Evening shadows encircled Boston's Logan Express as it wove its way towards the airport. I felt a little sick but still blamed the heat on the bus, which was turned up too high, and not the alcohol I had imbibed.

The way to the airport was jammed with Saturday-evening traffic backed up through the Callahan Tunnel. It had begun to spit rain and the covering of snow was turning to slush, slowing things down even more.

"Aer Lingus. I'm travelling Aer Lingus," I told the driver when he asked me for the number of my terminal. "Sorry I've forgotten the number." I masked the irritation in my tone. When David was with me, I let him negotiate the luggage, check in, and find the way to the boarding gate. It made him feel important, buttressed his ego. I was unusually judgemental that day.

I wondered if I would have been better to have stayed at home and spent my Halloween concentrating on my family. There were times when missing them had so affected me that even when I was in front of a studio audience, I was diverted by thoughts of how content we all had been when David and I were agreeing.

"Aer Lingus." The driver stopped the bus. A skinny man near the aisle stood to allow me to pass. He had knees like my husband's. That was the first time I'd experienced David's self-deprecating humour – when he made fun of his bony knees.

A line of porters waited. Choosing an Eddie Murphy lookalike, I followed him into departures. When we arrived at the Aer Lingus desk, I tipped him and waited in line. Passports, tickets, money. Nothing too bad could go wrong as long as you had those, David said.

A second check-in desk opened and the line moved faster.

"A window seat if possible," I told the lady. I could better visualise David, Esther and Rachael waiting for me if I were looking out as I landed.

I would get David a box of chunky cigars. He liked a smoke when he was mellowed by good food and good company. I would resist buying alcohol.

I added the cigars to my hand luggage, boarded the plane, found my seat and took off my raincoat, bruising it into the overhead bin. The woman in the aisle seat stood up to let me take my place beside the window. I wasn't in the mood for conversation so I flicked through *Cara*, the inflight magazine.

I was drawn to an article headed 'Breaking the Pattern'. It suggested that if you were worried about your relationship with alcohol you should terminate it as you would any other destructive dependence. I quickly closed the magazine and tucked it into its net pocket.

Rain punched rhythmic blows against the glass. I took my carry-on bits and pieces off my knees and crushed them under the seat in front of me. I rested against the headrest and closed my eyes and ears to the turmoil around me. Words of welcome to boarding passengers faded as I replaced them with David's face. He had phoned me only once since I'd left, when he knew I'd be staying with his mother. He had been curt.

He found my participation in talk shows challenging. That was the reason he had begun to retreat from me. I found myself searching for excuses to explain his behaviour. He resented my preoccupation with my writing. He hated ...

My restless feet kicked something hard. The invisible fence Granny Goldstein had bought for Roamy was in a bag on the floor. If he went outside his boundaries, the transformer on his collar would give him an electric shock. If only there were invisible fences for humans, I could buy one for David. Keep him away from pretty women and within the perimeters of my life. The dark thoughts made me edgy.

I reached down to retrieve the bag I had disturbed. My face flushed as I thought of the peignoir and nightgown I had splurged on in Filenes. David loved frills and flounces and I liked to please him. When he was happy, I was happy. Suddenly I longed for a drink.

The crew would soon be serving spirits and wine. But thoughts of David when he'd last seen me drunk, his face drawn, his eyes hollow, his trembling voice asking me to stop guzzling gin, the defeated set of his shoulders when I refused, spoilt my pleasure at the idea of having more liquor. I closed my eyes and ignored the drinks trolley when it came along.

The words, *They're mine, too*, were on my lips when the air hostess woke me for orange juice and tea. In my dreams, David had run away from me with Esther and Rachel. My tracksuit felt damp. Disturbing dream.

Granny Goldstein would have advised me to talk to a therapist about it and, if I were still living in America, would have offered me her own. 'Hon, she was a great help to me when Aaron died,' she'd say. But I'd have refused. To me it was all psychobabble. I've always had the strength and determination to solve my problems myself.

The sound of the engine changed. A voice through the tannoy told us to fasten our seat belts and make sure our tray tables and seats were upright. When we landed, I realised I had overlooked putting my watch forward. I changed it. It felt good to be back in the same time zone as David, Esther and Rachael.

As I waited by the carousel, I threw on my raincoat and pondered the opportunity that had allowed me to write a sex manual. David hadn't been sure whether he wished to settle permanently in Ireland. I had availed of a pilot career break scheme from teaching and gone to America with him for five years to help him decide. I felt glad when he chose to settle in Mayo.

While we were living in the States, he had been disappointed that I hadn't devoted my time exclusively to the care of five-year-old Esther and three-year-old Rachel. It was Granny Goldstein's 'go for it' that had spurred me to write. She provided the support I needed. Now, I felt fortunate to be back in my home county teaching, and drafting *Teenage Sexuality Part Two*. My suitcase on the conveyor belt jolted me back to the present.

When I had passed through the 'nothing to declare' area, I scanned the excited faces of people waiting for returnees but there was no one there for me. Lonely, I took a deep breath to keep from crying. I'd hire a taxi. It would cost. Too bad. If David were here, I wouldn't have had to spend the money.

A bank of heavy cloud loomed over Shannon. The taxi man backed up his car and fitted my case into the boot, empty except for a spanner. "I hope the rain holds off," he said.

Not in the mood for making conversation, I climbed into the back seat. My eyes were gritty with tiredness and I was reeling with disappointment that David had failed to meet me. The taxi man, after telling me his name was Johnny and asking me my destination, mouthed more platitudes about the weather, and drove on in silence.

We saw Daniel O'Connell on his perch in the Square in Ennis, a statue commemorating his winning the Clare election. I thought of Repeal and monster meetings. Primarily, I taught History and English and only volunteered to teach Health Education, euphemism for sex education, because of the indisputable need for it. I wanted pupils in the 1980s to have a different experience to when I was at school. Then sex education had been lumped in with religion. Now I had written a book on the subject. Life took strange twists.

When I was living in America, a publisher friend of Granny Goldstein's read my book, declared it 'charmingly old-fashioned' and targeted conservative religious groups as my market. After three years, the first part of my *opus* had become an option on the curriculum of Catholic American high schools. In Ireland, the Department of Education had deemed my book too liberal. Despite this, Atilla Press published it, thinking that its censure as a textbook would increase its sales.

It was then David began to withdraw from me. There I was again. Linking my success with the change in David's behaviour. My jaw settled into its stubborn jut. That had to be the reason he hadn't met me at the airport.

As we passed through Crusheen, there was a smell of fresh tar. Pity I couldn't get the County Council to do a bit of work on the surface of our drive, I thought.

The low-lying fields around Gort were flooded, trees and

stone walls were rooted in the grey water. Johnny looked over his shoulder. "Another excuse for the farmers to whine." I didn't answer him. Instead, I tried to invent the lives behind the bungalow walls – some with landscaped gardens and children's swings, others with grimy stables surrounded by hens and geese.

Sheep had broken through a fence and were straying on the road. Johnny broke his silence again and held forth about whether it would have been he or the farmer who would have to pay if he hit one of them.

I hadn't a clue. David was the lawyer in our family.

The gloom of the open countryside had a soporific effect and I dozed. Almost immediately, it seemed, the car hit a pothole and I was jolted towards the car roof.

"Have a little snooze, did we?" Johnny asked in a tone reserved for children.

I felt my hackles rise. "Yes. I was tired."

"Himself not with you, I notice." I caught him staring at me in the front mirror.

"No. He let me off the leash for a while."

He didn't say anymore until we arrived at my house. He told me the 'damage' and added, "Petrol is gone to the devil."

I searched in my purse.

"I'll get rid of the bags while you count the cash. No hurry."

I handed him some notes and waited. "Wouldn't dare let you keep the change without the boss being here." My voice was saccharine. "He takes care of the bills."

"Right. So long so." He left subdued.

I had mentioned the bills trying to be sardonic, but suddenly I became aware that what I said was true. David controlled our finances. I winced at the thought. Then to add to my disquiet I realised that my Mitsubishi Tradia, the car I had shipped from America when we came home to live here permanently, was the only one outside the house.

I opened the door quietly and felt the house snuggle round me. It was lovely to be back in my own space. But, although I was delighted to be home, the familiar surroundings made me think again of the sinister mail I had been getting for months to this address. My radio interview, the drama of my having hidden the gin in the washing machine, and my American trip had quelled my concern about it temporarily. Involuntarily, I looked towards the hall table where a pile of letters lay.

I prodded each envelope until I was satisfied that none of them contained a calendar of the type I'd been getting lately. The last one I received had come two weeks ago. Dates from the middle of June and end of August were ringed in red pen with a large question mark beside each circle.

Relieved that there were no new calendars, I took off my raincoat and hung it over Esther's jacket on the hallstand.

Then I looked towards the guest room. David would have summoned Carmel, our baby-sitter, to mind Esther and Rachael while he was away. The door was ajar. Carmel usually left it like that if the kids were playing in a neighbour's house and she was studying. She would then be able to hear them when they came back.

"It's me, Carmel, I'm back. Talk to you later."

She stuck her head around the door. "Welcome home Mrs Goldstein. Esther and Rachael are next door. Want me to go get them?"

"No, no, it's fine. Carmel. I'll relax for a while first." Though I was tempted to ask her to tell them I was home, I resisted. I felt grubby and irritable. Better to wait until I could savour being back before I met anyone. Decision made, I tiptoed up the stairs and walked towards our bedroom, with its adjoining bathroom, to have a shower.

Though the high-ceilinged room was small, David used to use it as a place to leave his books. Volumes ranging from Tort to Family Law to Liquidation could sometimes be found on the cistern, the weighing scale, the edge of the bath, everywhere. But not anymore, he seldom came in here now and never to unwind and read.

I undressed quickly and got into the shower where the hot water eased my tiredness. After luxuriating in the flow for a while, I dried myself and went into the bedroom. From the wardrobe, I snatched denim jeans and a check shirt. The jeans wouldn't zip on me until I lay on the bed to close them. When I straightened, my stomach put so much pressure on the waistband, I unzipped them again. Too many high-calorie dinners and sugary cocktails in the States. I opened the wardrobe again and selected a tracksuit bottom, pink and loose, similar to the one I had worn on the flight.

When I went downstairs, Esther and Rachael had returned. Both of them were eating a yogurt and pretended not to see me. I had experienced this before after being away for a while. This time, I didn't feel I deserved to be punished for my holiday, which hadn't really been a holiday. I felt as stressed now as I had before I left.

After a few minutes, Rachael sidled up to me and put her hands round my waist. When I went down on my hunkers, she pulled my head towards hers and whispered in my ear. "Mom, I didn't, you know, wet the bed since you left."

"Let's rub noses." Rachael liked to kiss the way Eskimos do. Since she had first seen Igloo children doing it in the television series *Far and Away*, while we were in America, she refused to kiss either her father or me the conventional way. We would start very gently, work up to a crescendo and end up laughing. Esther enjoyed watching but even when David cajoled her to try, she refused.

"What did you bring me, Mom?" Rachael asked. "Anything nice? Did Granny Goldstein send anything?"

"I brought you leggings and a top."

She skipped into the hallway to where I had left my bag. Esther and I followed more slowly.

"Which?"

I gestured towards the navy bag.

"Can I look?" She threw the contents of the bag out on the floor. "Are these them?"

"Yes."

"I'll try them on." Minutes later she came from the front room dressed in the new outfit, a navy sweatshirt, flowered leggings and a matching beret. She twirled.

"Lovely. Suits you," I said.

"Did you bring me anything or are they all for the baby?"

"You can borrow these if you want, Essie," Rachael stood still.

"Did you bring *me* anything?"

"Yes, Esther. I did. If you look in the case, you'll find a top and three books."

"It's not fair. How come I didn't get any leggings?"

My airline headache started again. "When did you last see your Dad?" I tried to keep my tone light though I heard a tremor in my voice. I had chosen not to ask Carmel as I wanted to minimise the chance of my students knowing that I was unable to keep track of my husband.

"Carmel gave us our tea, breakfast, dinner, tea, and breakfast again this morning," Rachael explained by way of an answer.

I knew that Rachael counted time by the number of meals she had eaten. Cora, our regular housekeeper, always put special store by mealtimes and Rachael liked routine. Tea-evening. Breakfast-morning. Dinner-midday. Tea-another evening. Breakfast- I had been in the taxi travelling from Shannon while they were eating that. It was now Sunday morning. David had been gone since Friday evening. No wonder he hadn't answered the phone.

Esther said, "Dad took his jeans with him. Said he needed

some casual clothes. I don't know why. He had a funny look on his face when he said he'd be working. He was a bit cross."

I rubbed my hand along my forehead. I'd been gasping for a drink since I came out of the shower. I had last done my relaxing techniques in Granny Goldstein's apartment in America and needed to do them again. It would help with the jet lag too. I couldn't afford to get fidgety, not now.

"Esther, take these." I pulled Granny Goldstein's multicoloured parcels out of the case. "Why don't you see what's in them. Then you can watch a video. I'll pay Carmel, then go into the bedroom for a while."

"To do your deep breathing. Can I come in after I've opened the parcels? I'll be quiet. Promise."

"Not today, Rachael."

"Okay." She pouted but knew enough not to make a fuss. Both my children knew when Mom needed to do these techniques she needed to do them.

"We'll watch *The Little Mermaid*. Okay, Essie?"

"Oh, alright. Go on. I can watch Anne later."

I smiled. Esther was as fond of *Anne of Green Gables* as Rachael was of *The Little Mermaid*.

My stopwatch was on the locker. I sat on David's side of our king-sized bed, removed my shoes and re-set the timer to go off in fifteen minutes. The muscles in my left leg and my left foot are getting heavier and heavier … I tried to concentrate. The hardest time to practise this method was when you needed it most.

Maybe David had been killed. I had visions of his Ascona being mangled and he dead. The relaxations had failed.

After unpacking, I folded my clean sweaters and put them back on the shelves of the wardrobe; I always packed too much when I was going away. I hung the suit I had worn on television in the walk-in closet and stacked away the empty case.

Or he could be alive and have a bloody gash on his head. "Don't be daft. You're totally over-reacting." The room filled with my mutter.

My mother always maintained that bad news travelled fast or was it Granny Goldstein who said that? Granny Goldstein. She'd asked me to let her know when I arrived. Glad of the diversion, I called Southborough, Massachusetts.

"May I speak to Mrs. Goldstein, please?" I assumed I was speaking to the concierge. My pulse raced. I imagined myself walking into the reception area, checking in with him and waiting for him to buzz Granny Goldstein.

"Yes, Miriam Goldstein. Apartment One."

"I'll put you through."

Though Granny Goldstein's first husband, David's father, was dead for many years, she still kept his name. He'd been 'filthy rich and a philanderer,' according to her, 'but I've always loved him the best.' She'd had two husbands since and divorced both of them. During our stay in America she had a lover, but had since tired of him. 'I picked up my first husband's bad habits,' she used to joke.

The attraction of her ex, she told me, was that he was called James. She liked to moan, "Oh James" to him in moments of passion, in imitation of the many blondes, brunettes and red heads who had panted the same to James Bond.

I was glad that I was not actually going to come face to face with the concierge, her latest Sean Connery. A hot blush warmed my face and neck when I remembered the way he looked at me. Though I failed to get pleasure from all the 'pawing' (as my mother put it) involved in lovemaking, I enjoyed when men showed they were attracted to me.

"This is Miriam," the voice on the phone said.

"Granny Goldstein, it's me."

"Suah. Suah. I know it's you. How could I mistake the accent? And no one else would dare to call me Granny Goldstein. I was expecting your call, though not at this unearthly hour."

"Sorry for getting you up so early. Forgot the time difference."

"No, no. Good to know you're home. Time I stirred myself. I'll be long enough dead." She hesitated. "Is there anything up, Tess? You sound a bit weird. Don't say David didn't meet you.

You're always telling me how much he adores you and you him. Such romance in ones so young." She laughed.

Why did the tinkle sound false? The dull headache, which up to now had been merely annoying, was becoming more acute, nipping and cutting, scissors-like, behind my forehead.

I remained silent.

"Tess," Granny Goldstein spoke slowly. "You know I envy you and David like crazy. He's so like his father." Her tone became rueful. "Or what I remember of his father."

When we first met, David had introduced me to his mother as Tess. From then on she, too, used the abbreviation. I hadn't the heart to tell her that I would have preferred if it remained exclusively his. Today I found her use of it especially irritating.

Sure that Granny Goldstein had picked up something untoward in my voice, I imagined her round face creasing in anxiety. "This has nothing to do with David," I assured her. "I just wanted to let you know that I'm home …"

She continued to rattle on but I had lost the inclination to chat.

I was putting the receiver back in its place when I heard the sound of wheels outside. It was David. I placed a smile on my face as I went into the hall to open the door. He pre-empted me. I'd forgotten that he had a key. "You're back." My voice sounded as flat as the steamrolled tarmacadam outside Crusheen.

"Hi, kiddo. Didn't expect you until tonight."

"You didn't! Why? For Godsakes."

"Why? Because you told me when I called that you didn't want me to meet you." His tone changed when he saw my genuine bewilderment. "Rita was to pick you up. Then you said you would stop off in Galway on the way back to check out the bookstores."

I had a couple of Granny Goldstein's vodka martinis on the night I had spoken to David on the phone. Books! I didn't need any books. My shelves were stacked with unread books.

Rachael must have heard the door open. As she was coming downstairs, she said, "You did say that to Dad on the phone,

Mom. I was filling my diary at the time and I wrote it down." She put her hand into the pocket of her jeans and took out her ever-present companion. "See. Here."

I took the little book. I had bought it for her one Saturday when we were in town.

"There."

I was left with no choice but to read the damning words:

mom told dad on the phone that Rita is picking her up on the way on the way back from massatutis. I'm disappointed. thought we were going to Shannon to meet her.

"Sorry, I do remember saying that now. With all the rushing around, I forgot. But that doesn't explain why I didn't hear from you after that one call, or why you didn't take my call when I phoned." I pushed back my shoulders. "Then you didn't bother to call me back. Not that I expected you would." I tasted the acid on my tongue. Why had I said that? Of course I had expected him to call me back.

He spoke slowly. "I did call you."

"On the Monday. To make sure I had arrived. Bully for you."

Esther emerged from the kitchen where she'd been absorbed in a book. She looked from my face to David's. Her shoulders slumped. "What's wrong? You're not fighting already, are you?"

David moved further away from the door into the hall and hugged her, a tight grasping. Then he pulled Rachael to him and kissed the top of her head.

"Where were you, David?" My fists clenched with tension. He dropped his eyes. "I was away," he paused, "on business." When I didn't have to collect you at the airport, it gave me more time."

"Away. Where?"

"Westport. I stayed in my usual hotel. Check if you want. As I said, I was on business."

His voice had an 'I do not want to be questioned further' tone.

I loved David. Of this I was sure. The possibility that he would lie, or God forbid be unfaithful, horrified me. I knuckled my eyes. "I'm tired. I'm over-reacting." That word again. I was becoming a habitual over-reactor.

"Come here." He took both my hands in his and pulled me to him. "It's good to have you back. I missed you."

Hearing the sincerity in his words, I let myself unwind.

Rachael and Esther smiled. We were standing in the middle of the hallway in a four-way embrace when I noticed the shopping bag David had left down when he came in. Written in bold letters across its centre was The Man Shop, Dublin.

Poised on the hard seat of a chair designed for someone with a well-cushioned ass, I pressed myself against its back. Beside me, too close, Kieran Crawley straddled a chair backwards. Though he was talking generally to the other teachers, I felt that he was looking for an opportunity to single me out. Blatantly I turned to look out the staff room window and pretended to be interested in the empty tennis court, with its pitted tarmacadam and its winter accumulation of rotting leaves, uprooted weeds and stagnant water. But he still inched his chair sideways until I could feel his leg pressing against me.

I turned away from the window and toyed with the idea of moving seats but I didn't want to give him the satisfaction of knowing the disturbing effect he was having on me. Instead I continued to ignore him and concentrated on the staffroom, its walls lined by squares of shelving, one for each of the teachers and each filled with books. To divert myself from his nearness, I examined what we called our 'cubby holes.' I could tell from the way the tomes were organised which shelf belonged to whom. Mine was tidy; Rita's was a mess but nicely so, almost as if there were a design to the jumble; Kieran Crawley's with its scientific hardbacks looked impressive. For show, I thought. I suddenly fancied giving him a quick kick in the balls to send him on his way. Granny Goldstein's influence showing.

Fortunately the entrance of Sr. Maureen Ruane made such a drastic action unthinkable. The thought struck me that we never called the principal by her first name only. "Sr. Maureen," I whispered to myself, testing it. But it didn't sit well on the stern woman with smooth skin, tortoise-rimmed glasses and perfectly coiffured hair who had come in. When she sat at the table furthest away from the window, Kieran Crawley jumped up, righted the chair, put it back behind the table and edged up to sit beside her.

The arrangement of the staff-room tables, where spare copies of the meeting's agenda were scattered, always reminded me of a typical Irish wedding reception. The tables were long. Teachers sat either side of them. Those who considered themselves important were at the top table.

Rita came in, spotted the vacant seat beside me and made a beeline for it. The first thing I noticed was that, though she wasn't wearing a bra, her large breasts showed no hint of sagging.

There was a hubbub of voices as, now that everyone was here, we caught up on the week's news. Kieran Crawley was a safe distance away so I felt more at ease.

"You're welcome back. How did the States go, Teresa?" The chorus was friendly.

"Hope Halloween went well. Today's agenda is short. We should be finished by half twelve," Sr. Maureen Ruane said in a casual tone to Kieran Crawley.

Paul Walsh looked up from perusing his timetable. A smile spread across several faces at the thought of a short meeting. I felt my own lips stretch. I loved teaching, hated the trivia attached to it.

"I hope they don't deviate from the agenda and start talking about crisp bags, discarded on the walks today," I said in a low tone that only Rita could hear.

Sr. Maureen Ruane, sitting with her hands facing downwards on the desk, wet her lips and waited. Bit by bit silence took hold. "It's time to get down to business." Her tone was neutral. "To start proceedings we'll say our usual 'Hail Mary.'" There was a scraping sound as everybody pulled back their chairs and stood up. I rose with them.

"Now and at the hour of our death, Amen." Shuffle. Shuffle. Shuffle.

We had listened to the minutes of the September meeting,

most of which we had forgotten, when Sr. Maureen Ruane said, "First item. Should we or should we not have a Debs this year?" She looked towards Paul Walsh. "Paul, it was you who wished this to be discussed." She smiled.

Everyone sat straight as Paul's voice filled the room. He finished his speech by saying, "I think there should be no Debs this year …"

"No matter who talks in favour of it now, there *will* be no Debs," Rita whispered. "But," she added breathlessly, "he's such a hunk, I understand why Sr. Maureen Ruane allows him to dictate policy."

After much digression and discussion, we got through to the third item, Subject Options. The talk was predictable until Rita said, "Why shouldn't Science and Home Economics be compulsory?" Her tone was childlike, unthreatening.

The Science teachers came awake. I felt my spine stiffen. They would hate this suggestion.

Rita continued, "Why are weak students encouraged to pick Home Ec.? It gives the wrong message. They should be allowed to do both."

"We don't have the personnel. Classes would be too big." Kieran Crawley reddened with indignation.

"I teach thirty-four in my Irish class. Mixed ability." Rita's voice, low in her throat, sounded impartial. Not for the first time, I marvelled at her ability to sound inoffensive.

Mary Martin, a science teacher, said, "It may cause timetable problems, but it is the 80s Every student should be exposed to Science."

Kieran Crawley said, "It's a nonsense idea."

He was so busy preparing for the post of vice principal, soon to be vacated, that extra hassle in his classes would be as welcome as a toothache. I was surprised. It was unusual for any of the men to be dismissive of an idea introduced by Rita.

"Thank you, Rita. I think more research needs to be done on the feasibility of this proposal." The principal's eyes peered bleakly through her glasses.

"Sr. Maureen is right. More research needs to be done on the proposal." Kieran Crawley's sage-like pronouncement held a finality that discouraged further discussion.

I quipped quietly, "Forget the research. Just get a sex change."

Rita laughed. We understood each other so well sometimes.

Over the next forty minutes, we got through the unsuitability of an upstairs classroom for a prospective wheel-chair-bound student, fundraising ideas for Transition Year, and the need to expand our numbers, plus two other items.

Health Education was last on the agenda. "Sr. Pius has some reservations about the course she'd like to share with us. Would you like to tell us about them, Pius?"

"Just as well posts of responsibility are given on seniority or there is no way you would have one. All that sex you write about," Rita murmured to me.

Sr. Pius pushed a strand of hair under her veil and said, "Yes, well. Ahem. They are not reservations exactly. They're concerns."

"We'll not go into semantics, Pius." Sr. Maureen Ruane, had noticed Kieran Crawley looking at his watch and was trying to speed things up.

Sr. Pius bit her lower lip. "Well..."

Over her pile of notes, Sr. Maureen Ruane as if conscious of her brusqueness, smiled encouragingly at Sr. Pius. Between them there was complicity, a silent acknowledgement that the lay staff could not be expected to share their superior view of morality. To give Sr. Pius time to think out her thoughts, Sr. Maureen Ruane turned her attention to me. "Perhaps Teresa, fresh from her sojourn in the States, would like to say something to alleviate Sr. Pius' concerns."

I wanted to say that I was unaware what her concerns were but Pius was a decent skin. I said nothing.

"How can Teresa comment if she doesn't know what Pius is going to say?" Sr. Annunciata found the opportunity to undermine the principal irresistible.

"I don't think A C words should be mentioned at all," Sr. Pius ventured.

Agricultural Credit Corporation, I assumed quickly. A new one had opened here recently. But that was A C C Maybe, she wanted to take them to a farm to see the cows and the bulls.

"A C, Sister. I'm not sure what you mean," Kieran Crawley said.

"Henry Kissinger's at it again," Rita whispered. "Our first lay principal in the making. Forget vice principal. That's only buttons."

I kicked her under the table. "I'm trying to concentrate," I said.

"Sorr...y."

"God help us," Sr. Pius continued. "I mean pupils shouldn't be learning about *artificial contraception* at all. After all this is a Catholic school and it is against Catholic teaching to use condoms or any of those contraptions."

Stunned silence.

Eventually I said, "Surely a facet of education should be the transmission of knowledge." I thought I sounded impressive. "Information is not a burden. What you do with that information can of course be guided. I'm sure the sisters will do an excellent job in religion class teaching pupils how to appropriately control their sexuality." David would call me a hypocrite if he knew what I had said. I decided there and then not to tell him.

I looked sideways at the nuns. Sr. Alice smoothed her Steilmann skirt under her and nodded at me. Sr. Marie Goretti shifted in her seat and eyed the kettle longingly.

Our soon-to-retire vice-principal who was recording the meeting stopped writing. "I found Mary Jordan blowing up a yellow condom at the back of my class the other day," she said. "Maintained it was her father's; she found it lying around and thought it would be *hip* to bring it into school." She emphasised hip in imitation of the red-haired tearaway.

"Wish he had made some use of them himself. It would have saved us all a lot of trouble." Sr. Alice patted her hair. "There are Jordans like steps of stairs from Leaving Cert to first year. I think there's a boy in second year up the road in St. Christopher's and another one in starting off."

"I understand what you're saying, Sr. Alice but, God help us, it's easy to abide by the doctrines of our faith when they are easy to follow."

Sr. Pius was on a roll, I thought.

"Now take the footballers," she continued. "They're part of a team. They have to work together. Wouldn't do if the full back went his own way and ..."

"Mayo are finished. It wouldn't make much difference what the full back did." Paul Walsh had a face the length of a six-foot ruler.

"Thank you, Pius," Sr. Maureen Ruane said. "Now if you have nothing else to add ..."

"*I* have ... something else to say."

Pius must be angry. It was unlike her to be assertive.

"I want the Health Education teachers to tell the pupils to pull up their socks and keep the top buttons of their blouses closed. God help them, they will catch their death of cold."

"What is the real reason, Sister?" I asked. Enough was enough.

"They should be prevented from showing off all that dirty flesh."

I put my hand over my mouth to stifle the giggle that was starting deep inside me. "This is unreal."

When I heard Sr. Alice's intake of breath, I realised I had spoken aloud. Time to backtrack. I would get nowhere being truthful. Catholic moralists and their ilk were still linking marriage and sex too closely. If Pius had her way, my book would have read like a comic ... goodies and baddies. Goodies were celibate. Baddies had sex. Goodies didn't tempt men with 'dirty flesh'. Baddies sexed up their school uniforms. Goodies started their families immediately after marriage. Baddies planned their offspring.

"I think, Sister, when the weather is cold this year they will be wearing coloured stockings. They're all in. There will be very little flesh visible." I had a go at copying Rita's dulcet tone.

"So you see, Pius, there is nothing to worry about. Now I think that concludes the agenda so I'll close the meeting." Sr. Maureen Ruane raised her eyebrows questioningly.

"We have covered the important things," Kieran Crawley said, "I'm sure. Anything else can wait until tomorrow."

As we all stood, Kieran Crawley, having missed his chance to talk to me earlier, walked across the room and grabbed me by the elbow. I stared at him, I hoped discouragingly. He had a handsome face. Pity he spoiled it with a pout that made him look like a brooding adolescence. Creepy Crawley the students called him. My thoughts were of Uriah Heep as he said, "Welcome back, Yank."

When I first introduced Kieran Crawley and his wife to David, he wondered how he had managed to win the 'lovely Pamela.' When he realised that she was a psychiatrist, he often referred to her as the 'the shrink.' But since that first introduction, much to my amazement, Pamela and he had become friends.

"How did the trip go, Teresa?" Kieran Crawley asked. "You were very eloquent during the staff meeting."

I was glad that teachers were still putting on their coats or buttoning their jackets and that I was not alone with him. "I said what I had to say," I answered.

Kieran Crawley's eyes narrowed. "How is David doing? The unexpectedness of his question threw me. I felt as disconcerted as if my doctor had refused to renew my prescription for Valium. "He's well. Busy."

He stroked the thick eyebrows shading his eyes and angled his head sideways. "You'll not be travelling again for a while, will you, Teresa. Tell David ..." He hesitated. "Never mind. I'll tell him myself."

"Yes, tell him yourself." Witty retorts jumbled around in my head but remained unspoken. I longed to wipe the suggestive grin from his face.

"*Sláinte.*" He raised his hand as if he were holding a glass and making a toast.

As I turned my back to him, I felt like I could murder a drink.

Kieran Crawley and alcohol flowed together in my mind. Maybe, because he always said *Sláinte* to me instead of goodbye. *Teresa, go home to bed. Put on that night-gown and peignoir. David said he'd be back early this evening.* My inner voice counselled me.

"What's the hurry?" Rita complained as I ushered her out the staff-room door. "We have the whole afternoon. I wonder does anybody fancy a jar?"

When we had walked through the front door of the school, her eyes unconsciously strayed towards where the men usually parked. There were no cars there. She continued, "Let's go for lunch and adjourn to Jo' Joe's afterwards. Teresa, you can tell me about your American adventures. And, I wouldn't half mind a spritzer." Rita only drank *real* alcohol on special occasions.

My heart leapt in anticipation of booze. "We have to set a standard for the kids," I answered. "No cavorting around the town just because we've been let off the noose."

"We used to do it before and I didn't hear you complaining."

"I'm joking. I'm just getting old and staid." I looked down at my grey skirt which picked up the threads of grey in my burgundy blouse. "Rit. I'm not hungry and I don't want to go for a drink," I lied. "But I'll ring you tonight for a chat and tell you about my Halloween escapades."

Rita looked at me curiously. "Fine. No big deal. I'll go home and finish sewing up the *geansaís* I've made for Andy."

Rita loved to knit. As I admired her jumper, I thought that she was the only one I knew who could make ordinary plain and purl look glamorous. I left my hand on her shoulder for a minute before I got into the car and opened the window.

Rita stuck in her head. "See you so."

"Yeah. Regards to the kids. And Noel of course. Does he still phone you as often?"

Rita smiled a self-conscious smile. "Every second night. He says he has to hear our voices or he would go mad."

"I guess the North Sea is quite a change from Galway. Especially for someone like Noel."

"I hope that's a compliment."

"It is. You know he would prefer to be home with you and the

43

children."

"Sometimes I forget that he's gone and cook for seven. I made so much casserole on Friday night that we were still eating it on Sunday. Even the boys were at me to throw it out."

I thought of Rita's five healthy sons.

"Andy is sixteen now. He needs his father. You are so lucky to have David around all the time."

"I guess so."

"Bye." Rita pulled her head out of the window and walked towards her car.

Lucky. You can be lonelier with someone than without them. As I drove out the convent gate to drive to Claremorris to collect the kids at school, I wondered for the umpteenth time why David had lied about being in Westport when he'd actually been in Dublin.

At the school, Esther and Rachael were playing tag around a tree. Their faces were pinched with the cold and Rachael blew on her fingers. Her knee socks lay in crinkled folds around her ankles. There were red marks round her calves where the elastic had been too tight. I had gone to town two weeks ago with the intention of buying a larger pair for her but had ended up in the pub instead. She stopped running and motioned to Rachael. Together they ran towards Cora's car that had just arrived. Goddammit! I thought I had mentioned to Cora that I would be collecting them. Wait a minute! That was impossible. I had expected the staff meeting to go on until four.

I got out of the car and pulled on my jacket. Cora's bare ankle emerged from the driver's seat. I closed my buttons, tightened my belt and shivered. "Cora, it makes me cold to look at you," I said.

"Sure haven't I plenty of fat to keep me warm. Not like you. Skin and bone," she retorted in response to what I thought was a light-hearted query.

"It's hard enough getting these two to wear warm clothes without having you as a role model," I said.

"Model is it? They make a packet. That fella in *Pretty Woman*. His wife. What's her name?" Cora stood with her naked arms on her hips, her face puckered. "Cinders? Coal? Something to do with a fire." She made a circular gesture with her hand. Then she shrugged. "Never mind."

I should have known better than to set Cora off on one of her tangents.

Esther said, "Cindy Crawford. That's who you're trying to

think of, Cor. Remember, Mom. The two C's. When some first years couldn't remember what alliteration was, Dad gave you a picture of her to show them."

Which didn't explain it and had never been used, I thought. Nevertheless I'd been chuffed that he'd been trying to help.

"And what was a happily married man like your father doing with a picture of Cindy Crawford?" Cora asked. "That's what I'd like to know."

Rachael's hand slipped into mine. "Where are we going, Mom?"

I felt a flash of annoyance that I should have aimed at Cora. "How do you mean where are we going?"

"Well. We always go somewhere nice when you get time off." As she shook her ponytail, her voice lightened. "But I don't care if we go home. I have half a duplo house made that I was going to finish while Cora cooked the mince for the shepherd's pie." She looked hopefully at me. "You could do it instead."

I hated frying mince. My mother's instructions resonated in my head. *Get the pan. Turn on the cooker. Find the oil. Don't put in too much. Throw in the meat. Keep turning it or it will burn.* "I was thinking of picking up some panties and socks. You can have something to eat while we're in town."

Esther kicked at a pebble, her lips puckered.

"Keep that up and you'll need new shoes too," I said.

Esther copied Cora's earlier shrug and held out her palms in an expansive Jewish gesture she had inherited from her father.

Cora gave her a little push. "Off you go so. You'll have a great time entirely. We'll do a bit of mince tomorrow with the chops. Tuesday's and Wednesday's dinner together. Won't that be great craic?" They both nodded.

"You can have a bit of cheesecake after your lunch," I addressed Esther. "Strawberry. Your favourite."

"Fine."

"Can I have some too?"

I knew that Rachael didn't like cheesecake. I turned towards the car. It made me feel small that a kid of her age felt it necessary to humour me.

On the journey, I asked them about school and made an effort to be interested. No matter how hard I tried, a sparkling gin and tonic loomed in front of me.

Later, after a feed of sausages and chips, Esther poked at a lemon meringue; there had been no cheesecake available.

"This is brill. I love strawberries and cream more than anything else in the world." Rachael's Lithuanian eyes shone.

"More than rice crispy buns? You told Cora you like them, *better than anything else in the world.*"

"Don't copy people," I said. Esther had stuck out her chin and mimicked her sister's way of speaking.

"Mom, you said that copying someone is a compliment to them." Esther cocked her head like Roamy did when he was outside, heard noises coming up the rocky drive, and was awaiting someone's arrival. I massaged my temples. Lawyer material. David always joked that Esther was lawyer material like him. "I'll have a coffee," I said to nobody in particular.

"Mom. You did say that."

"Not now, Esther, please." I turned to the skinny waitress, sitting at the table opposite, examining her split ends. "Could I have a coffee, please? Decaf." The girl took her fingers away from her hair; it fell over her face. "Any decaf coffee?" she shouted towards the counter.

"Decaf? What's that?" a voice asked.

The girl shrugged.

"Never mind. I'll take regular." I glanced at my watch. Four o'clock. I wouldn't sleep a wink tonight. *Positive thinking, Teresa. Remember David and his positive thinking.* Where was he now? I wondered. He was appearing in court this morning but had promised to come home early.

As we left the restaurant, a group of boys, whom I knew went to the local secondary school, stood together outside the swimming pool. They were smoking in a mutinous way, glad to be free of their parents and teachers, savouring the last of their Halloween break. Tomorrow they'd don their school uniforms and become part of the establishment again. The thought that they would consider me part of the restrictive system only worsened my mood.

Mist enveloped us as we ran towards the car. I felt it burrow between my hair and the neck of my blouse. When the three of us were ensconced, Esther beside me in the front, I turned on the radio and listened to the middle-class accent of the presenter as he quizzed callers about songs from the sixties. If they knew the correct answers, he rewarded them with prizes – a toaster, an electric kettle, and general household appliances.

The pseudo-intimacy between the caller and the presenter, who would never have even met, amazed me; the ability to act like a sister or brother to total strangers seemed to be a prerequisite for hosting such programmes. It was a skill I knew I lacked. During my own media appearances it had been Teresa this, Teresa that, as if the presenters had known me all their lives. I changed the station to a news programme.

When I got out on the Balllinrobe road, the traffic was light, and the mist had cleared. It was now dark and I had the lights on; I travelled the short distance to our house at an even pace. By five I was nearly home.

"Dad's back," Rachael said, "I can see his car." As I negotiated the turn into the house, my heart beat rapidly.

"Hi, Tess."

I had the key in the lock when David opened the door. As I saw his smile shine through his beard, pleasure swelled within me like Rita's rising bread. My palms felt clammy as I took out my keys. "David."

He looked over my shoulder to Esther. "Hi there, Essie. Hi, Rach. I'll help you carry some of those." He swept past me and took a plastic bag from Esther. Then he put his free arm around Rachael's shoulders. "I thought you'd never come back," he said. "I spent the last half hour resisting finishing your house."

Rachael's cheeks had spots of red in the centre. "Can we do it now, Dad?"

48

"Suah we can."

She looked at me. "We didn't come home after school. I was going to finish it then but we went shopping!"

"So I see." He picked pink socks from one of the bags. "Very nice."

"Daad." Esther grabbed them from him, her annoyance only half-real.

Say something bland. I couldn't let him find out that I resented the attention he was giving to Esther and Rachael. "Are you long home?" Though I tried to appear pleasant, my voice sounded brittle.

"I'm just in," David said. "Got away from the courthouse before the rush but I have to go out again later."

My overused pasted smile pained my jaw bone. "I thought, maybe, we'd have an early night." *I'm prepared to make love. I want to bamboozle you into telling me where you were while I was in America.* But of course the presence of my daughters stopped me voicing any of my thoughts. It was scary to love someone as I loved David. At last, I had admitted it to myself. I was scared that he was not in love with me anymore.

How could I go on without him? I remembered how hairs on the backs of his fingers tickled my cheeks when he stroked my face. But he hadn't done that for months, I reminded myself. He would have a shower before he went out. I would seduce him then. I thought of Granny Goldstein's usual advice in a dilemma. "Don't agonise. Do something." I would get out the chiffon night attire I had purchased in the States especially to vamp him, entice him back to my bed.

"Tess, why don't you go to sleep for a while? I'll look after these monkeys. I haven't spent much time with them lately."

"Neither have I."

"*You* have some excuse. I have none. And you must be tired. Your supposed Halloween break wasn't a break for you at all this year."

Warmth surged through me. He was right. I felt exhausted. "I'll have a snooze so."

The three went into the front room and I went slowly upstairs.

The sign he had put on the bedroom door was still in place, a remembrance of happier times. It was a cartoon version of a figure sleeping on a bed with zzzz rising from her nostrils like fog. Underneath he had written 'Let sleeping Moms lie.' Down a little further was a drawing of two little girls, their fingers on their lips – shhh.

I lay for a minute on top of the duvet and relished the firmness of the orthopaedic mattress beneath. Normally David preferred a soft place to lie. Our four-poster period in Framingham had a dip in the middle into which he loved to sink. However, he had suggested our present one because it was good for my erratic back pain. I wondered if dislike of the mattress had contributed to his sleeping in the spare room. *Get a grip Teresa*, I admonished myself. *Futons are as hard as nails to sleep on. Find another excuse for his desertion.*

The thought so shook me I sat up in the bed. I had to do something. A bath. I needed to have a bath. A bath, not a shower. I also wished to sleep but I had better stay awake and try to wash away my anxiety. I went into the en suite, locked the door and turned on the hot water tap, then the cold. Using my elbow, I tested the water's temperature. David always laughed at me when I did this – said my caution was anathema to my true personality.

As I stripped, I fumbled with my blouse buttons and tried to ignore the bruise, shaped like a pork chop, decorating my arm. My tights were halfway down my legs when I snagged them with a jagged nail. I soaked until the water had lost its warmth and then washed and dried myself at top speed.

Re-entering the bedroom, I put on a pair of pink slippers and opened the wardrobe to take out my new nightgown, the folds of which cascaded over my body, enhancing my skinny frame. I bent forward and let my breasts fall into its cups. As I practised seductive poses in front of our full-length mirror a thought struck me. *Rita* would never need to rehearse a seduction scene. She was a natural.

50

I moved closer to the mirror, inspected my hair and noticed tell-tale grey at the part and the temples. I'd have to make an appointment at the hairdresser's to get it done. Thankfully, it wasn't obvious enough for David to notice. I would dye it on Saturday. "You dye clothes, hon. You colour hair." Granny Goldstein's words.

I was unsure why I preferred David not to know that I dyed my hair. His own had streaks of grey but it made him look distinguished. Mine made me look old. I had kept the secret for three years now. Touching the end of a lock, I remembered when I had a head of brown hair. If I had been that good at keeping a secret from him, he could be equally good at keeping one from me. My nerves must be frayed to be entertaining such thoughts.

In bed the cool sheets scrunched under my buttocks. I let my spine sag and traced my unease. The bruise on my arm had been caused by accident. David hadn't realised how tight his grip was and I marked easily. The necessity to have to dress provocatively to seduce my husband was also irritating. I was like Salome for Godsakes.

David's humming, as he climbed the stairs, woke me.

My nightdress crumpled around my back, the chiffon not as kind to my skin as my usual cotton; its sexiness had been my priority when I bought it. David was my husband. I needed him. Though I didn't enjoy lovemaking, I liked the closeness it brought. He would be in any minute to change into his tracksuit. I inched out of the bed, re-arranged the duvet and, feeling a little foolish, settled myself beneath it.

He padded into the room and shut the door quietly.

"David. It's okay. I'm awake." I tried to imagine what Rita would do in similar circumstances.

"Oh!" As he glanced at my expectant face, he opened the wardrobe, took out his tracksuit, chose a pair of trousers, then rummaged through his shirts.

"Cora washed and ironed your blue one," I said.

He draped the shirt over his arm with the tracksuit and

trousers. "The house took longer than I expected. Couldn't find some of the Lego."

I remained silent.

"I'm in a rush, Tess," he added defensively. "I still have to do my exercises. I'll change in the kids' bathroom."

For months he had been late home, always preoccupied, occasionally harassed. During school term, I was busy correcting copies in the evenings, fatigued from managing Rachael and Esther's bedtime without his help, and then attempting to research my book. We were leading separate lives.

"I'll throw this on. I should have done my exercises this morning." He flung the tracksuit top across his shoulder and took the stairs down two at a time. I could hear him working-out. I imagined his tongue protruding slightly between his teeth as he lifted a dumb-bell from midriff to shoulder, a lock of black hair falling into his eyes. Two years ago, David would have had my sexy nightdress off me by now and the groans I was hearing through the ceiling would have been from sexual excitement.

Running my fingertips over the duvet, I kept time with the pounding from downstairs. Warm-up over, he was now doing the run. I knew the routine by heart. Each day, for months, David had put on his tracksuit, got his training manual, the much-thumbed *Royal Canadian Air Force Handbook*, and with the seriousness of a rabbi about to say *Kaddish* had gone downstairs and done the exercises from it. He wanted to reach the top level of fitness designated for pilots who were the same age as himself. They needed fitness trainers in the kibbutz. He always said he wanted to keep fit in case ...

After half an hour the noises changed to toilet flushing, downstairs shower running, and then bathroom door slamming. "I'm off, Tess. Bye Esther. Bye Rachael." Sound of exaggerated lip smacking. "See you all in the morning."

"Where are you going, Dad?" Rachael's voice.

"I have to go to work. Someone has to keep us in the manner to which we've become accustomed."

That was our joke. During my career break, he had been the

only salary earner and always kidded me about it. As he pulled the door shut after him, I got out of bed, dressed in my old dressing gown and went barefoot down the stairs.

The sound of 'Peter Rabbit' carried from the kitchen/family room into the hall. "The television is awful loud," I complained. Even after one of them had turned it down, I could still hear the beginning of the jingle for some soft drink. "Esther, Rachael, don't forget to mute the ads."

"Okay, Mom," they chorused.

David was adamant that his kids wouldn't be a foil for slick advertising executives. He insisted that they turn down the sound when the advertisements came on. Esther and Rachael had done this since they were old enough to work the remote control. One way or another, we all seemed to do his will.

In the sitting room, I undid the tie-backs and drew the curtains. Quiet, quiet house. I should have left the television blaring. Brown spots were showing through the apple-green walls. A film of dust covered the picture over the fireplace. The curtains were a shade I no longer liked; I had intended changing them for months. It seemed everywhere I looked I saw evidence of procrastination and neglect.

We had lived in this house for a couple of years. But despite our short time here we could have done more to improve it. It seemed neither of us cared sufficiently to bother. Perhaps, I hated to admit it, we were as careless with our relationship as we were with our home.

I rushed towards the drinks cabinet and grabbed a glass. An Irish coffee was what I needed. Even David approved of that. He had one himself, on occasion.

I went into the kitchen/family room with a half-empty bottle of whiskey under my arm, filled the kettle from the tap and plugged it in. I was the only one in the house who drank tea, so I usually boiled a mug of water in the microwave and plopped in the tea bag. Even as I boiled the kettle I wondered if it was because I wanted to savour the moments before I felt the tang of whiskey on my tongue or because I hoped something would crop up to divert me from indulging.

Rachael said, "There's no decaf coffee, Mom. You finished it before you went to America, remember? You made that stuff where you poured the cream over the spoon."

Esther turned off the television. "Irish coffees. That's what they were Rachael. Irish coffees. They have whiskey in them too. That's where the decaf went." She eyed the bottle in the way only Esther could. "And the whiskey," she added.

"It's time for bed, girls."

"But it's not even ni ...," Esther protested.

"Now."

A hot whiskey, I thought. One hot whiskey would be okay. When I was a child, my mother used to give me punch anytime I had a cold. Even my father raised no objections to this. My head hurt. Perhaps I had a cold coming on. The automatic kettle switched off. I made my voice firm. "Bed!"

Esther seemed anxious, Rachael looked bewildered. "Come here." I held my arms wide. "Gimme a hug." Rachael's head reached my midriff. My arms tightened around her. I bent and kissed her on the hair.

Esther came more slowly but her hug was even tighter than her sister's. "Mom. Don't . . . don't drink the whiskey. Last time you fell and nearly broke your ankle. Please."

I let them walk out of the room and up the stairs without answering. Then I grabbed the bottle. As I unscrewed the top, Rachael's voice floated through the ceiling.

"Mom, will you read a chapter of *The Lion, The Witch And The Wardrobe*?

"Not tonight, Rachael."

I reflected a moment on David reading for Rita's son. Then on my earlier failure to seduce him. I hated having to entrap my husband. I yearned for the safety of a loving marriage. I poured whisky into a glass and drank it straight. To hell with punch. That was for wimps.

That night Rachael wet the bed again.

"She's comin', she's comin.'" The warning went around the class. First years too. They picked up bad habits quickly.

"Please, stand up for the prayer," I said when I came in. I always reeled off the 'Hail Mary' in the junior classes; I recite it for disciplinary reasons. "Stand up straight. Stop pulling her hair." It was a good way of calming students. They blessed themselves. The ritual over, I asked them to arrange the desks in a circle. Discarded lollipop sticks, an empty mineral bottle, and chewed pieces of gum appeared from beneath the desks. "Tidy the room, please," I ordered.

While they were cleaning up, I took work sheets from the bottom of my briefcase. "Everybody back to their desks." I felt happy as I handed a copy of the questionnaire to each girl. David's resentment at the success of my book, his failure to respond to my sexual overture, our lack of closeness were no longer problems. Last night he had returned to our bed and, though I was half-drunk, I had felt him caress the small of my back, bury his face in my shoulder blades, and murmur, "Love you."

My tongue felt crusty. Although I had taken a mint to mask the smell of alcohol on my breath, I was still conscious that I had swilled whiskey the night before. Never again. There was no need. David had returned. He was the old David. My fear about his lack of love for me was my mistrust.

I was sitting on the edge of one of the tables in the circle when I noticed that Fionnuala Jordan, one of the 'steps of stairs' Sr. Alice had mentioned at the staff meeting, was twirling her earring. "Your ear looks inflamed, Fionnuala. Is it painful?" I asked her.

"A bit." She looked crestfallen.

"Did you get them pierced recently?"

"Yes, Miss. A week ago. The man said to rub surgical spirits on it and twist it every evening or it will get stuck."

"And did you?"

"No, Miss."

"I know someone who had to have hers cut off when she forgot to do what she was supposed to," Kathleen Moran informed us. "There was all goo around it and because your ear is so fat it'll …"

"Kack. Shut up." Fionnuala's normally high colour rose even higher.

"Come here until I see it."

All eyes riveted on Fionnuala as she manoeuvred herself out of the seat.

My expression, I hoped, was appropriately serious. "It's very red. Why don't you go down to Sr. Alphonsus and she'll bathe it for you."

"Aw, Miss!"

Mine was about the only class in which they would prefer to stay. Health Education held potential for the unexpected. All that talk of sex turned them on, according to Rita.

"Make sure you bathe it when you go home so. If you don't, it will go septic."

"Yes, Miss."

"Ask her now. She's in good humour." It was Kathleen Moran again. "Kathleen, what is it you want Fionnuala to ask?" My voice was as sweet as candy. "Perhaps you could ask it yourself."

"Why do we have to do sex education? Why can't we just do it?" she said.

I kept my tone level, feigned interest. "Do what?"

Blotches sprouted on Kathleen's jowls. She breathed deeply. Her exhalation and a flurry of words came together. "Whatever it is Mammy and Daddy do when they go to bed."

"You mean sleep?" Fionnuala of the many siblings wanted to

be included. Her smile was sly. It was beginning to look as if Kathleen were the innocent here.

"Why would you go to bed when you're not even tired? Sunday, Daddy gets up at twelve o'clock for his dinner. He goes to Mass on Saturday night in case you think he doesn't," she added. "When he's eaten all his chops, he makes Mammy go back to bed with him. She was ironing a patch onto my shirt the other day when she had to drop everything."

It was on Saturdays that *my* father used to take my mother to bed. The thought skipped through my mind and was gone.

Kathleen's voice rose. "Imagine! I listened outside the bedroom door. I knew they'd kill me if I went in. The sounds!"

"You'd think we're back in High Infants telling teacher the news." Shirley Broderick's disdainful tone was like her mother's, whom I once had the dubious pleasure of talking to on the phone about her other daughter Jacinta.

Refusing to be highjacked, Kathleen continued. "It was disgusting. I think they were having sex."

As that precise moment the door opened. It was Sr. Pius. "There's a lovely air of learning here, Mrs. Goldstein. Everybody seems so interested."

"We are ..." I was stuck for words. "We are ..."

"My ear is sore again, Miss."

"Is it, Fionnuala? Let me see." I looked suitably scandalised as Fionnuala, unbeknownst to Sr. Pius, winked.

"Poor dear," Sr. Pius crooned.

"Carry on with your work," I said.

Sr. Pius spoke quietly to me. "I hope you don't mind the intrusion, Mrs Goldstein. But I'm collecting the tea money." She looked away. "And I have to admit I was curious to see for myself what went on in a Health Education class."

I only smiled.

"You can give me the money again." Then she said in a tone for all to hear, "On my way back to the staffroom, I'll take little Fionnuala down to Sr. Alphonsus to look after that ear." As the door closed behind them, the class erupted into laughter. Sr. Pius, with her earnest demeanour and old-fashioned ideas, was a figure of fun for many pupils.

I felt, for a moment, the sense of helplessness with which I had become familiar since returning from my career break. For the past few weeks I had begun to put a little gin into a Styrofoam cup and take a few sips during class, when required. I had been so euphoric about David's behaviour, I had forgotten to bring any this morning, "Put down your pens and we'll see what you've written," I said.

The laughing continued. "But, Miss. We haven't finished yet," said a voice from the back.

"Now. You start, Shirley."

"But, Miss ..."

Suddenly Sr. Maureen Ruane's voice sounded over the intercom. "Would Mrs. Goldstein come to the principal's office immediately. Thank you."

My heart palpitated.

"Free class," they chorused.

So much for Health Education being their favourite subject.

My mind went into overdrive. Rachael or Esther. Was it them? Or David ... had something happened to him? How could I go on if anything had befallen any of my family? My expression must have mirrored my thoughts. Kathleen Moran stood up and opened the door. "You'd better go, Miss. Leave your books here. I'll bring them to the staffroom."

"Lick. Kack is a lick," one of her classmates said. I pretended I didn't hear as I smiled my thanks at her and became re-absorbed by my thoughts. My heels taa-tooed on the terrazzo floor until the mat outside the principal's office cut off the sound.

Sr. Maureen Ruane was sitting at her desk, her office door ajar.

"Teresa. Come in, *a stoirín.*"

I felt a wobbly sensation in my stomach and my mouth felt dry.

She looked at me, her eyes almost hidden in the tortoise rims of her glasses. "My dear Teresa," she said after a moment, "your mother has taken a turn. She is in Beaumar hospital. They want you to come immediately." To give me time to compose myself, I supposed, she busied herself with the October lists, stacked on her desk.

She needn't have worried that I would fall apart. Despite her calling me '*a stoirín*', past experience had taught me to be wary. She could be nice as pie one minute, very bureaucratic the next. The thought fuelled my determination to remain calm. Behind her, I saw a stiff-backed woman, jaw aching from trying not to cry – my reflection in the glass door of the data room.

She put the papers to one side. "You haven't touched your personal days. Why don't you take one? I'll get a H. Dip. student to sub for you. She can count the hours as part of her teaching practice."

One day. Great! "Thanks, sister."

"*A stoirín*, I know it's a shock. Perhaps your mother has just had a minor setback," she said with a kindness that sounded so genuine I had trouble keeping my mask in place. "Go and find out how she is."

"I will," I mumbled.

My mind was blank as I stumbled out the double door of the main exit. The flowers that had cheered me on the way in this morning had begun to droop.

I had my key in the door of the car when I heard Rita exclaim from the opposite side of the car park, "I've just heard."

I waved absently. The school grapevine, where news passed through like a kind of osmosis, was alive and well. I had the car in first gear when Rita came abreast of it.

She reached to me through the open window; the purple paint on her fingernails reminded me of death. "Teresa." She hugged me awkwardly. "I don't know what to say except if there is anything I can do …"

"Thanks, Rit." My voice shook. "You'd better go or you'll be late for class.

I bit my lip to stop me crying. But I had no way of controlling my thoughts. I put my hands each side of my head and pressed as if I could squeeze my feelings into non-existence. When this failed, I jammed my palms against the cold glass of the windscreen and rubbed them on my burning face. Then I called through the car window for Rita to come back. I needed a diversion, someone to talk to, someone to empty my mind of my confused emotions. But she had gone back into the school.

I met my father in the waiting room, a recess on the corridor, ringed with green upholstered chairs and a long leatherette bench by the window. Dog-eared magazines were heaped on a small round table. The sign on the door opposite said, 'Intensive Care.' Though there was only my father and I there, the place still felt crowded. We sat side by side as if waiting to confess our sins. My father always fulfilled his Easter duty obligation, which meant he went to confession each year between Ash Wednesday and Trinity Sunday, so he should find the situation reasonably familiar.

"Daddy, tell me what happened."

He bent forward, elbows resting on his knees, hands clenched in front of him. His knuckles were white lumps. "Well you know Mammy had a stroke."

"Yes." A nurse had told me when I arrived at the hospital. "But I want to know the details. How? When?" The quiver in my voice surprised me.

"Just after the dinner."

That would be one o'clock.

"A slight stroke. She'd made a lovely dinner, too. Bacon and cabbage with potatoes – Kerr's pinks." His eyes livened at the memory. "As usual, she cleared the table and went out to the kitchen to do the washing up. I was sitting in the armchair reading. There wasn't much in the paper, so I nodded off. When I woke up, I heard a noise, as if something had fallen."

I drew in my breath. "Did you *do* anything?" My emphasis floated over his head.

"I shouted out to her, 'Lily, go and see who that is.' I thought it was Frank Maloney with the messages. He sometimes thumps the door with the box. I heard her answer, so I was convinced she had brought him into the kitchen. I must have dozed again. This time the thirst woke me. The bacon. I went out for a drink of water and found her on the floor."

For a minute he was silent. Then he clasped his hands as if he were praying, and shifted on the bench. "She must have grabbed onto the draining board when she felt herself falling and pulled all the dishes with her. That was the noise I heard. She was still speaking a little then."

"The ambulance?"

"It was she who told me to call 999."

Typical. I wanted to ask him how long my mother had lain on the kitchen tiles, but it would seem as if I were accusing him. On the other hand, he had a tendency towards self-delusion, so any criticism would have passed unnoticed.

"The ambulance came quickly. I helped to lift her in." He looked at me expectantly as if he deserved praise. No way, I thought.

"How did she seem?" I asked.

"I sat in front."

Comfortable for you.

"The ambulance man said she regained consciousness." My father rubbed a palm over his receding hair. "He said she was trying to speak. I wasn't able to see her when the men took her out." He put the heel of his shoe against the chair leg.

A nurse came out of 'Intensive Care' and told us that a doctor would be with us soon.

We waited. What was taking them so long? Surely someone could tell us something.

A woman, holding a newborn, and a man walked past. "Isn't he gorgeous?" the dad said to nobody in particular. They continued down the corridor oohing and aahing and laughing out loud.

"Shhh," a nurse cautioned them. "We try to keep this floor as quiet as possible."

Quiet because the patients on it are critically ill, I thought. Then the nurse said to my father, "Mr. Casey, you can see your wife for a little while."

My father looked a question.

"I'm her daughter," I said.

"Of course. Follow me."

My shoes squeaked on the polished floor as we followed her into 'Intensive Care.' There were four beds, two side by side against opposite walls. On the wall facing the door, there was a paper towel dispenser by a sink. The nurse led us towards my mother's bed; I tried not to look at the other patients. I was struggling to gather my wits before looking at Mammy, when my father, who had been following, bounded past me to the sink.

He turned on the hot tap and waved his hands under it. Then he reached for the paper towel, all the while talking incessantly. "This is the intensive care unit. She's in the best place she could be." He gestured towards a nurse who was injecting a frail figure in another bed. "They all look like good nurses." He sounded confused, weary. "They must deal with strokes every day."

The nurse who had been leading us showed remarkable composure in the face of my father's strange behaviour. She went over to him, took him by the arm and guided him towards my mother's bed.

Her eyes were closed; her face was as motionless as a death mask, and as blank. The air seemed unnaturally still. The sheets, folded over a blue bedspread, were a brilliant white. Blue and white, traditional colours of the Blessed Virgin.

My reaction to her frailty and thinness took me by surprise. I felt a disturbing kind of detachment. My mother reminded me of any sick old woman, blotched skin, creased hands clutching the covers, victim to all the lines, crumples and infirmities that age bestowed. Beneath her crown of lustreless grey hair, her neck looked sinewy and yellow. I recalled a line from Yeats I had been teaching that morning: 'A comfortable kind of old scarecrow.' But as I continued to gaze at her, my emotional objectivity disappeared, my heart raced; for a second I felt caught in the mesh of the past from which I had tried so hard to disentangle myself.

I unclasped one of her hands and grasped it. The skin was papery and her nails were blue, as if she had varnished them. I pressed her hand to my lips and was disquieted by its coldness.

Then aware that I had forgotten him, I looked at Daddy's troubled face and realised that he too was suffering. I was being selfish and insensitive. It was at that moment my mother opened her eyes.

"Pat," she looked towards my father. "Pat, are you alright? I must have given you an awful fright."

My father had been standing on the same side of the bed as me; now he rushed to the other side and moved closer to her. "I'm fine, Lily. Sure I called the ambulance like you told me."

My mother turned to me. "Teresa. How did you find out? Shouldn't you be at school?"

"Oh Mam."

"The nurse on reception phoned the school for me to let her know," my father said. "They're very nice, all the nurses."

"A mutual admiration society. What do you think, Mam?"

My mother's giggle was girlish and weak. Pat always gets someone to do his bidding, was her unspoken message.

The nurse, seeing my mother was awake, bent over her. "Mrs. Casey, it looks like you're on the mend."

"Nurse. Do you know where my teeth are?"

The nurse smiled. "Of course. I'll get them for you." She patted my mother's hand and beckoned to me with her eyes.

When we were outside the 'Intensive Care' room, the nurse spoke in an even lower tone than she had been using inside. "The doctor has said that we could move Mrs. Casey a few days after she regained consciousness. Depending of course on her progress. She will be going into a public ward." Her expression was impassive as she waited for my reply.

"Godammit." My father had never taken out health insurance. He used to boast that neither Lily nor himself had been sick a day in their lives so he should not have to waste money paying other people's bills. My mother would hate being in a public ward.

"I'll pay for a private room," I said. I wondered if David would mind, then hoped that he wouldn't. Uncharacteristically, David and my mother were allies; she was always saying how much she liked him. My father felt the opposite; he frowned on David as a non-Catholic and a foreigner. On the subject of David, my mother refused to compromise.

"How *is* my mother? She'll be alright, won't she?"

"You should ask the consultant," the nurse answered.

"If I could find one." The idea of my mother dying bewildered me. I knew everybody had to die. Sure she was seventy. She had a good innings. How often had I heard people say that about strangers. It was different when it was your own mother.

As if she had read my mind, a doctor materialised. "Mrs. Casey should have recovered in a couple of days, Mrs. Goldstein."

I concentrated on the spatter of broken veins high on the doctor's cheekbones.

"We have done a CT scan, monitored her heart and kidneys and as far as we can see at this stage there is no permanent damage."

Despite my best efforts, I again felt a level of detachment. I looked again at the purple threads only half disguised, and hoped the consultant was better at diagnosis than at applying makeup.

"She will have to take Wafarin but generally she should be able to lead a normal life."

"Thank you, Doctor."

My sense of reality returned. "She's going to recover. She's going to recover." I repeated the words over and over like a mantra. Now that the crisis was past, I felt like a puppet with its strings fraying, on the verge of collapse.

When I re-entered the 'Intensive Care', my father, his face drawn tight as a drum skin, had gone to the sink again and was sprinkling his hands. This second trip took me by surprise. I thought he had stopped all that nonsense. Now that he had started, he would make the pilgrimage six times in the next hour.

It was obsessive-compulsive behaviour. Our GP had put a name on it for my mother and helped her cope. 'Separate the behaviour from the individual,' she liked to tell me, advice I found hard to follow.

I called him back to the bedside and told him the good news that my mother would recover.

"She'll get well, Teresa. Isn't that wonderful?" he repeated in much the same manner as I had done myself.

I smiled and said, "Yes, Dad. It's wonderful. The only thing we have to make sure of now is that she stays well."

A cough from the bed disturbed our rare moment of shared understanding.

A half hour later, David came. He was wearing the Fair Isle sweater Rita had knit for him. She had chosen well; the coffee threads wandering through the wool complimented the golden flecks in his eyes. Immediately, he went over to my father, shook hands with him and addressed him in a low tone.

My father, obviously deciding to put his low opinion of my husband aside for the moment, held fast to David's hand. In his agitation, he was speaking loud enough for me to hear. "Who told you? How did you know? You were great to come." Syrup dripped from his voice.

"Rita." David took his hand away and looked towards me. "She rang from the secretary's office. I had little choice but to obey." His tone was playful. "You know teachers. Orders from on high."

To keep myself from smiling idiotically at him, I bit the inside of my lip. I wanted to run to him and pull him into an embrace. At the thought that I would soon be like Roamy, who stood on his hind legs begging for attention, my shoulders tightened. "If that was how you felt you should have stayed away," I retorted, deliberately choosing to misinterpret his attempt at levity.

In a stride, he came and hugged me briefly. Then he said, "How are you doing, kiddo? I couldn't believe it when Rita called. You must have got a godawful fright."

"I did a bit." His concern almost made my mother's illness

worthwhile. "Mam is much better. They think there's no damage done."

"There you go. She'll be fine." The sound of the tap running almost drowned his answer.

"Dad. That sink is not for general use. You will have all the paper towels used."

"Tess, you're being a bit testy." David placed his warm palm on my back. "If we don't cool it, we'll be thrown out."

As I looked towards the nurse, she put her finger to her lips the way I used to do to noisy pupils.

David said quietly, "Go home, Tess. Check on the girls. I phoned Cora so she will be with them. Pat and I will be here when your mother wakes up."

My father nodded. "You take care of the grandchildren, Teresa," he whispered. "David will look after me."

Back from the hospital two hours, I was tired and irritable. We were sitting eating at the kitchen table. Esther's mouth was puckered like a bulldog's from the excess cheese pizza she had stuffed into it. Beside me, Rachael was devouring a bowl of pasta. To keep them company, I nibbled a cracker.

Every few minutes Rachael's hand went down to rub Roamy, whimpering beside her. I knew that if I were not watching, she would have given him a few forkfuls at this stage. Looking deprived and woebegone, he trundled away to the living room and lay between the couch and the wall.

"I'd like to go back to the hospital to make sure Nana is really awake," I said. David had phoned to tell me she was out of 'Intensive Care,' and in a ward. The nurses had said she would sleep a lot so visitors were superfluous. But still I wanted to see for myself.

Esther said, "But who'll look after us if you go? We'll be all on our own. Cor won't be here long more."

"Esther. Did we ever leave you on your own?"

"Yes." She squared her shoulders. "*Dad* never left us alone but you did." Her finger stabbed in my direction.

"Don't point." Reflex response to a serious accusation.

"Remember the time Rach was in hospital getting her tonsils out. While I was watching telly, you went into Circle supermarket. You brought home three bottles, wine or whiskey or something."

You'd think from the way she was talking I was a bad parent. The pizza sauce smelled acrid, bitter, like Esther's tone. Had Cora heard? No. Thank God. The kitchen door was closed and she

68

had said she was going to tidy the nook under the stairs.

I remembered the time she was talking about well. I had spent a wakeful night at Rachael's bedside. When David relieved me the following evening, I was exhausted from worry, needing to relax. The alcohol had done the trick. After a few drinks, I had packed Esther off to bed and slept soundly through the night.

Cora came in from the hall and saved me from having to reply. "Letters for you." She turned them over in her hand. "I'm afraid Roamy got a hold of them. They must have been on the floor since the postman threw them in."

"I thought he had got out of the habit of chewing everything in sight," I said.

I focused on one, a large C4 envelope, now covered with teeth marks.

"Roamy." I pushed the biscuits away, got up and walked towards the living room and the couch. I guess I needed a diversion from the threat the letter held and poor Roamy was it. Smart dog that he is, he refused to budge.

"Roamy." My pitch rose. "Come here."

"He's giving us the two fingers," I said when he loudly emitted gas which stank the room to New Jerusalem.

"Two paws you mean," Esther said before she clamped her own two fingers to her nostrils. "Pee-you. Yuck."

I knew already how Esther reacted to untimely bodily emissions but this time I knew she was play-acting.

She got up from the table and threw a morsel of pizza into the bin. "Ugh. Smell is disgusting." She ran towards the tin box of clothes pegs sitting on the windowsill, and fastened one to her nostrils. Through nasal tones she said, "Mom, you've frikened the shit out of the poor dog."

Having done his worst, Roamy sidled out from behind the couch, his tongue lolling imploringly.

I suddenly experienced a surge of anger; I hadn't known the brush was within my reach until I felt it in my hand. As I held it above his head and saw him cower, I was conscious of a feeling of power. Here was something over which I *had* control.

Esther, the smirk wiped from her face, pulled the clothes peg off her nose and said, "Mom. Don't hit him, Mom." Her face had gone from being full of devilment to being pale with shock. "You didn't use the brush even when he chewed your good boot. Mom?"

"Bold dog." I lowered the brush.

He lay on his back for a tickle.

Rachael sank to her knees and played a tune on his breast. Then she planted a kiss on his nose and he slobbered all over her.

Cora had left the letters on top of the television set.

They lay piled there, the C4 on the bottom. On the day before my radio interview a similar one had arrived. It had been held together by a sticker picturing a large cabbage. One, before that, had a sticker with flowers splashed across it. I felt the colour drain from my face. My midriff tightened. Better get it over with and open it.

Esther said, "I wish Dad was here."

"Give it a rest, Essie." Rachael displayed an unusual asperity.

"Okay then. I won't open my mouth anymore. So there!"

"You're holding that letter funny, Mom. You'd think it was going to bite you." Rachael looked puzzled.

Cora was unusually authoritative. "Esther. Go up and change the water for the gerbils," she commanded. "Rachael, do the same for the hamster."

"Cora, you know their names. Mine is Thunderball and Rachael's is ..."

"Esther. Just go," I said, trying to appear normal.

"I *do* wish Dad was here," Esther said loudly as she left the living room. I heard her stomp up the stairs with Rachael trailing after her. "Even Roamy isn't safe in this house," she shouted.

Cora, her face screwed in a frown, left the room.

I was glad to be on my own. I took hold of the long white envelope I knew was our credit card statement. David had arranged that it would be paid directly from our bank account. When he was doing it himself, he ended up paying interest on late payments. The new arrangement meant that our account had always to be in credit.

Scanning through it, I noticed that it was quite high. It would be too soon for the bills from my American trip to have gone through. David had been spending while I was away.

Another envelope had a Mickey Mouse transfer and childish writing that told me it would be addressed to Esther or Rachael. I saw, *Esther Goldstein... Boston, MA...* scrawled on the left-hand corner of the letter. I liked getting letters from Granny Goldstein. Shoving it into my pocket, I put the others aside and went into the hall.

My breath caught. I would soon have no choice but to open the suspect letter. I felt as if I were about to fall over a precipice. Exercise was good for stress. "Esther, Rachael, we'll go for a walk with Roamy." My voice as it carried up the stairs was deliberately light.

"Who'll be here if Dad calls?" Esther's question was full of resentment.

"I will," Cora shouted back. She stopped cleaning under the stairs and came to stand in front of me. "But I'll have to leave when you get back." She looked at my expression. "Not bad news I hope?"

"No, No." I fancied her face fell.

"Thank God. We've enough bad news with the butcher."

"Sorry?"

"Surely you've heard about Jimmy Ford. Hasn't he a tumour the size of a golf ball in his head. Poor fella. His wife is expectin'. Think it's breach. And her mother only died last year. A lovely woman. His brother stole the five thousand from that poor eighty-year-old a couple of years ago. Goes to show you. No matter what they say, there's someone up there – watchin'."

David would consider such an idea *garbage*.

Esther stomped down the stairs. "I've fed Thunderball. As ordered. *And* I cleaned out his cage."

I murmured, "That was quick." She stank of urine-soaked sawdust. To make amends for the debacle with Roamy earlier, I smiled. "I'd say it needed it, Essie."

My banter won her over and she relaxed under my atoning hug. "While we're waiting for Rachael, you can go and wash your hands."

"So my hands are dirty now, are they?" Even before she went into the kitchen, my wayward daughter had contorted her face into a grimace. I heard a splurge of water, then the clanking of the paper-towel holder as it gyrated on the worktop from the fury of her pulling.

The rapid change in Esther's mood from compliance to resistance was like that between chrysalis and butterfly. My poor comparison was, I knew, prompted by the glimpse I had caught of a caterpillar on the flap of the letter I had yet to open.

After slamming the door of the kitchen after her, Esther stood before me and held her palms close enough to my nose for me to smell scented soap. "They're clean. Want to check?"

Before I could answer, Cora interrupted. "Murdered you should be, Esther." She had such an expression of disbelief that, despite her behaviour, I pitied my child. "Why did you have to put that gerbil beside the curtains? I've just been in your room this minute and he's them half chewed."

Esther's retort was swift. "It couldn't have been this minute Cora because I put his cage over by the radiator and he has now *eschewed* them. Get it. *Eschew* ..."

Cora drew in her breath in bewilderment.

"It means keeping clear ..."

"Yes Esther, we get it." My pretence at *bonhomie* was being sorely tested. I felt like strangling her.

Cora muttered something about the calamity of having an English teacher for a mother and children who were too *glic* by half. She heaved a sigh and her chest expanded like an inflated balloon. "Whatever about eschewing," she said, "he has sawdust all over the floor." Her voice became more guttural. "Who do you think will clean it up? James Bond?" With that parting shot she hurled open the door to the utility room.

I turned to Rachael, who had just come downstairs and had missed all the excitement. "Let's go, kiddies. A breath of fresh air will do us all good."

Esther said, "Wonder who the letters are from? Hope there's a birthday party. Half the people I invited to mine last year haven't invited me back."

If we opened one we would have to open them all. "They'll wait, Esther." My voice quaked and for a second I felt terribly alone. "They'll be still here when we get back from our walk."

"Your jacket is still on the top of your chest of drawers where you threw it yesterday. Get mine as well. It's on the bed in my room," Rachael shouted upstairs to Esther.

"And my trench. It's in my wardrobe. My blue scarf, too," I said. The shock of having received another ominous letter had made me feel cold.

I took the coat from Esther when she came downstairs and put it on, winding the scarf around the back of my neck and securing it under my chin.

"Take the short lead, Rachael. You know he hasn't sense enough to stay in from the cars." In a tone that mimicked her Nana, Esther continued, "We have chanced it once too often and still brought him back alive but 'he who loves danger will perish in it.'"

"Oh! Quit the editorialising, Esther." I sounded sharper than intended.

"Yeah. Nana used to say that to Mom when she was young. Didn't she, Mom?"

"She sure did." Deliberately I *eschewed* thoughts of my mother. After all, it was my childhood, not theirs.

"See you, Cora," we called as I pulled the door behind us.

It was a dull evening, low unbroken cloud; the light filtering through was charcoal, silver and grey, the colours of lead. Esther and Rachael skipped on ahead, Roamy loping behind them. Like a chameleon, Esther had changed back from an old woman to being a kid again.

I envied their ability to avoid floods and puddles as they hurried down the drive. Though I tried to pick my steps, I still squelched in mud. When I reached the road, I almost slipped on greasy dead leaves from an overhanging beech. I walked close to the ditch as cars sped by. Usually I loved this walk; oncoming cars hadn't scared me at all.

"Race ya," Esther challenged Rachael.

"Here, Mom. You hold Roamy," Rachael said and the two ran off.

The biting cold razed my skin. I had forgotten to bring my gloves and though I blew on my knuckles, my breath failed to warm them. I jammed my free hand into my pocket.

There, I felt the spare key of the box I usually leave in room seven at school. Some pupils were too shy to ask a question about sex in Health Education class so I had requested the handyman to make a box where they could put their queries, usually notes crumpled or sticky with chewing gum. I used to consult David about the more difficult ones. He had loved me so much then.

The key reminded me of the one to the booze cabinet in my parents' house. My father, though he didn't drink himself, insisted we have alcohol available for visitors. The cabinet had scarcely ever been opened and he had kept the key out of sight. At fifteen, I found it, used it and stole as much booze as I could without being found out. I had found a way to make my life tolerable.

Had that been the beginning or the end of my troubles? I didn't have a drink problem, I told myself. A tipple now and again helped me to unwind. I often gave it up for months. There were times when I drank too much, of course, but didn't everyone?

"I won. I won." Esther appeared and grabbed the dog's lead. "I'm going over to the sandpit to Rachael, Mom. I came back for him," She jerked Roamy. "See ya, Mom. Coming, Rach."

She forgot to look before crossing the road and ran into the path of a speeding car.

The driver jammed on the brakes and stopped within inches of her. He lowered the window and shouted, "Did nobody teach you to be careful crossing the road?" His exasperated look at me, her careless mother, spoke volumes. I waved at him, a pointless gesture that left my hand hovering in the air for a couple of seconds.

Then delight replaced embarrassment as I looked at the driver of the car coming in the opposite direction. My pleasure at seeing David behind the wheel changed to uncertainty; the curling blonde hair visible from the back seat belonged to a female, busy talking to a child.

David with another woman made all my fears real, confirmed my distrust of my husband. I stood very still, as if not moving would make me invisible.

The whole incident took place very quickly. One minute they were speeding past, and then they were gone. Unanswered questions I had tried to banish about David's whereabouts the weekend I had returned from America came back full force. I felt sick. "Rachael, Esther," I said, "let's go home."

"Coming, Mom."

My feet dragged. I used to trust David implicitly. He always said that one woman was enough to handle. Though occasionally I had entertained the idea of his being unfaithful, I had never really believed it. Nor, I determined, would I believe it now. He was my David. We had entrusted ourselves to each other for better or for worse. There was a letter waiting to be opened. I had enough real worries.

I turned to chat to Rachael and Esther but they were too busy arguing.

"Snail. Rachael is a snai...l."

"Oh, shut up about it, Essie. It was only a race." Rachael's voice shook. "You're a snail. Rachael is a s ..."

Rachael grabbed a lump of clay and flung it into Esther's face. "There. That should shut you up."

Quick as lightning, Esther scooped mud from a puddle and threw it.

Too bad for me that her aim was terrible; a dollop of oozy mud landed on my cheek, ran onto my chin and into my scarf.

Roamy circled around barking and yapping like a mad dog.

Though we must have looked a sorry sight as we trudged home, I was glad in a way that Esther and Rachael had had a tussle. It was good to see Rachael standing up for herself. It was only my face that was dirty because of their mud fight, but I could use it as an excuse to delay opening the post for another while.

They followed me upstairs. Esther went into their bathroom. Rachael disappeared into her bedroom and closed the door. I went into the en suite and showered.

Later, when the three of us were back downstairs in the kitchen/living room, resplendent in clean clothes, Rachael held up the post. "Can we open ours now? Esther really wants to see if she's been invited to ..."

"Okay."

Friends again, the girls lost interest in my letter as soon as they had their own. "Mom, we're going to watch telly."

Rachael ran back. "Oh, nearly forgot." She presented me with my oversized envelope. The coloured sticker of a caterpillar, used as a seal, made my heart career crossways.

I focused on the caterpillar's wormlike resemblance, its infinite pairs of legs, its strong jaw, and deemed it ugly. Ugly and menacing. My hands trembled as I ripped the correspondence open.

The calendar was similar to the one I had received in the middle of October. Again, dates that meant nothing to me were circled in red pen with a question mark beside each circle. I shivered. 'A goose walked over your grave,' my mother would have said. I wished my discomfort could be explained away that easily.

Rita sometimes sent humorous cards that only made sense to both of us. Once, when I was in the middle of revising Keats's poem 'Ode To a Nightingale' with a Leaving Cert class, I had received a picture in the post of a man, who looked a bit like David, hollering that he couldn't see 'what flowers were at his feet'. I understood immediately that she was joking about David's keep fit regime. But weeks ago, when they had first arrived, my instincts told me that these calendars were not a joking note from a friend.

It had been a long day, endless; I was bone tired. So much had happened since I got up this morning. Images of the woman who had been in the car with David reappeared. I imagined the scenario when he returned. I would say to him, "You'll never guess what happened today."

"With your father in the hospital?" he'd say in an uninterested tone. "You mean the way he was washing his hands?"

"No, not that."

"Something at school? The principal was reluctant to give you the time off." He would stifle a yawn. Or then again, maybe he'd be attentive and interested like he had been in the hospital. Months of his unpredictable reactions had left me jumpy about how he would behave.

I felt fearful at the thought of pursuing the conversation, afraid that he would think me unreasonable. An unreasonable wife who was not worth loving. *We were out walking and you passed in the car. There was a woman with you.* The words echoed in my mind, but would remain unspoken; I hadn't the guts to confront him.

He was moody because he was going through a mid-life crisis. It was patronising, I knew, to use such a tag to explain his behaviour but it was the only way I could deal with his refusal to talk about work, his desire always to be on the go instead of being at home.

So what if he were having an affair, I told myself. It would end. Men were like big toddlers; they played with novelty toys but in the end went back to the teddy with the gouged eye and one leg. Not very flattering, I knew, but I wanted him no matter how unsteady our relationship. He was as much a part of me as my spine.

The house seemed empty as I climbed the stairs. In our bedroom, I hunted through my panties and took out the envelopes I had put there. I would take them downstairs, tear them up and throw them in the rubbish. Tomorrow was bin day. Decision made, I decided to have a drink. To celebrate!

My mouth was dry as I reached into the cavernous drawer where I stored my summer clothes and, from beneath them, took out a bottle of gin. The liquid was reduced by an eighth when I took it from my lips. *Feck* the begrudgers. I was not going to feel guilty about a little *deorum*. I was holding down a good job and living a normal life. My mind locked onto the consoling thoughts like the vice grip in David's toolbox.

Those with drink problems, alcoholics, were people you passed guzzling wine on the street or sprawled drunk on the path. There was nothing to be concerned about. Soothed by the alcohol, I changed my mind about ridding myself of the calendars. I would keep them. Maybe I'd show them to David sometime and we would laugh about all this.

I folded the envelopes, put them back under my panties and took another slug of the gin.

Alcoholic? I wasn't an alcoholic. I wasn't that stupid. I had a first-class honours degree, and had a book published. My drinking was under control. My husband was the only one who thought it wasn't.

Jo Joe's pub was dim and comforting, lit only by a turf fire. A bar faced customers as they came in. The walls were covered with old billboards and handbills advertising goods from a penny to a shilling. A corridor led to the toilets.

An old man with his hat on wheezed over to the fire from where he had been standing by the bar, opened his mouth and shot a lump of mucus into the flames.

"He thinks it's a spittoon," I joked.

"Poor fellow," Rita said.

Following her gaze, I saw a half-consumed pint, a short beside it, in front of where he'd been standing.

"A bit too fond of the jar, I'd say," she said. "It's a bit early to be having a chaser."

I ordered a glass of beer though I longed for something stronger. "What'll you have?" I asked.

"Spritzer." I'm going to get a table by the fire.

The jukebox in the corner playing 'You Took a Fine Time to Leave me, Lucille,' began to get on my nerves. "Joe, could you turn that down?"

Joe, co-owner of the pub with his wife Josephine (Jo for short), came out from behind the bar, touched me on the shoulder and said, "Anything for a good customer, Mrs. Goldstein."

Was he implying that I was a heavy drinker? I used to like Joe. Thought him an amiable person, a good businessman. But now I felt like telling him to 'Begone, Joe.' Biblical language. 'Begone, Satan.' David's Jewish influence breaking through!

The drinks in my hand, I sat next to Rita. Perched beside me, with her legs crossed, she looked settled on her chair while I fidgeted on the edge of mine. Her red hair, partially pinned up, shone like a beacon in the dimness.

Though conscious that a wrong word from her could cause me to crack like an eggshell, I blurted out, "Rit, things are bad between me and David."

She looked at me for a second. "Hold that thought. I have to go to the loo. Back in a few minutes."

Her abrupt departure told me that she was unsure what to say and needed time to think.

While she was gone, I re-enacted the scene uppermost in my mind – last night's confrontation with David.

I was the one who should have had the high moral ground when he came back, supposedly from the hospital. Ironically, I had ended up feeling guilty. He accused me of being drunk and out of control. I'm forced to admit that my words were slurring a little, but I knew what I was doing. It got interesting when I mentioned seeing him in the car.

"Yes. You did see me in the car with a woman ..."

"Who was she?" On hearing my anxious tone, his softened.

"Pamela Crawley."

"What the hell were you doing with her?"

"I needed some advice."

I had heard of erring husbands coming up with novel excuses but this one took the biscuit. "Why her? Advice on what, for Godsakes? If she were dumpy and grey haired would you have been as quick to seek her out?"

His eyes held a look of desperation. If I had been less perplexed and angry, I would have felt sorry for him.

He spoke slowly, chose his words carefully. "Remember when you were in America?"

Remember? How could I forget? I wanted him to stop. If he were going to make a confession, I didn't want to hear it.

"When I told you I was in Westport ..."

"David. Tell me." I had changed from not wanting to hear, to not being able to wait.

When he did manage to make the announcement, I found it anti-climactic.

"I was in Dublin. At a course on addiction."

"Addiction?" I was genuinely flummoxed. "Why?"

He threw his hands in the air. "Because of you. Why do you think? That you have to ask proves my point. You've no idea that you have a drink problem."

The shopping bag with Dublin scrawled across it haunted my dreams.

"You know the saying. If you're not part of the solution, you're part of the problem. I had to do something. Otherwise there's no point in hanging around."

It was the first time he'd ever mentioned, even indirectly, the possibility of leaving. "First time I have ever heard you suggest there was something you couldn't solve." The hateful assertion reverberated in my head.

Rita, interrupting my thoughts, regained her seat and continued as if there had been no break in the conversation. "I'm sorry you're having problems, Teresa."

I felt myself steady under the influence of her normality.

"I've noticed recently that you were more tense. When I'm with David and you now, I feel as if I'm walking on thin ice. Afraid I'll say something wrong." She reached over and touched my hand.

"I think he's going to leave me." There, I'd said the unmentionable and, unlike Lot's wife, had failed to dissolve into a pillar of salt.

Rita, who usually only drank a spritzer, said, "I'll join you in a beer."

"I'm changing. I can't stomach this." I slid the empty glass to one side. "Get me a gin. No tonic."

Rita threw me a strange look.

I opened my bag, took money from my purse and handed it to her. "I'll pay for it."

Her face turned white. "You know it's not that, Teresa." She tilted her head to one side and appraised me from under her long eyelashes. "It's just that you always say you don't like to drink during the day. Remember the last time when ..."

"If it's a problem, I'll get it myself."

"Okay. Okay. I'll get it." She went up to order.

Who was she to question my drinking habits? It was nobody's business how much I drank. I knew my limits. And it was now after three o'clock; I had resolved not to drink before three o'clock no matter what happened.

"Thanks, Rit," I said as she plonked the drinks on the table and sat down.

"What makes you think he's going to leave? Is he interested in anybody else?"

Trust Rita to be tactful. 'Interested' had an academic feel. David is interested in the Torah. Granny Goldstein would have said, "Is he screwing somebody else? or "Is he getting laid?"

"He's been out a lot lately. There's always some excuse. You know he's a trainer for the under-sixteen football team. Some drivel about wanting to belong. Wanting to do something for the community." The straight gin I was gulping softened the edges of things. The pub, Rita, and Jo became the nicest people in the world, David the nastiest. "I used to think it cute that a Bostonian Jew had got involved in life in Claremorris but now I just find it a pain."

Rita opened her mouth to say something but I pre-empted her.

"Any night he's not home I'm on tenterhooks wondering what time he'll appear. I've stopped keeping Esther and Rachael up to see him. One time it was midnight and they were still waiting for him to come in."

Rita's eyes registered disappointment. There was her usual take-stock pause. "I'm surprised at David. It seems unlike him. He was always so," she paused, "dependable."

"I thought things would improve after I came back from my American book tour but they haven't."

"You isolated yourself a little when you were writing the book, Teresa. Maybe he just got fed up of it all."

"Whose side are you on for Chrissakes?" The gin had lost its soothing effect. Rita was being nasty. "Do you want another?"

"I've to go. We'll talk about this again tomorrow. Somewhere more private."

"Not in a pub, you mean." I took pity on her. "Alright, off you go home to your kids. I'll just have one more."

"Teresa, you're driving."

"So? If the cops catch me, I'll use Fintan's name. What's the good of having a cousin in the guards otherwise?"

"Teresa, stop acting tough. You might kill someone."

I knew her concern was genuine when she added, "My clan can wait for me for a while. I'll hang on; we can have a coffee and leave together."

There was no more talk about David. We both drank strong coffees and ate a chocolate *éclair* each. Rita told me about the recent bonus Noel had and of his ambition to come home permanently.

Her car was parked in the school grounds so we parted outside the pub, Rita to drive over the border through Milltown to Tuam, me to remain in Mayo.

The caffeine so invigorated me that I forgot I had alcohol taken until I emerged into the air. The blast of cold made me feel a little woozy. I used to be able to drink three times as much as this and not be affected.

At the end of the street, behind the commemoration plaque to the men of 1916, was another pub called The Pit where candles were the only light. Where you could steal in unnoticed for a quickie. Unnerved by the temptation, I walked in the other direction and took a roundabout way to my car.

I was marvelling at the lack of food hygiene in a butcher's window, where cooked food was side by side with raw meat when, from the corner of my eye, I noticed Kieran Crawley across the street. He was walking in the same direction. Afraid that he had seen me, I resisted the urge to retreat into a hardware shop selling galvanised buckets and clothes pegs and headed, instead, for a second-hand bookshop further on.

Inside, the shelves were chock-a-block, mostly with outdated paperbacks of best-selling authors, plus shelves on crime and romance, as-good-as-new volumes on self-improvement, and some detective stories. Anxious to appear nonchalant, I picked up a tattered Ruth Rendell and promptly left it down again.

A copy of 'The L Shaped Room', and beside it the other two books in the trilogy, caught my eye. This was an unexpected surprise; I had wanted the final volume for ages. I was flicking through it when I heard the door open.

The newcomer said, "I'm searching for a copy of *Papillon*. Someone borrowed mine and forgot to return it. "

The voice, silky and deferential, was Kieran Crawley's.

"Crime section, Sir." I knew that Kieran Crawley collected butterflies. Caught them with his net or bred them, classified them into genus, set and arranged them in drawers. I had seen his Irish collection once, Red Admirals, Peacocks, and Small Whites. l remembered him pointing them out to me, but I was unable to place when or where it had happened.

He smiled, a twist of his mouth. "Teresa, my dear. What are *you* doing here?"

"Buying books." I waved my paperback.

When he heard my glib response, he straightened his shoulders. "Of course," he said softly. "Of course."

"I really have to get going." I paid for my book and as I waited for the assistant to put it in a bag, he came behind me again.

"My darling Teresa, let me buy you a drink. It's not often we meet this early." He put his hand on my arm.

"Sorry, Kieran, it's not a good time for me. I have to go home." I had to work with the creep. Couldn't be too rude. I was glad I had so little to drink.

"Come on. Just one."

"I don't feel like it," I repeated.

"The Pit. One?"

"No. I said no. Thank you."

He shrugged. His bulbous eyes swept over me. I felt like one of his winged victims.

"Fair enough. Another time." Then he mouthed what had

become his usual jibe, "*Sláinte.*"

I had hurried towards the bookshop, now I ran towards the car park.

My hand was shaky as I pulled down the rear view mirror and looked at my face that was blotched and grey. The skin under my eyes was transparent and there was flakiness at the tip of my nose. I looked my age with a few years added on. Sighing, I turned the key in the ignition, pressed my foot on the accelerator and zoomed into Sloane Street.

The sky darkened and there was a sudden downpour. Rain pounded so heavily on the windscreen that the wipers became sluggish. I slowed. Although I was going at a snail's pace, I could hardly see anything. I barely recognised the library where I went most Saturdays with Rachael and Esther.

As I drove towards a zebra crossing, the flashing lights seemed to dribble down the windscreen. I found it difficult to know whether the woman standing at its edge wanted to cross or not. She put her foot on the white line, then changed her mind and walked away. I was about to drive off when she reappeared and, without any dawdling, rushed across the road. I didn't honk; she reminded me of my mother whom, in my anxiety about David, I hadn't thought about since last night.

I was heading towards the open road when the rain changed to hailstones. About four miles on, a woman wearing a cloth handkerchief, knotted at the corners, on her head, a padded khaki jacket and a man's trousers, held up her hand to stop oncoming traffic. A teenager held a paper the size of *The Farmer's Journal*, over his hair with one hand while with the other he waved a stick at a herd of sorrowful cows with udders down to their knees.

I thought of the carcass in the butcher's window. Perhaps I should consider following David's example and become a vegetarian. David! My cheeks warmed in anticipation. I wondered if he would be there when I got home.

As abruptly as it had started, the shower ended. The watery sun, that had been low in the sky when I headed towards

Claremorris, had fallen further into shadow behind the roadside trees and streaked the sky with seashell pink.

The light weakened gradually. Trees merged with the black. I switched on the headlights to full.

I was twenty minutes from home. This part of the road was narrow, pot holed, unlit and flanked by dark woods. Rounding a bend, I found myself tailgating a tractor and trailer loaded with cement jumbo bags. The farmer plunged the tractor into a pothole. Mud splattered my windscreen, forcing me to brake.

The wipers smeared dirt across the glass. I pumped the knob at the top of the indicator switch but the reservoir was empty. My hands tightly gripped the steering wheel.

I was tired. The sojourn in the pub seemed long ago. "Goddamnit." I envied the farmer when he turned into his comfortable house while I had to continue my journey peering through filth.

Up ahead, a couple of miles from the sharp bend, I knew there was a petrol station and an adjoining shop where I could get some windscreen washer and pick up a couple of bottles of wine.

After I turned the corner, I felt more relaxed. Unboxed cassettes lay in the pocket of the dash; I knew exactly which one was where. Reaching for an original recording of Marlene Dietrich, *The Best of Times*, I put it into the player. 'Underneath The Lamplight,' she crooned. On the straight again and soothed by the music, I kept my speed under forty.

The neon sign over the pumps lit up the night. I parked directly in front of the window and walked towards the entrance. A bell trilled as I opened the door.

A young man in a designer tracksuit sat behind the counter reading a magazine. He looked up as I approached. "Can I help you?" he asked.

"Windscreen washer," he repeated after me. "Right. Won't be a minute." He opened a door into the adjoining garage, letting an unpleasant smell of oil and petrol drift into the shop. I longed to be home, reading a book with a drink in my hand.

The young man re-appeared carrying a large bottle. "No concentrate," he muttered. "You'll have to do with this."

David usually bought this stuff. I hadn't a clue what my options were so I took what I was given. I picked out two bottles of wine and paid him. The bells cheeped again as he opened the door for me.

I left the bottles on the passenger seat, opened the bonnet and poured water into the windscreen washer container. Back in the car, I pushed the washer button, turned on the wipers and, feeling relieved, checked for oncoming traffic before pulling onto the road.

The motorbike seemed to come from nowhere, tyres screaming, shimmying from side to side like a drunk, trying to avoid me.

The Tradia shuddered as the bike hit me at an angle on the passenger side. The driver and pillion passenger were thrown to the ground. Fear thick in my throat, I jammed on the brakes.

I switched off the engine and unbuckled my seat belt. Sickened by the thought that I may have seriously injured somebody, I got out of the car and stood in the darkness trying to assess the situation.

A young woman lay in a foetal position on the ground, her eyes closed as if she were in bed. The fanciful notion that the mist could turn out to be her shroud galloped through my mind.

The motorbike driver got to his feet immediately and took off his helmet; he turned towards the girl and knelt on the ground beside her. "Eibhlin, are you alright? Jesus Christ, are you alright?"

She opened her eyes, straightened her body and touched her arm. Then she smiled an uncertain, tremulous smile.

Relief surged through me when I saw that she was conscious and seemed to have suffered only minor injuries.

"I'll call an ambulance and the cops," the young shop assistant said with an authority that belied his youth.

A man carrying a pitchfork ran from the barn beside a nearby house. "Eibhlin? Holy mother of God, what happened?"

He towered over her. "Don't move. You might have something broken. Stay put until help comes."

When she said, "I'm fine, Jimmy. Got a shock. That's all," and put out her hand for her boyfriend to help her up, my thinking of a shroud seemed absurd.

"Will you stay where you are, I'm tellin' ya. The ambulance will be here in a minute."

The pitchfork man, countenance like the devil, then turned his attention to me.

"Bet you're the returned Yank who teaches in the convent down the road. Heard about the *gluaisteán*. Couldn't be two of you with the wheel on the wrong side, I'm thinking."

I remained silent.

Cars dipped their headlights and slowed. Motorists peered through their side windows.

The ambulance came quickly and stopped in front of the garage. A man in the passenger seat got out and went over to the young woman. His examination of her was, to me, perfunctory but seemed to satisfy him. He said in a no-nonsense tone, "Come on young lady. There are no bones broken that I can see but we'll take you in for a thorough check-up." He and the driver strapped her into a stretcher. In a few moments, she was settled in the ambulance.

A blue light shone; the engine revved and, as the ambulance sped off, the siren sounded.

I heard the pitchfork man say to the boy, "I'll go and get the car. We'll follow her in as soon as the guards have talked to you." He sounded kind but after his comments about my left-hand drive, I chose not to get into a conversation with him.

I leant against the back of the car. The smell of petrol strong in my nostrils acted like smelling salts and revived me.

Twenty minutes later, two guards came on the scene. They parked the *Garda* car in the space vacated by the ambulance, left the engine running and the lights still turning.

The older man, whom I recognised as Sergeant Ivers, said to his companion, "Let's keep these good people moving."

The guard dutifully directed stalled traffic quickly past the obstruction.

After taking notes of the skid marks and the position of the vehicles, Sergeant Ivers spoke to the motorcyclist and, with orders to call into the *garda* station in the morning, permitted him to go to the hospital.

Next he turned to me. "Your particulars?" He pulled at his crotch. "Kevin's a nice lad. He could have been killed." He looked at the car. "How could you have missed the motorbike?"

I felt suddenly cold. I stood up straight. "I'm always careful when I'm pulling out onto a road. When I looked through the passenger window, there was nothing coming." I heard the quiver in my voice. "Please could we get this over with? I want to go home."

The sergeant raised his notebook to the ready position, then changed his mind and went over to where the motorbike lay on its side on the ground.

I noticed for the first time that it was big and heavy.

His face took on a more serious expression. "A lighter bike and it would have been worse. That's probably what saved them." Then he raised his official notebook again and asked me for accident details.

As clearly and concisely as I could, I told him what had happened. While I was speaking, his patient demeanour reminded me of a psychotherapist. My account ended with the assertion that the motorcyclist was going too fast.

"That as may be." He appraised me. "Any drink taken?"

He noticed my hesitation. "Right. I'll have to breathalyse you," he said. Before I quite knew what was happening he was shoving a tube towards me. After I had breathed into it, he examined it with narrowed eyes.

What if it were positive? I thought.

A barely audible sigh escaped Sergeant Ivers' lips. "At least you're sober. That's something."

I breathed deeply, hoping oxygen would calm me.

The sergeant shifted on his feet. "You'll be hearing from us," he said.

When I got back into the car and turned on the ignition, Marlene Dietrich resumed where she had left off. I stopped the tape.

Though I had realised that Cora would be in a tizzy about my being late, I drove at a steady twenty mph. When I arrived home, I looked more closely at the damage to my car. It was worse than I had imagined. The passenger door would have to be replaced. The greeting I got when I opened the door of the house did nothing to comfort me.

"I thought it would be at Mass I'd be this minute, not sitting here waiting for you." Cora rushed from the sitting room. "I've been watching for the car for the last hour. I thought you'd never come. I'll won't make Knock now before the vigil is over." Her coat was on, ready for flight.

"Sorry, Cora. I got delayed."

A slammed door was her reply.

"Is there anything wrong, Mom? You look awful pale." Rachael perched on my knee when I sat on the settee.

"No, I'm fine." I felt a consuming need to crush her to me. Her muscles felt pliable under my arms.

"Mo...m?"

"Sorry, I don't know my own strength."

I turned to Esther watching from another chair. "Essie. You next."

She came slowly but her face broke into a smile so wide it revealed her gums and was enchanting in its spontaneity. "No mauling, right?"

I pulled her to me. The smell of talcum powder was strong. It struck me that I hadn't known she used anything other than soap. Of late, there was a lot I didn't know.

I let her slip from me as unwillingly as if she were a life raft and I was drowning. In as normal a tone as I could muster, I said, "Why don't you go and do your homework. Then you can watch a video."

"Oh, goody. Which one will we watch, Rachael?"

As soon as they were gone, the shock of the accident hit me again. I had to have a drink. I thought of the bottles of wine in the front of the car but felt like something stronger.

The bottle of brandy was exactly where I had left it after my last swilling episode. David could not begrudge me a drink after such a nightmare. He was already late home, which usually meant that he wouldn't be in for hours.

The amber liquid slid down my throat and deadened the coldness inside me.

Five minutes later David opened the front door.

"Hi, Tess! Where are you?" He stuck his head round the door of the sitting room. "Oh! You're here."

My eyebrows lifted in surprise and delight at his timely homecoming. He was wearing the green and royal blue jacket I had bought for him when we were living in the States.

"I know it's ages since I've been home this early but all that's going to change." His tone was upbeat.

"Oh, David." I reached out my arms to him in much the same way as I had done to Esther and Rachael. He came slowly into them. "Thank God you're here."

"I'm glad I'm here too."

His arms wrapped around me and, for a few seconds, I felt as if I were in a cocoon. Needing to feel the touch of his lips, I slackened my hold on him and inclined my head backwards inviting him to kiss me.

He dropped his arms to his side and stepped away from me.

I winced at his expression of distaste.

"You smell like a brewery. God, Teresa, have you no shame?"

I grabbed his arm. "David, David. You don't understand. A motorbike ..."

"Where did you go after school? You were supposed to be getting off early." His eyes sparked with anger.

"I came home. I ..."

"I called you at three o'clock; there was nobody here. When I called again at five, Cora answered."

"I went to the pub after school with Rita but it's not what you think."

"Isn't it?" He shook off my arm.

He was jeering at me and, somehow, I knew he was jeering at himself too. For having come home early. For thinking we could start again. "I had only one gin and then we had coffee. Ask Rita if you don't believe me."

He wrinkled his nose. "That's why you stink of brandy," he said without inflection.

I realised that the force rising in me was an angry hurt. "David. Will you let me explain?"

He rubbed his hand over his face. "Okay. Go on."

"You know the petrol station on the way from Ballindine? I was pulling out from there and a motorbike ran into me. Two people were knocked down."

"I don't believe this. You were pissed and you knocked someone down. And you will expect me to defend you. Are they dead?" His face was raw, contorted by rage, and for a moment I thought he was going to hit me.

We stood within inches of each other but were miles apart. My voice, even to my own ears, was coldly polite. "It was not my fault and I was not pissed, as you so graphically put it. And no. Nobody is dead."

I wanted to bolt from the room and get out from under his glare but I knew that he wouldn't let me. David had lost his temper before and it wasn't something I wanted to experience again. I made myself stand still.

"It doesn't matter anymore. You've become a lush. I have had as much as I can take." His white lips flared from under his beard. "Where are the kids? Fobbed off with a video as usual?"

"Fobbed off? That's rich coming from someone who's never home."

"Teresa, I don't want to get into another slanging match. But I will say this and no more. Unless you do something about your drinking, I'll take Esther and Rachael and we'll be outa here."

So I'd been right when I told Rita I thought David was going to leave. Lucky Rita! She would be at home knitting her cardigan, lips pursed, counting stitches. He couldn't leave me. I fumbled for words as I grasped him by the arm again. "David."

He pushed my hand away and went to join my daughters.

I traipsed sluggishly up the stairs to the bedroom. Tears jabbed at my eyes as I uncorked my faithful bottle of gin.

The following morning the alarm clock woke me at the usual time but I pressed 'snooze', to keep the sound at bay for ten minutes. When it jingled again, I switched it off. The ceiling slowly tilted; I knew I had been right to put off facing the day.

My head collapsed back on the pillow. In an attempt to blot out the moving walls and ceiling, I shut my eyes again. But when I heard Cora's key in the door, I knew I would have to move or suffer an interrogation as to why I was not up. Taking a deep breath, I hauled myself out of bed and fled, slipper less, to the en suite.

After a shower, I felt a little better. At least the room decided to remain steady. But as I sat on the edge of the bed, I wondered if I ought to stretch out for another half-hour.

There was a pounding on the door; Rachael put her head round and shouted, "Mom, cooked breakfast, if you want some."

Scrambled eggs mixed with brandy and gin in the stomach of my imagination and both threatened to re-appear. "No, thanks, Rach. I'll pass."

I pulled on a green jumper over woollen slacks. In front of my wardrobe mirror, I plastered make-up onto my telltale red nose.

A cup of strong tea and a slice of toast would make me feel better, but this morning I was unable to face playing happy families. I decided to make a getaway. As I pulled the hall door after me, I could hear the hiss of the downstairs shower.

I lowered myself into the car, inserted the key in the ignition and turned it. The engine wouldn't start. It growled like Roamy when he is protecting his food, made a sputtering noise and died. I switched it on again but the sound was weaker so I turned it off.

94

I had no choice. I would have to seek David's help. It would take me half an hour to get to school and it was already a quarter to nine. I jumped out of the car and ran towards the house.

"Mom. I knew I heard the door close. Rachael's face crumbled like a chucked sweet paper. "Did you forget to say goodbye?"

"The bloody car won't start," I said.

"Language, Mom. Language," Esther scolded.

"Oh shut up," Rachael said, "Mom's late for school." She ran down the hall and knocked on the bathroom door. "Dad, Mom's car won't start."

"Be there in a minute."

Cora appeared, scowling, a dishcloth in her hand. "This house has gone mad," she said.

I retreated to the open air. Seconds later, David emerged, his hair still wet, wearing only a vest, trousers and socks. The sight of his tight muscles, flat stomach and bulging biceps made me feel unfit, middle-aged, cross. "What's wrong with it?"

"I'll have to look and see first." As he walked around to the driver's side of the car, he exclaimed, "No wonder the battery's flat. You left the lights on."

"I was upset after the accident and must have forgotten to turn them off."

"Suah." He shivered in the crisp morning cold. "I'll have to get jump leads."

"But I'll miss my first class."

He relented a little. "Okay. I'll run you to school,"

"What about work?"

"Vera will hold the fort."

"You're a saint," I said, without thinking.

"Only you could call a Jew a saint and think it a compliment."

"We'd better hurry," I said, "or my second years will be screaming their heads off."

A short while later, fully dressed and wearing a warm jacket, he was ready to go.

When I got into his car, I was determined to keep our exchanges civilised; I didn't speak except to answer the few words he directed to me.

The atmosphere became tenser as we passed the petrol station where the accident had happened.

"Were you breathalysed?" David's jaw was set in a grim line.

"I told you I was sober. You can check with the sergeant. You obviously don't believe me."

"Are there any other complications?"

"The man who came along was an uncle of the pillion passenger on the bike that crashed into me."

"There's nothing unusual about that. The country's so small everybody is related to everybody else."

"Very funny."

"I'm serious. Settling here was a madass stupid thing for me to have done. Goddammit, I'm still a stranger. No matter how hard I try, I'm treated as an outsider."

"David, I get that you're cheesed off with me. But would you stop blaming the whole country for something I've done."

But he was on a roll.

"Maybe if we were in Dublin or some big town, things would be different. If I weren't a lawyer, I wouldn't get a look in at all. The way things are looking I can see us hightailing it back to Boston."

"I lacked the courage to ask whom he meant by us. The kids and himself, or us, as in me too.

He continued, "In small towns everybody minds everybody's business."

That's it. Blame everybody except yourself, I thought. I felt the colour drain from my face; I knew it would return in angry blotches. "You're the ideal husband," I said, but my tone was empty of the teasing we used to engage in a year ago. "Everybody sees us as a couple, but we're not. People can be fooled. We hardly open our mouths to each other anymore. Except in a crisis."

"*You* may not open your mouth to talk, but you certainly open it to drink."

When we stopped at a T-junction near the school, I hissed, "I'll walk from here."

"Aren't we the big independent Miss, now that you're a few minutes away from work?" He turned and looked me in the eye. "Grab a cab this evening. I won't be collecting you."

Resolutely I got out of the car. From the pavement I barked, "Grab a cab my ass. You'd think we were in downtown Boston instead of the asshole of nowhere." I slammed the door before he had a chance to reply.

The day now appeared a darker grey. My briefcase felt full of rocks as I trudged the rest of the way to school.

Country girls, passengers from an early school bus, still wearing their coats, walked around the grounds in twos and threes, chatting and laughing. Others, books in hand, memorised their homework, their lips moving like the lips of nuns reciting Divine Office.

"Morning, morning." I pretended to be cheerful as I greeted those I met. A psychologist once told me that when the divide becomes too big between the public and the private self, it's time to take stock. Yet here I was, feeling like shit, acting like a *Bord Fáilte* representative. Once I allowed that negative reflection to intrude, others followed.

I worried about the accident.

Then agonised about David saying he regretted coming back to Ireland.

Also, my mother was coming home from hospital either today or tomorrow. My father was going to phone David at work when he knew for sure she was being discharged. With a jolt, I realised that, apart from the times I had set aside to visit her, I hadn't thought much about my mother.

The accident, David's discontent, my unease regarding my parents lingered all day when I went to class, when I ate my lasagne lunch, when I half listened to the principal discuss students who had broken the rule by going down to the village at dinnertime, when I tried to contribute a solution. By four o'clock, my mind was a blob of problems, real and imagined.

To add to my distress, I realised that I had no car. Rita would surely run me home, I consoled myself. I would be able to tell her about the accident, ask her opinion about David's behaviour.

As I walked from my Leaving Cert class, I came upon students lounging with their backs to the wall of the assembly area. "Who should you have now?" I was more curious than annoyed.

"Miss Canny," they chorused. "She's gone to Esker, Miss."

Rita. It was then I realised that I hadn't seen her all day. She was absent from lunch but she usually supervised that time on a Thursday. Now I recalled that she had taken the Transition Years for an overnight stay in the retreat house.

One girl said, "Miss, we had a free class. We didn't leave 'till the bell went."

"That's alright." She had misinterpreted my disappointment at Rita's absence for disapproval.

Suddenly a crowd of students, less restrained than the ones I had talked to, ran past carrying banners. They were dressed in blazing rainbow hues reminiscent of butterflies, their faces streaked with the 'colours of creation,' ready to take part in the ecology rally organised by the Mayo schools.

I recognised a little one from second year, dressed in brown and green, whose banner read, *Leaf me alone.* Another declared, *The sun has 5,000 million years to go, how long has the earth?* The lady proclaiming that particular message was dressed as a sunflower in bright saffron. Butterflies and flowers reminded me of the calendars in my drawer at home. My head began to throb. Calm down, I told myself. You're all over the place, having a bad day. Concentrate on getting a lift home.

Kieran Crawley lived sixteen miles from me and I was on his route. He was the obvious person to ask but I was reluctant to seek him out. A half hour in the car listening to him rabbit on about rare Fritillaries like the Heath and the Glanville failed to appeal to me. Also, there was the matter of my rudeness to him in the bookshop and of David being Pamela's patient.

David must have been furious with me to suggest getting a taxi when he knew how expensive it would be. Maliciously, I thought, of course, he's a Jew. I remembered a joke I heard as a child. Why are there so many corners in a synagogue? So that the Jews can hide when the collection plate comes round. "Stop it," I told myself. You're being nasty. This morning I had called him a saint. Now I was calling him a miser when neither was the truth.

Most teachers were gone when I reached the staff room. Once upon a time, we used to have a cup of tea and review the day's events. Not anymore. Unwashed cups sat on the tables beside mugs caked with strong smelling soup.

Kieran Crawley had left. His briefcase was gone from beside his cubbyhole so my option of asking him for a lift was gone. I decided to walk down to The Pit and ask them to ring a hackney. Also a drink would relax me for the inevitable confrontation at home.

I pushed open the door and stepped into the gloom of the pub. Tommy the barman saw me coming and assumed I would have my usual.

I gulped three drinks. By the time my transport arrived, I had drunk four more. For the road.

When I got home, David had reorganised the furniture in Esther and Rachael's room.

"You know, Tess, it's pretty crazy Esther having two dressing tables in her room when Rachael has none." He deliberately ignored that I was late and spoke to me as if I had been there all evening. The subterfuge suited me fine.

"Dad suggested we do a swap." Esther took her sister and me by the hand and led us into her room.

"See. I have Rachael's chest of drawers now."

My first thought was that they were very quick to do their father's bidding. If it were me who suggested such a solution, they would have fought against it and then against each other.

"Isn't that neat?" Esther's laugh halted when she noticed my lack of enthusiasm. "Oh Mom, you're not in a bad mood again?"

Rachael joined in, "We thought you'd be pleased."

I felt queasy from all the alcohol but how could I tell my kids that? I left the room and came face to face with David.

"Well," he smiled, "what do you think of the new arrangement?"

I felt that he was making an effort to put the morning's conflict behind us. It was up to me to do the same. I moved closer to him.

He took a step backwards.

"So! I've been drinking. Shoot me." I heard my voice slur.

In a resigned voice, he said, "Go sleep it off. You'll need to be wide awake when Nana and Granddad come."

"They're coming this evening?" The thought of having to put up with my mother and father for the night was the last straw in what had been a horrible day. "I thought they were coming tomorrow. Why didn't you tell me?"

"What am I doing now? Telling you."

"That's why you came home so early, wasn't it, Dad? Didn't a nurse ring from the hospital?" Rachael and Esther had emerged from the bedroom.

"Yes, Rach." He turned towards me. "I intended to be home early anyway. I wanted to talk to you."

"When exactly are they coming?"

"I was supposed to go and collect them half an hour ago. I called and left a message that I would be late but that I *would* be there."

"Because I could have come home any time of the day or night?" I knew I was being painful but couldn't control myself.

Rachael took my hand. "Mom. You're nearly always home. It's Dad who's usually out."

David chucked his younger daughter under the chin. "What does the holy bible say? Honour thy father and thy mother..."

"That thy days may be long unto the land which the lord thy God giveth thee," Rachael and Esther said in unison.

The ease with which they quoted the bible floored me.

"Seems as if some of my wisdom is sticking," David joked.

Esther and Rachael smiled at each other.

"Time to go. You two can come with me. Entertain me with bible stories."

"Daad."

"I'm teasing." He sidestepped me. "I'll have to drive like crazy to get there at a respectable hour. Come on, you two."

"Bye, Mom." They ran down the stairs.

He turned to me and said, "Try to be sober when your mother and father get here."

My father's voice penetrated my fuzzy brain and I woke. The scent of the lavender essential oil I had doused on the pillow to help me sleep lingered. I felt the cotton sheet beneath me and wished I could remain where I was, snuggled under the peach duvet, confident as a badger in her set.

I looked at my watch. It was three hours since David, Esther and Rachael had left. I must have slept for about two of them but I still felt unrefreshed and headachy. I stuck my hand out from under the bedclothes to stroke the touch lamp on the locker.

When I heard my father's voice again, I put my skates on, as Rachael would say, and jumped out of bed. The room was lit with a glow that softened the harsh green of my St. Patrick's Day tracksuit, making it look pallid. Grabbing it from the end of the bed, I threw it on, bottoms first. I was pulling the sweatshirt over my head, when my father's words made sense. Before this, his assertions had just been a confusion of sounds, a jumble.

He said, "I have a touch of *Féar Gorta.*" He used this phrase when he was feeling ravenous. I was never sure quite what it meant. *Gorta* was the Irish for famine and *féar* for grass. Hungry grass, I guess.

"A few sardines and a bit of toast would be lovely," he added.

I remembered times when he devoured lashings of Irish stew in the middle of the night while my mother, shivering in her dressing gown, agonised about whether he 'would like anything to go with it.' She meant dessert.

The cadence echoed in my ears as I dragged my feet downstairs to greet everybody. When I saw Esther and Rachael hanging their jackets on the hallstand, I knew they were obeying my mother's orders. She couldn't be that sick if she were worried about keeping *my* house tidy.

I tugged at Rachael's ponytail and patted Esther on the head before I kissed them quickly. There were blots of tiredness on Esther's cheek and Rachael looked like a wrung-out dishcloth. "Say goodnight to Nana and Granddad and Dad and go to bed."

While I lingered in the hall, they did what I told them without demur.

I still felt tired and irritable. *You were drunk going to bed,* I reminded myself. *You always feel like this when you get up after a feed of drink. That is why you have taken to having an odd gin in the morning. The hair of the dog.*

"Goodnight, kids." Heavy-lidded, the two plodded by me and climbed the stairs.

I ventured into the kitchen and lingered, unnoticed, by the door; I wanted to get myself together before I was forced to muck in.

"*I'll* do that for you, Mrs. Casey." David was taking bread from my mother's hand and putting it in the toaster when my father got up from the table and headed towards the cooker.

"Not that way, David. Lily knows what I like. You do it, can't you?" His eyes looked too big for his glasses as he impaled my mother with them.

"I don't feel great, Pat." My mother sounded as frail as Rachael's talking doll when her batteries are low.

"What is there to do? Turn on the grill and put in the toast. Turn it over, put the sardines on the other side and grill them."

"Daddy, we *have* no sardines." I felt so triumphant that his plans would be thwarted I forgot my intention to remain in the background for a while.

"Where did you spring from?" he asked.

My mother, standing with one hand clutching the sink and one hand trembling by her side, noticed me at the same time. She looked at me lovingly, expectantly. I didn't even ask her how she was feeling.

"We have some sardines now." David held up a tin for my

inspection. "We stopped at an Eight Till Late in Castlebar."

Suddenly my father's body went rigid. The air around him became charged with something akin to electrical energy. Up to now, I had thought it was only the car door and Esther's hair that discharged static in our family. Galvanised by his dismay, his vocal cords went into overdrive and he shouted, "What time is it?" Although he sported a Rotary himself, which was never a second wrong, he repeated an octave higher, "What time is it?"

David looked at his watch. "Eleven o'clock on the nose."

My father relaxed. His stomach muscles returned to their normal sagging position, evidence, if needed, of how well my mother fed him. "Plenty of time so." The air in his environs became normal.

David's nose and mouth crinkled in puzzled unison.

"Did I never tell you?" my father was expansive in his relief, "I don't eat after twelve o'clock on a Saturday night when I'm receiving communion on the Sunday. The abstinence rule has changed, but *I* don't agree with it."

I felt a knot in my stomach. "How often do you eat at this hour of the night? Hardly ever."

David's expression changed from puzzlement to humour. "Guess as tomorrow is Saturday you'll have a helluva long fast this time."

"Maybe it's preparing for the Jewish Sabbath you are, Daddy. That's tomorrow alright."

My father's resentment draped the room like a curtain. Ignoring us, he barked, "Lily, time we were going to bed. Remember, you've just come out of hospital."

David waved the sardines. "No fishy on the dishy then?"

My father shifted from foot to foot. "Same room as usual?"

"Yes, but it's David's office now. We sold the bed and put a futon there instead. I hope you find it comfortable. It's what the Japanese sleep in."

He pretended not to hear me.

"Lily, are you coming? I thought you were half dying a while ago. Now it looks like it'll take a JCB to shift you."

My mother shrugged in my direction and shuffled behind him.

To make up for overlooking her earlier, I reached towards her. Beneath my touch, her bones felt brittle. Afraid I'd crumble them to pulp, I hugged her lightly. Anger, aggravated by my hangover, swelled through me. Why was she always the stoic, the victim, always pandering to my father's needs? In case she would read my mind, I kissed her on the cheek but didn't make eye contact. "Goodnight, Mammy."

"She thinks that at the age of seventy your father will change," David observed. "And she is as mistaken as the New Testament."

"Forget the bible, David. We'll have enough religious bullshit for the next week." To take the sting out of what I'd said, I returned to stand beside him at the cooker where he was turning on the grill to toast the bread and sardines. "I'm wrecked." I checked my watch. "It's nearly midnight."

"The bewitching hour."

What would happen when it came to going to bed, I wondered. Would he put up the folding bed in Esther's room or sleep with me?

I divided the toast and sardines between us and we sat side by side at the table and ate them. I felt deflated, like a pricked balloon. At one o'clock, after I had yawned several times, David suggested we retire.

"I'll put Roamy to bed. I just want to finish looking over a brief. I didn't get time this evening. I'll follow you up."

I hauled myself upstairs. Despite taking my time undressing, taking off my make-up, putting on moisturiser and brushing my teeth, when I climbed into bed he still hadn't come. He had mentioned the bewitching hour. I needed a spell alright - to dissolve the loneliness swamping me.

I lay rigid, awake, agitated. My eyelids kept snapping open like blinds on a faulty roller. I buffeted the pillow. Weary to desperation, the unaccustomed hum of the radiators, left on all night because of my mother's need for heat, buzzed in my head. I would never sleep.

There I lay like a lovesick fool waiting for my husband to honour me with his presence. Goddammit. My blood rose until I found myself groping beneath the valance for my slippers. A few days ago, I had shoved them under the bed. "Gotcha." My hand pulled one out. Empty. Second time lucky. The bottle of gin jutted from my left slipper. A few gulps would help me unwind. I cradled the bottle. "Hi, lover boy."

Next morning I felt like I had the flu and searched in the medicine cabinet for a thermometer. My temperature was normal. Dismissing the thought that the headache was caused by dehydration from gin, I took two painkillers with a glass of water.

In the kitchen I was taken aback to see David standing at the top of the table buttering bread and my mother sitting at the other end talking to Rachael and Esther.

I stood beside him and said good morning to all.

"I was getting the breakfast ready myself," my mother said, "but David insisted."

David's voice was low as he explained that he was preparing food for my father. "Isn't it crazy? She brings him his breakfast in bed. I'd feel like crowning him with it, but I guess we won't be around when she goes home. Any change will have to come from her. Doesn't he see that she's sick?"

"My father sees what he wants to see."

David widened his eyes. "Runs in the family."

"Mammy," I felt I had to negate his comment, "we're going to spoil you for the rest of the day."

"Thanks, Teresa. I do feel a bit tired."

"Mom, if you get the dinner," Esther said, "I'll get the tea. Granddad likes his tea."

"I'll help you with it, Essie," Rachael offered.

Though I was surprised by their willingness to work together, I just said, "Right. That's decided."

"Teresa. Don't have anything but free-range chicken for dinner. Lately Pat refuses to eat any other kind of meat. He says they're full of chemicals."

I thought, free-range chicken my ass. I said, "But Mammy, you detest chicken."

My mother nodded. "I'll do with a bit of bread and butter."

Before I could answer, my father was at my elbow. "You're up." I sounded like I was accusing him of a crime. "Thought you were in bed."

"I could hardly expect Lily to bring me breakfast now, could I? No. I was going to get it myself," he answered.

"Here it is, Mr. Casey. Ready to be eaten."

"I'll pull up a chair so." As my father tucked into slice after slice of bread, liberally spread with butter and marmalade, my mother, deprived of her martyr's role, resumed talking to her granddaughters.

Three cups of tea later, my father looked critically at his wide girth as he got up from the table. "You know Lil, I weighed myself on Teresa's weighing scales. I've lost two pounds since you went into hospital. I'm fading away."

"There's no paper, Pat." My mother wrung her hands. She looked apologetically towards David. "Teresa must remember how much Pat likes his paper in the morning."

I did indeed remember.

My father turned towards me, pleased with himself. "I've been walking down to Tom's for it myself for the last couple of months so that Lily could stay in bed late."

He mistook my surprise for doubt.

"If you don't believe me, ask her. Lil, haven't I brought you your breakfast in bed every morning since you started complaining of being tired?"

"Oh," she said, evidently disconcerted. "Oh. Well that's true. You did."

Happy that he had set the record straight, he said, "I'll have a look at the *Irish Times*." He smiled. "I might learn something from these bigwigs."

"Speaking of bigwigs," David said, "I'm going to be gone most of the day. I've an important case coming up that I have to research." He looked at us all but I felt that his words were aimed at me. "I'll be late home so don't worry."

"Aw, Dad."

Esther had said what I wanted to say. I wanted David around all day. I tried to be open-minded and liberal and let him have his space but in the last year I had become an anxious and possessive wife. I resisted asking him if he were really going to work.

"Granddad will be here to play with you today," David consoled Esther. "You can beat him at Scrabble."

When David drove away, we settled to a day of relaxation. Well, relaxation in so far as I could get away with it. I knew that dinner would have to be served at two, which meant that we were unable to plan anything else. This had always been the ritual when I was growing up. We ate bacon, lamb chops or roast pork, heavy meals. Weekdays my father went back to work while I went back to school. Weekends I was expected to help my mother clean up while my father read the paper. Tradition without good reason is but ancient error. Even now, I lacked the guts to rebel.

At noon, I put a chicken in the oven to roast. The girls were on the verge of fisticuffs about who would butter the bread and who would make the roast beef and salad sandwiches. I was about to intervene when their Nana, with her instructions, united them both. As I listened to her issuing orders, I was transported back to my teenage self. Ironic that my mother only played the stoic victim where my father was concerned.

"Rachael, put the beetroot back in the jar. Esther, wrap the roast beef. No, not in aluminium foil. In cling film. How will we know what it is otherwise? No, Rachael. Throw away the lettuce with the dressing on it; it gets soggy. If you want to save salad, you must wash off the mayonnaise gently and then pat it dry. At this rate you'll never make a housewife."

Though the only effect she was having on Esther and Rachael was to make them giggle, I said, "They're just kids, Mammy. What do you expect? They shouldn't even be asked to make sandwiches."

My mother, in her element, pretended not to hear me. She

reminded me of a despotic teacher who revelled in having found some new students to boss. When Esther said sweetly, "It's okay Mom," I realised that I was the only one taking umbrage.

My mother monitored every chore I did around the kitchen when I lived at home so I guess I was oversensitive. For her there were three ways of doing everything: her way, my father's way and the wrong way. My father had been uninterested in what went on in the kitchen so my mother had free reign there. Everything had its place in her fiefdom. The bottom shelf of the dresser was loaded with cups, saucers and plates, second shelf with glassware and bowls according to a precise pattern. God help me if I left a cup beside the statue of the Infant of Prague that stood alone on the third shelf.

In my house, my family put boxes of breakfast cereal beside tins of tuna, beside packets of soup all on the one shelf, squeezing them in anywhere they could find room. I gave them hell about it.

My mother had racks of saucepans of all shapes and depths, drawers full of matching cutlery, sets of china in pristine display cases. She had been unhappy. Time I realised that an ordered kitchen or regular meals were not that important.

At two o'clock, we sat down to eat. Afterwards, when the washing up was done, my mother dozed on the couch while my father played 'strip Jack' with Rachael and Esther.

Later, we all watched the episode of *Coronation Street* we had taped the night before.

"That Mike Baldwin," my mother said, "shot he should be. He should have more sense. And will you look at Mavis? She's a right ditherer. Do you see what that pair are doing, Pat? Bad enough carrying on like that if they were married."

"Nana, why are you always giving out about *Coronation Street*? They're only acting you know."

"How many times have I told you the same thing, Lily?" my father chimed in, "even an eleven year old notices the way you go on. It's bad enough when you do it at home but at least there, there's no one but me to hear."

110

"I think it's cute," Rachael said.

"Nothing but sex, sex and more sex," my mother continued, while running her fingers distractedly through her hair. She criticised everyone for the rest of the programme.

When *Coronation Street* was over, Rachael asked if anybody wanted sandwiches.

"Now that Nana has shown us how to make them right," Esther quipped.

"I'll do it," I said, glad of the diversion. My mother and father, I thought, have been here less than twenty-four hours and I already feel on edge. As I put mustard on the ham, I tried to banish the vision of a sparkling gin.

The following morning, Sunday, David was sitting on the couch in the front room, reading, Rachael snuggled up beside him. I was sitting upright on an armchair opposite him, trying to relax. Esther was ensconced on a low stool half hidden by Roamy, standing in front of her.

My father stuck his head in the door. "Did anybody see my tie? I left it on the cistern in the bathroom."

"Why are you talking funny, Granddad?" Esther asked. Then, a flash of inspiration. "I know. You forgot to put in your teeth."

"I'll get them for you," Rachael offered.

He came into the room. "It's my tie I'm looking for not my teeth." This time he pronounced each word clearly.

Esther stood and unwound the tie from around her neck. "The cistern was a stupid place to have left it. It could've fallen into the bowl. Imagine the stench, especially if you'd forgotten to flush." She patted Roamy on the head. "You're not as silly as that, are you, Roam?"

"Esther, go and get ready for Mass. You too, Rachael. Neither of you have your coats on yet."

Amid a cry of, "it's not fair," they did as they were told. After they'd left David and I alone, tension, a relict from our recent rows and his absence all day yesterday, vibrated the room.

He looked up from his book and shook his head as if bewildered. "You and your Dad are so alike."

"Why?"

"He takes out his teeth in case he bites the yeast they pass around at the altar in your church at half time. Right?"

"Yes you're right but I've tried to talk him out of that idiocy for years." I wasn't in the mood for another confrontation but it seemed to be the main way we communicated these days. "And David. Half time is for football matches. You're talking about the consecration, the most important part of the Mass."

"Yeah. The consecration. When you eat your God." He gave a mock shudder. "Weird."

"Can't see why you're talking about this now and we just about to go out the door … But now that you've started … Tell me why I'm like my father."

He hesitated, took a breath and plunged in. "Remember when I met you. You were as thin as a pin. You told me yourself that you were eating apples and yogurt for every meal, that you saw yourself as fat. After several bouts of sickness, you went back to eating normally. You beat what could, in modern parlance, have turned into anorexia on your own."

I felt a mixture of vanity and apprehension. This was leading to something. "It's true. I did start eating. I don't think Daddy will ever be in danger of starving himself. Why does that make me like him?"

"Your personalities are the same."

I laughed. "You're mad in the head. Me? I don't practise a letter-of-the-law religion, I don't think women were born to serve, I don't ..."

"Both your personalities are obsessive." Your father smoked forty cigarettes a day but he gave them up immediately when the doctor told him he was in danger of contracting lung cancer and scared the shit out of him."

I knew he was borrowing his notes from the same old tune, my 'over indulgence in the bottle.' But the timing threw me.

My thoughts raced. In the past year my relationship with David had deteriorated. I was unsure which had started first, my marriage problems or the heavy drinking. The only way I could find out was to give up the gargle.

"I'm going to stop drinking," I said. My statement was as simple, spontaneous and straightforward as that.

"I'll believe it when I see it," David muttered. Then he looked straight at me.

Something about my demeanour must have forced him to take me seriously. He hesitated before he got up from the couch, held my hand and squeezed it. "I'm not perfect either." His smile was wry. "Don't forget I need the wisdom of Pamela Crawley to keep me on an even keel."

I felt grateful for his sensitivity but the mention of the Crawley name shocked me. Inexplicably I thought of the sinister calendars hidden in my drawer upstairs. Again without forethought, I said, "David, I've been getting strange ..."

From the hall my father shouted upstairs to my mother, interrupting my confession.

"What the hell is keeping you, Lily?" he asked. "Mass starts at ten. It's that now. We'll be dead late. And Teresa is still nattering away to David as if they'd never met before in their lives."

"Granddad, chill. We'll be a few minutes late. Big deal," the intrepid Esther shouted back.

David and I left the room and joined my father. Esther and Rachael, followed by my mother, came downstairs and completed the family.

"We'll wait until eleven o'clock Mass," I said.

"We have nearly an hour to wait. We may as well get comfortable," my mother suggested. "Tea for you all. Coffee for David." She went into the kitchen and the five of us traipsed after her. Soon a smell of coffee filled the kitchen.

The coffee my mother handed to David was steaming and looked appetising.

Cup in hand, David, smacking his lips in appreciation, sat at the table.

My mother spoke to my father. "I suppose there's no point in asking you to have anything."

"Don't you know, Lil, that I cannot eat or drink anything until after Mass?"

I knew that my father became irritable when he had an empty stomach but I was surprised by what followed.

He pulled a chair from under the table, sat opposite David

and fiddled with his cap. "David, do you go to any service at all?" He looked at him speculatively. "Even Protestants have some kind of a thingamabob they go to."

David sat very still.

My mother busied herself with pouring tea.

Esther broke the silence. "Granddad, do you like my Dad?"

"Course he likes him, Essie. Don't be daft." Rachael threw her sister a pleading look.

"Then how come he told me not to talk to him about religion. And *never* to mention Jesus." For my father's benefit, she bowed her head as she said *His* name.

"He never said that." My mother was adamant. "Did you, Pat?"

"Don't tell lies, Esther," I admonished.

"He did too say that. I told him I could talk to my Dad about anything, and he said not to be too open or he might go after me with a hammer and nails."

I had always hated the notion that Christians blamed Jews for murdering their saviour. Now I was learning that my father believed it. I was at a loss what to say or do.

Esther filled the stunned silence with an explanation. "Hammer and nails, get it? Calvary. Jesus on the cross! Jews!"

"Esther!" Rachael said.

My mother's face turned puce. "Esther and Rachael, would you leave the room? Please."

Esther was reluctant to move but Rachael pushed her towards the door. "Come on, Essie. You've caused enough trouble."

"What did I do?"

Their voices faded as they went into the front room.

My father screwed up his cap. "It was a joke."

David stood up and dwarfed us all. He caught my mother by the elbow. "Let it drop, Mrs. Casey."

"*I* will be the judge of what to do, David."

My heart thumped. I had never heard my mother speak to a man like that before.

"Pat was out of line. He shouldn't say something like that to anyone. And besides, they're your children, not his. It will not happen again."

A nerve jumped on my father's temple. "Don't you talk for me, Lily or I will ..."

"You'll what, Pat?" The question lay in the room like a time bomb.

"I'll ..." His voice drained away. Sweat glistened on his face. He was still dressed for ten o'clock Mass in his overcoat, scarf and gloves.

"You'll go out and ring a hackney to take us to Mass. Teresa. Name of a hackney." My mother's voice held a steel edge.

"Tommy Gilmore Ballyhaunis Road. You'll find it in the book," I answered.

"The children can come with us." My mother issued the edict through stiff lips. "Teresa and David could do with some time on their own."

"A hackney? Are you mad, woman?" my father said. "You expect me to ring it?"

"I do."

He slunk away, like the cat next door who cowers when she sees Roamy. At the door he looked back to make sure my mother was in earnest. Then we heard him fumble with the telephone book.

"Lily, I don't know which one to use."

"There's a booklet there from the Chamber of Commerce headed *Claremorris Directory*. All the local numbers are in it." I was enjoying myself but I was sensible enough to keep the satisfaction out of my voice. "Just look up hackneys. Or it might be under taxis."

For five minutes we talked about the awful weather, the need to get the drive finished and had started on Esther and Rachael's homework when my father's angry voice put a stop to our conversation.

"Lily. Will *you* do it for me?" His tension infected the room.

My mother's face twisted in a half smile. She returned my gaze. A coldness, that had nothing to do with the temperature of the morning, ran up my spine.

Slowly she got up and walked out to the hall, leaving the door ajar. She took the book and found the appropriate name in a matter of seconds.

"David." My father sidled back into the kitchen and snorted into his snow-white cloth hanky. When he had finished clearing his nostrils, he held it in front of his chest like a shield. "I know Esther and Rachael don't go to Mass every Sunday. I'm just worried about their immortal souls. I shouldn't have said about the hammer and nails to Esther."

"It's fine, Mr. Casey. Don't worry about it."

My father took his misshapen cap from his pocket, plonked it on his head and hurried away.

Amid goodbyes from the kids, the door slammed.

"I've constantly heard your father talk about eternal life after death," David said, "and yet he is bored if there is nothing good on television." His eyes were hard as if they were chiselled from the Empire State's limestone.

Now, seeing his anger, I realised what it must have cost him to remain calm while my parents were here. "Fair dues to you," I said, "accepting my father's apology like that. You must have felt like punching him."

He looked at me, a lengthy look, harsh and judgemental, and said, "Fair what? Fair Jews? What exactly does that mean?"

"I said fair dues. You've heard me say that before. It's another way of saying good for you."

"It's a helluva way of saying it. If you said, 'fair game,' I'd have understood that you meant Jews."

"David. That's all I meant. It's to me you're talking. My father's not here now. I've said that a million times before. You're being unreasonable."

"I guess I am but it's hard to deal with bigots, especially when they're your own family. The garbage your father was spouting has clarified what I've always guessed." He glare at me challengingly and waited.

I remained silent.

He went over to a photograph, on the wall, of Esther that he had taken in the States on the day she first got the knack of balancing her bike. He traced her outline with his finger.

The silence seemed to go on forever.

At last he turned his attention from the photograph and voiced what to me was a non sequitur. "I was born a Jew. No need for ritual to admit me to the community of Jewish people. But just like your father, you considered our children pagans until you got a priest to baptise them and make them Catholic. Calling them biblical names was a meaningless gesture in case I protested."

I thought, he is as unyielding as Pharaoh, refusing to let the Israelites leave Egypt. "What are you saying exactly?"

"That you and your mother and father like to forget that our children are half Jewish like me."

"Then maybe you should have reminded us."

"It's always my fault.

"David, I ..."

"My father was right. I should have known that if I married out, my kids would be Gentiles." He hesitated. "It was your drinking that made me go to Pamela Crawley for help. In the process I realised I had my own problems."

"You mean we have problems?"

"I think you have problems that are separate to you, and I have problems that are separate to me." He continued. "If the girls don't know anything about Judaism, they'll think Catholicism is their only heritage. How many Jews are there in Ireland? Two thousand? Crazy to think three more would be a threat."

I felt dismayed. This was unfamiliar territory. A while ago, during the debacle with my father, I said I was at a loss as to what to say or do, now I was at a loss what to feel. Most of my colleagues at school were unaware that David was Jewish. If they suspected it from his name, they had assumed he was a convert. Did that mean I was ashamed of his religion? "I never said the girls shouldn't be conversant with Judaism."

"I'm talking about being more than conversant with it. I want to tell them how the Jewish year is divided, how ..."

I felt a sudden anger; I had decided to stop drinking and realign with David. Now he was shifting the goalposts. "My father has had more of an effect on you than I thought."

"That's not fair."

Unconsciously he had copied Esther's favourite phrase.

"I understand why your father hates that you and the kids don't attend Mass regularly. Some Jews put a helluva store by religious ritual also. In the past three months I've felt the need to attend some prayer services at the synagogue in Herbert Road."

My anger drained away like water down a plughole. He shouldn't have had to hide his desire to practise his religion from me. When I married David, his being a Jew had added to his attractiveness but I had taken it for granted that the children would be baptised. We had seldom discussed religion.

I was standing close enough to him to smell his coffee breath, warm and flavoured. My fingers itched to touch his fingers, to pull them over my face, to tell me by touch how much he loved me. "David. Everybody's gone. Will we go back to bed for a while?" I was sober, no alcohol to mask my distaste for sex. Because it felt so out of character for me to be making such a suggestion, I felt awkward. "You can test your stamina. Check if your fitness regime is working."

Silence.

I finished with an embarrassed squawk. "That's if you want, of course."

"If *I* want," he said, his eyes suddenly cold and bleak like winter weather. "That's rich coming from you, Teresa. If *I* want! You're suggesting sex as a balm for my hurt ego. Unusual as the offer is, it would solve nothing. I'm surprised that you think it would."

Guilty as charged, I thought. That he was justified in what he was saying annoyed me. I called him a pompous ass.

"Maybe I am a pompous ass."

His resigned air alarmed. I felt an unexpected icy fear. What would we do, David and I, if he voiced the untellable, that I was undersexed, passionless, inhibited? Perspiration trickled somewhere on my body.

Sitting on a chair outside the principal's office, I began looking at my watch at two thirty. I expected the meeting regarding Jacinta Broderick's ability to take a higher-level Leaving Cert paper in English to take place at two o'clock. Now it was almost three and Jacinta and her mother were still talking with Sr. Maureen Ruane. I had to be at the hospital at four thirty.

It was exactly two months ago since my mother had her first stroke. Despite the doctors' optimistic prognosis then, they were discharging her today following her second one. I felt as I often did recently that I should be in three places at the one time, guilt-ridden wherever I was.

Expecting to be cross-examined (David's terminology) immediately after lunch, I had rushed my food in order to get here at five minutes to two. Onions, part of the liver dish I'd eaten, were coming up my throat. "Shakespeare never repeats except after onions." Every year pupils came up with that one. I certainly knew how he felt today.

I looked at my watch again. What a waste of time. A teacher with a free class was supervising mine while I was sitting here doing nothing. If the principal didn't send for me before four o'clock, I'd have to excuse myself. I promised my father that I'd collect my mother rather than have her travel home by ambulance. My impatience had to do with a fear of being late collecting her and little to do with anxiety about my impending meeting.

I was confident of my capacity to think quickly on my feet. David maintained that my sharpness resulted from my years of teaching. I suppose he was right. I gave the impression that I knew more than I did even when I had only read the material for the first time the night before. It had to do with voice control, my gift for ad-libbing and for disarming awkward pupils with a sense of humour. But to be on the safe side, and to distract me from worrying about the time, I decided to recheck Jacinta Broderick's details.

Opening my 'Teacher's Organiser,' I flicked through it until I came to my Leaving Certs. Broderick Jacinta was second on the list after Ansboro Mary. The pages were laid out with headings, *Name, Attendance, Oral work, Written work, Behaviour.* Her lack of progress throughout the year was obvious. Jacinta Broderick had been a pupil of mine for Health Education while a Junior and had been in my English class since she had gone into the Leaving Cert cycle. Closing the book, I got up from the bench and started to pace.

My mother's first stroke two months ago; my accident with the motor bike – two months ago; last time I had imbibed an alcoholic drink – two months ago. A couple of weeks ago I had acknowledged that David was a David I didn't know.

When I stopped drinking alcohol, it would appease David and life would go back to normal, or so I'd hoped. I had stomach cramps the first few days after giving it up and I was constantly sweating. Fighting with David, Esther, Rachael or the kids at school had become the norm. David's assertion that I was going through classic withdrawal symptoms highlighted that it was self-inflicted and aggravated the situation.

However, as I persevered, the tiredness I had so often complained about disappeared. I no longer forgot things but, just in case, I wrote lists. Several books on how to please your partner had given me the illusion that all was well. I stopped badgering Cora about dust behind the radiators, and I no longer scrubbed the side of the stairs with a nailbrush.

My pacing had begun to resemble a soldier on point duty outside a military installation when I heard raised voices from the office and stopped in my tracks. The door opened and the principal stuck her head out. "Mrs. Goldstein. Would you please come in?"

Jacinta and her mother were sitting in front of Sr. Maureen's desk. Mrs. Broderick passed her daughter a tissue. "Clean your nose." Almost in the same breath, she added, looking at me, "Why can't my Jacinta do honours English? I done honours in the Inter Cert."

"Mrs. Goldstein. I would like you to meet Mrs. Broderick." Sr. Maureen spoke in a silky tone.

"Good afternoon, Mrs Broderick," I smiled.

Her face reddened. She gave an almost imperceptible nod as I sat beside Jacinta. "I know who she is. She's the one who phoned me about Jacinta. Wants her to change to pass." She paused. "Returned Yank. Wheel is on the wrong side of her car, Sister. Did you ever see the like?"

"I beg your pardon?" Sr. Maureen's voice was less silky now.

"Mrs. Broderick, I don't think this is relevant. I have given you a lot of my time already so I would like you to stick to the point."

"If you ask me, it drives on the wrong side too."

"Mrs. Broderick!"

Sr. Maureen tried her best but she found it difficult to deal with recalcitrant parents. No matter what accusations Mrs. Broderick made regarding me, this was the most assertive she would become.

"Jacinta said Mrs. Goldstein was always excusing that Shylock fellow in English class. Wasn't she, Jacinta?"

On hearing this unlikely literary allusion from Mrs. Broderick, I tried to keep my expression blank. I realised I had failed when she inclined her head in my direction, her eyes glittering and said, "Surprised ya, that. Didn't it? I remember the bastard because he was a money lender." Her mouth twisted. "My mother, God rest her, had her share of those shilling a week fellas when I was growing up. Bleed you dry they would. Then there's that Jewish woman auntie Kathleen is minding in New York. Filthy rich and pays her a pittance."

Shakespeare had created Shylock when he was living in an England where there were no Jews and without ever having met

122

one; a woman like Mrs. Broderick could be forgiven her anti-Semitic feelings. The thought helped me maintain my equilibrium.

"Mrs. Broderick," I said, "all I do is advise pupils of their capabilities." I turned to Jacinta. "What grade did you get in English in your exam when Miss Brogan was teaching you, Jacinta?"

She shuffled, pulled at her lip and remained silent.

I opened my organiser and pointed to her name with my finger. "Never mind. I have the information here."

"I got an f," she mumbled.

I felt sorry for the kid. Making a valiant effort to be nice, I turned to the mother. "You're correct Mrs. Broderick. Jacinta took a higher level paper at Junior level but Leaving Cert is much more demanding."

"She has the right to do honours if she wants. That's all I'm saying."

I knew only too well that if she failed she would blame me. If she did well, it would be her genius. "Certainly any pupil can persevere with higher level. All I can give is my professional opinion." Even to my own ears I was beginning to sound like Sr. Maureen.

"Suppose it wasn't your fault neither that you knocked the brother's child off her bike on the wet road," Mrs Broderick said.

My quick thinking came in useful. Niece. This woman's niece was the girl I knocked down. Her uncle, Mrs Broderick's brother, had said he'd heard about me. Probably from her, I realised now. "I'll presume then," I said, "that Jacinta wishes to continue with higher level."

"Devil of an enquiry about her afterwards. She could've been dead for all you cared."

I remembered David phoning the sergeant the next morning. He would have told me if there were anything seriously wrong with her.

"I don't think this is the time or the place to discuss this, Mrs. Broderick." Sr Maureen's voice was a scouring pad. Perhaps I had misjudged her ability to direct the conversation.

"Went into shock, she did. Spent two days sleeping. My brother, ignorant bugger, didn't even call the doctor again. A neighbour's girl is a nurse in Dublin. She said she probably had concussion. Could have got a packet out of you, she could."

In an artificially modulated tone I said, "If you'll excuse me I have to go back to class."

"Think you're smart, don't ya? Just because your husband is a big solicitor and poor Eibhlin has nothing." Mrs. Broderick turned to Sr. Maureen. "She won't get a penny. The husband will see to that. Doesn't want his insurance to go through the roof."

I stared at her.

"Good at handling his own interests he is, but from what I heard from Paddy Joe Gilmore, he's not too good at handling his client's' He ..."

Sister. Maureen said slowly, "Mrs. Broderick, I will have to ask you to refrain ..."

Brrrring! The telephone on the desk rang. Sr. Maureen said, in what I thought was a relieved tone, into the receiver, "Yes, Sr. Pius, I know I'm way behind schedule ... Yes, you may come in. The meeting is just breaking up ..."

Sr Pius, not known for her patience, was obviously phoning from the phone extension in the staff room. From what I could gather from the one-sided conversation, she was in a hurry to get some forms signed.

A few minutes later she pushed the door open. "Sorry to interrupt."

Her eyes rested on each of us in turn. Then she said, "Dolores Broderick. I don't believe it. Good to see you."

"Nice to see you too Sr. Pius. I'm causing trouble as usual." Mrs Broderick's face wreathed in smiles.

"Sure didn't I put up with you in my class for three years. I should be well used to your shenanigans. How's your mother these days?"

She's nearly ninety. Lost a bit of her spirit, she has." Mrs. Broderick looked across at me as I edged towards the door.

"Remember the day she came in complaining that our class had no good teachers."

Sr. Pius nodded, smiling, understanding what she meant.

To enlighten Sr. Maureen and me, Mrs Broderick added, "Except for Sr. Pius I had only lay teachers teaching me. Lord have mercy on my mother, she loved the nuns." She wagged her finger in my direction. "I think she had it down pat."

"Jacinta. Return to class please." Sr. Maureen Ruane levelled her gaze at Sr. Pius. "Let's get these signed." She said to Mrs Broderick, "Thank you for coming."

"Goodbye, Mrs. Broderick." I nodded towards Jacinta. I felt my head was at a perfect angle to make a dignified exit.

Annoyed, I walked down the corridor, opened the door of the staff room, manoeuvred my way around the tables and went to my shelf to take out my books. The bent heads of teachers, correcting homework, didn't lift as I pulled a battered copy of *Soundings* from the pile. My mind was working overtime. I was unsure which of the insults hurled at me had hurt me most. None, I decided, but Mrs Broderick's references to David had perturbed me.

I understood why he had omitted to tell me about the claim from Eibhlin. He was a solicitor. It was his job to deal with stuff like that. What I failed to understand was Mrs Broderick's veiled accusation that he was mishandling a client's business. Once upon a time, he used to talk to me about his work but that had all stopped long ago, part of the strain between us.

My former excessive drinking had shaken him, I knew. But was there something more sinister, another worry to add to my list of anxieties? When I'd been sitting outside the principal's office to await my interview with the Brodericks, my main concern had been my commitment to take my mother home from hospital. It seemed an eternity ago.

The reception area of Beaumar hospital was bright, its yellow walls reminiscent of sunshine and optimism. Corridors led away from the main area. A young woman sat, the space in front of her barricaded from intrusion by a long desk. My father handed me the invoice for my mother's stay in hospital. "It's like an inventory, it's so long." His voice held a note of awe and appreciation.

"No wonder," I smiled so that he would not feel indebted that I was footing the bill, "they charge you for everything. Remember when Esther got her tonsils out, they told me I could come into the theatre with her until she was anaesthetised, then they charged me for the cap and gown and shoes."

"Same when they offer you tea. They forget to mention that you have to pay for it." My father's eyes glinted with cunning. "But I fooled them; I used to order a big dinner for Lily and then *I* would eat it myself. Cost nothing extra."

An orderly, dressed in a green uniform, brushed past us pushing a wheelchair.

"That chair may be for Lily. They said we would have to wheel her to the car." My father was speaking in such a calm voice that I wondered where his usual jittery self had gone. "I'll go up and organise things," he continued, "while you settle the bill."

"Right so." I walked over to the reception trying not to let shock, that my mother would be unable to walk, show; I gripped the counter. The receptionist was talking on the phone.

I thought of my father. There was a composure about him that was new. Perhaps my mother's dependence on him since her relapse had improved his confidence.

The receptionist was still talking on the phone.

A discharged patient was wheeled out of the lift, flanked by her two daughters and son. I continued to watch them when they left. An older man, her husband, had a car waiting for her at the front door.

I wished that woman was my mother, that I was one of the sisters instead of an only child, that my father could drive us home, where I would find another sister or brother waiting for me when I stepped out of the car, who would say, 'Everything is ready, radiators on, fire down, beds made, fridge full, minding

126

rota in place. Four of us plus Dad. We'll manage.'

"Don't be daft," I muttered, ridding myself of the fantasy.

Still the receptionist talked on the phone.

Tired of being polite, I stared at her so hard that I could see coffee stains in her brown eyes.

Uncomfortable under the scrutiny, the young woman finished her phone call and took the bill. Her voice was cold. "Access or Visa?"

"Visa." She took the card from my outstretched hand and went into an adjoining office to process my card. I looked at my watch. It was now five minutes since I first approached the desk. My mother would be down soon.

The lift door opened as the receptionist returned. "Visa won't authorise the transaction. You'll have to pay cash."

"I don't believe this. There must be some mistake."

"I'm sorry, Mrs. Goldstein." Her voice had softened and the edges of her mouth drooped in sympathy.

"But the Visa bill is automatically paid out of our account every month. The bank must have ..." The creak of a wheelchair and my mother's laboured breathing made me turn around.

"Ready to go, Teresa?"

"Wait there, Daddy. I'll be with you in a minute."

"I'm in a quandary," the woman said quietly. "Your mother has no insurance and she has been in a private room for three weeks." She looked towards my parents, then back at me. "I'll have to notify the manager." Then she said mysteriously, "But I'll get in contact with someone first. Check if they're free."

My father looked quizzically at me. "Daddy, sit down in that green chair over there. You can pull Mammy up beside you. There's some problem here."

"I never did trust those plastic credit gadgets." He settled the plaid shawl around my mother's legs and manoeuvred her in beside the armchair. After he sat down, he touched her face before he took her hand and put it in his lap. Through her twisted lips, I hoped it was a smile I spied.

The manager, a middle-aged man, wore a double-breasted

grey suit, a flowery tie, and a plain blue shirt, the kind worn by guards. The receptionist said a few words to him before he turned to me. When he shook hands, he barely touched my palm.

"Mrs. Goldstein, how are you?" He looked away from me. "Seems to be a problem with this." He waved the bill.

"I cannot understand it. This has never happened before."

"But it has happened now and we must deal with it." His voice was an octave higher.

Patronising little git. I had an itch to land him a swift kick in his scrawny buttocks and put him through the glass doors. My voice was syrup. "I'll give you my home address and phone number."

"I don't think that will suffice. It's quite a large sum we are discussing here, Mrs. Goldstein.

A young woman entered the reception area from one of the corridors and approached the desk. A silent message flowed between her and the secretary before she turned to me. "Mrs. Goldstein, good to see you."

When she smiled, showing improved but, in spite of having worn braces, irregular teeth, I recognised Una Loughnane, Dr Una Loughnane, now; she had often left my class to go to the Orthodontist. She still had a sister in the school.

"Helen shares a flat with me." Una looked towards her friend, the receptionist. "She recognised your name. My baby sister is in Leaving Cert. She was telling us about the sexy book you wrote. She couldn't believe that a teacher would admit that a French kiss was not a mortal sin. And my mother saw you on the *Late Late*, in May. You're famous."

"You never lost your gift for exaggeration," I said in a playful tone.

The receptionist laughed, "She exaggerates alright. She's always telling us how hard doctors work."

Una shrugged and looked towards the hospital manager. "Paudie, it's a wonder you didn't see her on Gaybo."

"I was in Medjugorje in May."

"Oh!" Una's eyes sparkled. "Still, you must be impressed. This woman is breaking moulds."

Paudie dismissed her comment with a disdainful wave but his voice was ingratiating. "Leave your name and address with Helen, Mrs. Goldstein. I'm sure we'll hear from you promptly."

"Her husband is a solicitor," Una said helpfully. "No danger of her falling foul of the law."

"Thank you both, I said."

They flashed me a smile as I waved goodbye and turned towards my father and mother, the thought, 'how will I pay for my mother's treatment?' uppermost in my mind.

When I smelled a mixture of cow dung, I knew I was in the right area. I had asked Rita to leave the lights on so that I wouldn't miss the house. The suggestion that I stay with her for the night had come from me. I figured we could both do with the company. I needed some time apart from David. I had been waiting for an opportunity to broach the subject of the unpaid hospital bill with him. One hadn't presented itself yet. As a result, I was constantly on edge. I would soon have to summon my courage and confront him. These were my thoughts as I drove in the open gates, parked in the yard, hopped out and walked towards the house.

Rita and Noel lived in a well-kept two storey on the outskirts of Tuam. Behind it lay a garden, plant strewn, and then a grove of horse chestnuts, oaks and aspens.

Before I had even knocked, I could hear Rita warbling inside: *home again across the sea. I am sailing stormy waters to be with you ...* She threw open the door. Poured into a pair of denims and one of her home knits, she was in her stocking feet, and was holding Tiddles, her fat yellow tabby, under her arm.

"I thought you'd never come."

There was something about her delighted laugh and the timbre of her voice that made me realise something good had happened.

"Welcome to my humble abode."

We walked through the hallway, scattered with boots and Wellingtons, and into the terracotta-tiled kitchen where a fire sputtered in an open hearth. No matter how many times I visited Rita's house there was always something new to admire or to

130

envy. This time it was the heavy deal chairs standing around a deal table, anchored in the centre of the room. It bestowed an air of permanence that I always failed to achieve in my own house.

"Like them?" Rita asked coming behind me, holding a glass of red wine. Bought them second hand. We haven't a penny but, as you know, I could never resist a bargain."

I nodded. "They're very nice."

Andy, the oldest of Rita's sons, stood at a worktop carving a joint on the bone.

Rita said, "This is the only one of my offspring you'll see tonight and he's going out to the front room in a few minutes. Aren't you, Andy?" Her smile was self-indulgent. "This is a strictly no children night. The other four are in bed ... well, they are in their rooms, at least."

"Rit. I have eaten." I had deliberately stuffed myself with pasta before leaving home knowing that Rita's delicious food went very well with wine.

"That's okay." She took a large gulp of her drink, almost finishing it. "Beef is delicious cold with chutney. The boys love it for their lunch. When you said you would prefer not to eat, I had it already bought. It can be their treat for being so good tonight."

I felt annoyed with myself. Rita had gone to a lot of trouble to make the night enjoyable and I was being a stick in the mud.

"Don't worry," she reassured me again. "Food never goes to waste in this house." She smiled her winsome smile.

The warmth and the lingering smells of dry mustard with freshly milled peppers lulled my senses.

Rita replenished her wine from the dregs of a bottle. "Want a drink? There's plenty where this came from. I splurged."

I sat on the couch before the fire. "Feeling a ball of wool under me, I got up and retrieved it. "Water, please." Tiddles, soft and plump, rubbed against my legs. I put down my hand to stroke her and laughed. Beside her was another bedraggled ball, its threads clinging to her claws.

"Nothing but balls in this place," Rita's voice slurred. "That happens when you're the only woman in the house."

For a surreal moment, I fancied I was the plant in *Little Shop of Horrors*. Feed me. Give me to drink. No. I had done with all that. If I were to go back drinking alcohol this quickly, David would say he had been right about my being addicted. And *I* knew he was wrong.

"You're staying tonight, aren't you? Have a real drink. There's duty free there as well. I'm only startin.'"

I said, "Will you get me some water, then sit down and be quiet."

Her throaty laugh told me she was not offended. While she busied herself at the fridge, I relaxed in the glow of the firelight that bathed the old wood and the brass coal scuttle. Faded rugs lay like islands on the floor. A Busy Lizzie thrived in a deep ceramic pot. The wickerwork basket bulged with piles of jumpers. Rita had become a contract knitter for a woollen factory while Noel was out of work but I had not realised she still did it. For a second I remembered the Visa card debacle at the hospital. It was the 80's Nobody had much money.

Rita was seldom intoxicated. Pity it had to happen tonight. I was afraid I would be unable to resist the temptation to join her. I knew exactly how long it was since I had my last drink, had measured the time in craving, and resentment. But I consoled myself with the thought that I would have been unable to stay away from it all this time if I had been addicted.

The cushions were luxuriously soft under me. Each time I came here, I marvelled at how much the kitchen was the core of the house and the core of the committed living that Noel, Rita and their five sons shared. I couldn't quite analyse my feelings as I contemplated my friend's life. They were a confusion of admiration and yearning.

Rita bounced back with my glass of water in a robust pottery goblet. She had abandoned the wine and was now drinking from a hefty measure of whiskey and ginger ale. "I cannot believe I haven't told you my news yet. I've been dying to tell someone. The boys know of course but only an adult understands the loneliness."

132

I said, "Will you tell me what it is you're talking about before I choke it out of you?"

"I'm resurrecting all Noel's stuff."

For the first time I noticed a mug emblazoned with his name in the middle of the coffee table.

"You should see our bedroom! When I heard the news, I robbed the kitty and drove into Galway to buy psychedelic material to make new curtains." She took another swig from her glass. The alcohol had deepened her voice even more. The tip of her tongue appeared between her teeth. "I thought of buying a mirror for the bedroom ceiling but I restrained myself."

"Will you," I fisted my hand, "tell me the goddamned news?"

"Noel is coming home for good next week. Isn't that wonderful?"

"Oh, that *is* wonderful, Rit. Really good news. How come?"

She beamed. "He's been working overtime for a year now. We have paid off most of what we owed. He has saved enough to start a small cable company. He thinks he'll be able to get a contract with Digital." As she swung around, I noticed how her jeans made the best of her ample ass and minimised the width of her hips.

She had left her hair loose and now she pushed it out of slightly glazed eyes. "I don't care as long as he's home." Her eyes narrowed. "I don't know how long more I would have lasted without sex." Her statement was matter of fact. "I don't think poor Mammy, who made me chant three 'Hail Marys' for purity every night, would be impressed if she knew that masturbation is my saviour."

Conversations about mothers and their teaching on sexuality made me anxious. Where had Rita the diplomat gone? David always maintained, without irony, that she was a loss to the diplomatic service.

"Teresa, you don't know what it's like with Noel. Nobody does. I'm on a permanent high when he's around. I know we don't always have money but who cares."

She took a photograph from the mantelpiece and handed it to

me. "Remember that. It's of Noel cutting the grass. It was taken on the second of June, fifteen years ago, by me. Imagine! We were ten years married and he had forgotten. All he was interested in was getting the lawn mowed before it rained." Her eyes, bright as Tiddles', wrinkled in glee. "I've just to point to the photograph when it's coming near our wedding anniversary and it jogs his memory," she winked beguilingly, "now I get the full treatment every year. No more memory lapses." She hesitated. "When he's here." She made a thumbs up sign. "Which will be always, from now on."

I looked at the photograph. It was out of focus but Noel's face and smile were still visible. He was looking away from the camera, at Rita I presumed. He never could tear his eyes from her. I put my fingers to my eyelids and took them away damp. David had felt like that about me once.

Rita made herself another drink and replenished mine. "Sure you won't have something stronger?"

"I'm tempted but I know I won't stop if I start. No. I'll stick with water. I don't want to have a hangover."

"Please." She put her hand to her forehead. "I'll probably have a whopper of a headache tomorrow."

Then she left her drink on the floor and pulled me up by the hands. "Let's go out for a walk."

"Where?"

"Oh! Down the road. We can look at the stars and smell the *cac bó*. When Noel makes his millions, the only mud I'll see will be in the beauty masks I'll plaster on my face."

I laughed. "What about the boys?"

"No hassle. Andy's here, remember. I'll just tell them where we're going."

Five minutes later we were walking along a country road. "Hope no car comes." I looked at our dark clothes. "The driver wouldn't see us for diamonds."

Rita had her eyes towards the sky, looking at the stars. "Do like me. Walk along the ditch."

"Walk along the ditch." David had used similar words to me

the night we escaped my parents' house to walk around Ballymoate, a country road like this. We had kissed and cuddled like teenagers. The memory made me nostalgic. "Rita, do you think David has changed?"

Rita stopped, turned around and faced me. Her face was almost as rosy as her hair. "I thought things were better between you. You haven't complained about him for ages. Anytime I see him he's in good humour."

I knew I should have kept my mouth shut. "When do you see him?"

Despite the amount of alcohol she had consumed, Rita seemed to sense the tension behind the question. She gave me a sideways look. "I'm sure he tells you where he's going when he's out."

"If he did, I wouldn't be asking."

"He was here three times last week. He gets here around nine o'clock. In time to read to the boys before they go to bed."

Feeling angry, I turned and began walking down the road in a different direction to Rita.

"Teresa, hang on."

"These are not walking shoes. I'm going back." I heard the squeak in my voice, but Rita was satisfied with my answer.

"I'll go with you."

"Don't bother. I'm able to walk a few hundred yards on my own." My hostile tone was wasted on her.

"I'm getting a bit cold. Anyway I could do with another *deorum*."

Rita, when we came abreast, stared right at me. The look on her face changed from doubt to speculation to comprehension. "You didn't know he called to me so often, did you? I didn't want to mention it at school and I haven't seen you alone since the night in the pub. Remember the night of the accident?"

"Could I forget?"

Rita's eyes remained fixed on mine. "I don't believe he's having a relationship. With a woman, that is."

"With a man?"

"With Judaism. David's trying to establish his identity as a Jew."

"Big deal." Echoes of Esther again.

"It *is* a big deal to him." Her voice grew louder. "He feels you don't know what he's trying to say or do. He wanted to talk to you when your father was there, but you were so interested in your own drinking habits you scarcely listened to what he said."

I flinched as if she'd kicked me. Tears softened my eyes and my mouth quivered with the bruise of betrayal and its unexpectedness. I felt a pain beneath my rib cage. "Up to now I was naive enough to think that any arguments I had with David were between us and not for general consumption."

"Teresa, he only spoke to me and that's not exactly general consumption. And we weren't talking about you." Her voice was breathless. "Well, not in the way you think. It just came up by accident."

"Oh yeah!"

All trace of drunkenness left Rita's voice. "David asked me how much you drank on the night you knocked the girl down. He told me you were giving it up entirely and mentioned how it came about." She tossed her red mane. "It was a monologue, not a discussion."

"I see." But I did not see. Not really. If Rita weren't to blame, then David was. I'd have preferred if it were the other way around. Rita's Noel was coming home. We would meet at school and on the occasional night out. David, Noel, Rita and I used go to the pub, the cinema, the odd concert, for dinner.

But my whole life, emotional and physical, was bound up with David. Since his desertion I had been floundering. He still came home but he had deserted us, his family. Rachael's assertion that her Dad didn't have enough time to read to her was a symptom of the malaise.

We all have the same amount of time. It's what we choose to do with it that's important. I heard David's words of wisdom in my head. He chose to confide his innermost thoughts to Rita instead of me. He chose to read for her kids rather than his own. And he did not have the excuse anymore that my drinking was driving him away. If I had subconsciously harboured a doubt that there was anything physical between my David and Rita, an affair in the dictionary sense of the word, I knew now that I was wrong. The conviction failed to lighten my mood.

I got back from Rita's the next morning brimming with ideas but unsure how to implement them. After a night of lying rigid on Rita's pine divan bed, or alternately dreaming bad dreams, I was sure of one thing. My love for David was separate from the love I had for Rachael and Esther but both were of equal value.

David must feel strongly about Judaism to have broached it with Rita. I would have to make an effort to share his enthusiasm. Next time he went to the synagogue the children and I would go with him. I did not love him enough. He was the best of husbands.

I felt fat although I knew the mirror would show me the lie. Since I shed weight in my twenties, I was careful about what I ate. There was a pimple on my chin and my eyes, my best feature, were bloodshot from want of sleep. I would have to abandon my writing for a while. I couldn't live the rest of my life with a book.

I was trying to be a good abstemious wife but the strain was getting to me. My inner voice, reliable as usual, counselled that it would take two to mend this marriage.

My mother had been the mainstay of our house. My father hated his job and let that hatred dictate our lives. He was in good humour on a Friday evening, stayed in bed until six o'clock on Saturday, went to twelve o'clock Mass on Sunday and came home depressed. Monday morning and work was fast approaching.

My mother and I had lived our lives in his life. I had no memories of Sunday walks, picnics, football matches. My father was uninterested and my mother wanted to be there to get his tea in the evening. My smile felt bitter. I was progressing. Before this, I would have said my mother *had* to be there to get his tea. My mother chose to be there. As I was choosing to be there for David.

The following morning sounds of laughter greeted me as I drove up the drive to home. A red bucket, part of a bubble-making pack we had bought for the kids, stood before the open door. A large watery bubble, followed by Rachael holding the bubble blower aloft, came around the corner of the house.

"It's my turn. You've had two goes. It's not fair. Give it to me." Esther, and Roamy, careered after her.

David appeared in the doorway dressed in my plastic apron. He said, "They have me drenched." He looked towards his torso. "In spite of what I'm wearing."

I felt the usual tenderness well inside me. To cover my vulnerability I asked the inane question, "Any post? It hadn't come before I left for school yesterday."

Rachael, having handed over the bubble blower to Esther, hugged me around the thighs. "There's a big package. Like the one you got the day Nana got sick the first time."

"Mail? It's on the stairs. I was afraid we'd forget to give it to you." David's comment was one of a man in a comfortable relationship. 'All that glisters is not gold.' Appropriate that the line in my head was from *The Merchant of Venice*. Jacinta Broderick's mother had already accused me of being partial to Shylock. Jacinta Broderick! That was opening another poke of pigs.

The envelope was the same size as the previous anonymous calendars. My swallow sounded loud to my ears. I felt a tightness in my chest.

"I know who it's from. I wanted to open it but Dad wouldn't let me. He knows who it's from too." Esther handed me the bubble maker. "Here, you have a go."

My hand shook and my breath came in such short gasps I was incapable of gusting a decent bubble.

"Mom! Give it back."

In spite of my trepidation, I gave a small smile at Esther's disgust.

Feel the fear and do it anyway. Where did I hear that? Some self-help book somewhere. I took the envelope from the stairs; its weave felt luxurious. Whoever sent this was not short of a dollar. I thought dollar because I had spotted the sender's address and zip code on a printed sticker on the envelope's corner. I didn't expect it was from Granny Goldstein; for a long time she had handwritten that information "because," as she so eloquently put it, "I forget to order those darn thingamajigs."

"It's from Granny Goldstein," Esther said. "I knew all the time." She pointed at the left-hand corner of the envelope. "She must have ordered these ... at last."

"You should have told me."

"We didn't want to burst your bubble. Get it? Bubble? Burst?"

Rachael said, "Essie, we're not all thick you know."

"Sure?" Esther legged it out the door before Rachael could respond.

David said, "Open it, Tess. It must be something important for Goldfinger to write twice in a month."

I slit open the envelope, took out a brochure and handed it to him. I unfolded the letter, which, unusually for Granny Goldstein, was handwritten. My own mother had never seen a computer except on television and regarded them as newfangled objects from another age, whereas Granny Goldstein was a whiz at word processing.

Darlings, the letter began. Her writing was unwieldy. *I'm coming to visit.* After those first lines, I was too bamboozled to absorb her meandering. Until I came to the part where she said she had addressed the letter to me because she wanted me to have the chance to refuse. David wouldn't, even if he wanted to, because of his *Jewish thing about family.* She asked if relations were *kosher* between us. Would her coming add to the strain?

She stressed that she wanted an honest answer.

What had David been telling her? I had told her nothing untoward about our marriage. Any phone call I had made had been upbeat. "What's in the brochure?"

"Pictures and a glowing description of Ashford Castle. Look! Here's one of President Reagan when he stayed there. Wow! Cong sure looks scenic." David laughed. "No wonder Mom is impressed. There is a low-down on how *The Quiet Man* was made. You know that, since I have come to live in Ireland, it rates almost as high as *Dr. No*, with her. He rolled his eyes and scratched his beard. His face creased in a broad smile. "Wait until she hears that some of the locals from the movie are still alive."

David's spontaneous reaction made it feel like old times. I used to love him for his unpredictability. Our out-of-doors shenanigans, that I had recalled at Rita's, re-surfaced, making me blush. When had his freedom of mood and movement become an encumbrance? "David, we will have to give her a good time. I'm looking forward to it already."

He came towards me and took the letter. His eyes were soft as they rested on mine. "The kids will love having Goldfinger around. Won't you, kids?"

Esther and Rachael understood David's nickname for his mother. Not only did she sport gold rings on each finger of her right hand but, on two occasions when she was babysitting for us in the States, she had allowed them to watch 'Pussy Galore' cavort with James Bond in *Goldfinger*. As well as Sean Connery, Honor Blackman was her idol. Ursula Andress and now, it seems, Maureen O'Sullivan!

"When's she coming?" Esther asked. "I hope she's gone before my birthday. It's me who'll be twelve but she'll be the one hogging all the attention."

Rachael, David and I looked in unison at Esther's woebegone face.

David said, "Your birthday will still be a month away by the time she goes back. She's coming two weeks Saturday."

I said, "Which reminds me. 'Midst the bubbles and Granny Goldstein excitement, I forgot to tell you. Rita's Noel is coming home for good. He'll be here next Saturday."

The Saturday of Noel's proposed homecoming we woke to grey sombre clouds. David, having reluctantly set the fire and lit it, came in from the shed carrying coal. He said that he had heard on the radio earlier that showers were promised in the afternoon. "You chose a good time to order a fire, Teresa. It's just the day for sitting beside one and reading the paper." He sprawled on the settee in front of the flames he had kindled.

After my sojourn in Rita's, I had been determined to bring some of the comfort of a real home into my own four walls. Warmth, artificial or not, would be a change. In the end it had been Esther and Rachael who had persuaded him to do my bidding and get the fire going.

"You've changed your tune," I said. "I thought you considered making a fire a madass idea."

"Man's privilege to change his mind and all that stuff."

Rita usually had brown bread baked for David on Fridays; she knew how much David liked my mother's, and that she would not be able to make it for him anymore. I had just cleared up after we had demolished three quarters of it for breakfast.

He started to read the paper. Rachael and Esther lolled on the floor playing Scrabble.

"You can't use proper names. Are you stupid or something?"

"I can use what I like, can't I, Dad? Esther is just being a pain." Rachael sounded unusually plaintive.

David's tone was light. "Is that Junior Scrabble?"

"Daad! Junior Scrabble is for babies."

"Then I'll be a baby." Without hesitation, he put aside the paper, barely opened, and added, "Rach. Get the other one and we'll have a game."

"Oh! alright. I'll play too." Esther rubbed her hands through her hair, apprehensive for a minute. "May I?"

"Course you can, Essie. Can't she Dad?"

"Suah."

A working silence followed. I went upstairs. I was pulling the duvet up on the beds in Rachael's room when I heard the phone shrill. It was the oddest thing. I had never noticed its loudness before.

"Tess, will you get it? These two are disgracing me," David said, good humour restored. "I cannot afford to lose my concentration."

"Okay." I walked into our room, sat on the bed and picked up the white extension.

"Teresa?"

"Rita." I smiled. "How are you?"

"I don't know how I am."

"Your voice. It sounds strange. You couldn't be still hungover."

Ominous silence.

"Has something upset you?"

Silence.

Rita's lack of response made me realise that something was seriously wrong. "Rita, what's the matter?"

"I don't know how to tell you. Oh God!"

Was she going to confess that there was something more between her and David than a close friendship, I wondered. Teresa, forget the paranoia. My voice, even to my own ears sounded strained when I said, "For Godsakes, Rit, spit it out. It can't be that bad."

"It's Noel." She seemed further away than Tuam.

I calmed down, remembering how worried she got when Noel was travelling. "Should he have been home by now? I'm sure he's just got delayed."

Sobs sounded hollowly in my ear.

"Rit! Is it something else? Are the kids okay?" I heard my voice scale. "Are *you* alright?"

142

Silence.

"For Chrissakes talk to me."

"The boys are still asleep. They were up late last night making welcome home banners for their daddy. Oh God! How am I going to tell them?"

"Rita?"

"Noel is dead."

I mustn't react. Howling like a banshee wouldn't help.

"Please come. I don't know what to do."

She is now a free agent, free to pursue my David. The thought, nasty and unwarranted, caught me by surprise. "Is there anybody there with you?"

"The guards have gone down to get my mother. I was making queen cakes when they knocked. I thought it was Mary from down the road. She said she would help me hang the curtains in the bedroom before he came."

A myriad of emotions churned inside me. To think I had been envious of her. Jealous of her voluptuous figure and her winning ways with men. With David. "We'll leave immediately." I didn't know what else to say. When I put down the phone, I wandered about like the biblical Job.

I staggered downstairs, glad David and the kids were in the kitchen. The bottles in the drinks cabinet in the front room stood like soldiers in a guard of honour. The morning sun eyed the bottle of gin and made it shine. Sweat seeped through my palms. The brown bread was a lump in my stomach. There was a pain behind my eyes. Unpleasant phantoms of bartenders' whispers, forgotten hours, knowing glances, were what helped me totter from the room without opening a bottle.

David's face was bleached white when I had finished telling him. Before I went to warn my father that we were coming, he took me by the arm but we didn't embrace.

"Let's go," he said, "come on, kids."

"But we haven't finished the game and I was winning."

"Come on, Esther," Rachael shouted.

"Run upstairs and get your pyjamas. You'll be staying the

night in Nana's."

"Esther, your father is talking to you."

"Going to Nana's now is a real bummer. She's no fun anymore."

David's face regained its colour and matched his reddened eyes. The flush across his cheekbones made the straggling hairs in his beard stand out. His grip on Esther's arm was tight and his voice shook. He reached out to hit her.

"David, leave it. It's not her fault." The shocked look left his eyes but he was unrepentant. "Spoiled brat."

An array of pictures muddled through my head of unpleasant imaginings, in which David lashed out and I was left black and blue. Admit it, Teresa. Don't be always trying to play happy families. The scenes in your mind are not all make believe, merely recalled.

After depositing Esther and Rachael in my parent's house, peace took hold. For the rest of the way to Tuam I didn't have to cope with the two squabbling in the back and was able to concentrate on my thoughts. As I looked at David, his face set like a Halloween mask, I knew he didn't wish to talk either.

I thought of the photograph of Noel mowing the lawn on his anniversary, then of a younger Noel – the Noel who could be funny and serious and who had met Rita, fallen in love and married her within a year. It is said that within a marriage one partner usually loves more than the other. Not in Rita's.

The door was open when we arrived but David still banged on it with the brass knocker. Voices inside lowered as Rita came to the doorway.

Her Titian-coloured hair highlighted the chalkiness of her face. The patterned cardigan she had pulled on clashed with her striped figure-hugging jumper. Her movements, which, despite her large frame, were usually fluid had now become heavy and cumbersome, reminding me of a trapped animal.

After the embraces were over, she said, "He insisted that I didn't collect him in Shannon. Wanted the six of us to welcome him here, at home. He got a heart attack in the taxi. Thank God he wasn't driving. Imagine he was as far as Claregalway. If only he had let me collect him, I'd have been there when he died. Oh God, I can't believe he's dead." She put the back of her hand to her mouth. "I only found out half an hour ago, when our doctor phoned, that he had a weak heart. How could he do this to the children and me? Why didn't he tell me? He shouldn't have been working at all, never mind on an oil rig." She looked towards David. "Why didn't he confide in me?"

Why was she asking David? I dismissed the thought as unworthy of me and moved to take her in my arms, but David was quicker. Rita left her head on his shoulder and he caressed her hair with rhythmic strokes. "Rit. You will come through this."

We walked like a cortège into the kitchen. Since I had last been here she had covered the table with an oilcloth which, in the circumstances, bestowed an inappropriately festive air on the room. In the centre of the table stood a mixing bowl, with yellow dough smeared on the sides. A wooden spoon was stuck in the mix; an opened tub of margarine, an empty egg carton and a baking tin lay askew beside the bowl. Pastry cases were in place on the tray but only some of them were full. Dough from others was splattered over the table.

Rita bent and picked up a dirty knife lying on the floor and left it on the table. Her eyes held a tormented look. "I had it in my hand going to the phone when I was told. I must have dropped it on the way back."

Her mother, a tall, robust woman, marched into the room. She looked helplessly at David and me standing in the middle of the floor. "I'll finish these off, Rita."

"Mammy, there's no need." She turned to me. "Look in the fridge. It's chock-a-block with food and drink. All from neighbours. In the time you took to get here, three different houses sent up stuff. Who do they think will eat it?" Her tone was wry. "I could have done with it when Noel left." She shook her head. "People think teachers are loaded."

I felt a stab of guilt. I knew, since the other night, that she was still knitting jumpers to bring in extra income, but I had not realised that she was that hard up. But then I had never bothered to find out.

She raked her hands down her face. "Were it not for David helping me out with the mortgage, I don't know what I would have done. Noel was out of work so long and we owed so much money."

The indebtedness in Rita's voice was a weight I could hardly bear. "David?"

She nodded assent in his direction.

I thought I howled but as I looked at Rita, her eyes moist, and at David's jaw set in a grim line, his eyes dark, guarded, I knew it had been an internal cry of rage. Realising that my humiliation at the hospital, when my Visa card had been rejected, was a consequence of David's generosity to Rita, I felt like a dam trying to hold back an overflowing river. But I was afraid if I started to scream and wail and lash out at David I would not be able to stop. Also, I like to think my innate decency took over and prevented a scene on such a tragic occasion. I yearned for Esther and Rachael. I needed to feel their love to restore my equilibrium. "I'm glad he was able to help." I averted my eyes from David's although I could feel him staring at me.

He said awkwardly, "Tess, I would have told you but Rita preferred ..."

A vice pinched my gut. "I understand." But I was confused. It was my money too. Rita was my friend. David was my husband. We should have decided something like this together. Kill. At that moment I felt capable of seriously injuring both of them.

Andy, Rita's eldest whom I met when I visited recently, came out of the room. His face was the colour of the orange juice he was carrying. When he saw David, he squared his shoulders and, tilting his head, gritted his teeth. His swollen eyes betrayed him.

"Come here." David's face was closed as he pulled Andy into an embrace.

To quell my desire for an alcoholic drink, I focused on Rita's mother. "Where are the other kids?"

"They're with the Barrets down the road. They have children

of their own so they will have company. Poor little things. What will become of them?"

Before I could answer, David said, "Tess, Andy has asked me to go to the funeral home with him and Rita. They are meeting the director and seeing the body at five o'clock."

He was behaving as if nothing untoward had been revealed. In the scheme of things I supposed he was right. It was only money after all. The problem minimised in the face of death. I went along with the subterfuge.

Rita came from behind. "You could come to the morgue too, Teresa, but I thought you would stay here with Mammy until my sister and brother come. There will be hundreds of people calling." She sounded matter of fact, brittle, unlike her usual self.

"Fine, whatever makes sense."

By the time they left, the house was full. Six-packs of beer and bottles of whiskey stood on the table. Glasses had run out and drinkers were using mugs. Noel. I couldn't take my eyes off the one with the name Noel on it.

The pipe, left on a shelf, reminded me of Christmas. Many times, on the 22nd of December, the four of us had dinner together to celebrate Noel's birthday. He used to smoke the pipe afterwards.

My headache, which had started at home by the drinks cabinet, worsened. I would miss Noel but I had known him more as part of a twosome. Noel and Rita. Their names went together in my head like Romeo and Juliet.

Rita had been alone for months and I had neglected her. It was easier to socialise with her when she was one of a couple. Again, I was thinking the unthinkable. I didn't relish the thought of Rita, a loose wire, electrifying my David. "Have a drink. It will ease things." My internal voice bullied itself into my distress.

Many people came to the door to express their condolences. Rose Varley owned a flower business in the town. She dropped in with a dejected face and a thirst for a sale. Over a sherry she distributed printed accounts of the floral tributes to be got in her shop. One of Rita's brothers ordered a wreath and another put a deposit on a marble flowerpot for the grave.

A woman who introduced herself as Rita's immediate neighbour on the left brought a chicken casserole and her neighbour on the right had made a pot of vegetable soup. They all said, "It's such bad news." Each of them told me where they were when they heard and asked me to remind Rita that if there were anything she needed, she had only to ask.

If only I had my car with me. Rita's family were all there and I could have easily gone home. I couldn't bear the thought of hanging around for the evening without a drink. Just one. I would stop then; I tried to fool myself with tall stories.

The door opened and a colleague who lived near Claremorris came in. After half an hour we left together. I gave a message to Rita's mother for David. He would find me in my mother's house with the kids. I had to bite my tongue to stop myself from adding something nasty.

The next evening I left David, Esther and Rachael in the car and joined the queue that was waiting outside the morgue to view Noel's corpse. It was David who suggested I go alone to the 'funeral parlour' while he stayed with Esther and Rachael. He had been there yesterday and did not feel a need to go again.

It started to drizzle. There were three people in front of me, and a festoon of coloured umbrellas behind me. Though people talked less loudly when they came nearer to the door, their conversations were still audible.

My stomach lurched when it came to my turn to move inside. A plain casket, mounted on a chrome dolly, stood in the centre of the room. Relations, Noel's grandmother among them, her face withered like an old apple, were sitting on benches covered with leatherette, the kind you'd find in a dingy pub, and were reciting a decade of the rosary. A large cross hanging on one of the walls broke the monotony of the peeling paint.

Rita was standing flanked by her five sons. Noel's siblings and mother stood further down the line and then Rita's mother and family.

I felt as if I were drunk. Wishful thinking. I had the feeling that I was looking at this bizarre scene from a distance. Taking a deep breath, I prepared to do the rounds of hand-shaking.

Some of the people in front of me studied their shoes as one by one they shook Rita's limp hand and mouthed their patter. When someone she knew well came, Rita embraced her tearfully. More than her tears, the tautness of her neck and the strain in her shoulders showed the trauma she was going through.

The litanous 'sorry for your trouble' had the effect of a mantra on me. Fatigue from last night's sleeplessness caught up. Pity ran through me. Rita had lost a loving husband. Five children had lost a loving father. I hugged my friend. Her body, usually soft and pliable, was tense and rigid in my embrace, her lips cold and dry on my cheek.

After I had sympathised with the two families I stood beside the coffin, blessed myself and pretended to say a prayer. The waxen figure in the coffin, thinned by hard work and an obsession to return to his family, was like a stranger. I forced myself to touch his cold hand.

Talk seeped in from outside. "Who would ever have thought the pint would go so dear?" or "Did you hear about the bugger of a heifer who escaped onto the main road on me?" The words of the first sorrowful mystery of 'The Agony in the Garden' and "I can't get anything done in this awful weather" mingled in my mind. I went to one side to wait.

I wondered how David was coping with the kids. Had they been a welcome excuse for him to remain outside? I wondered if it would have been too painful for him to witness Rita's grief for another man. The thought, ugly, obtrusive and so wrong, shocked me. I was falling into the trap women fall into when their marriage is in trouble. Blame someone else. The fault couldn't be mine. There had to be another woman involved.

I stood with my legs apart for balance, took deep breaths and felt myself uncoil.

At last we streamed out of the room allowing the chief mourners to remain while the undertaker closed the coffin. The hearse was parked outside the door of the morgue. Crowds, still nattering, waited for the coffin to emerge.

I hurried back to the car and sat in the passenger seat. Although it was a gloomy day, David had donned sunglasses to hide his tears, I guessed. Esther and Rachael were unusually quiet.

"What's wrong with you?" I asked, more to fill the silence than to find out.

"Dad hit me." Esther turned her bruised face for inspection.

Rachael had her hand around Esther's shoulder.

"Don't exaggerate, Esther." David's words were clipped. "I hit her with my elbow. By mistake."

"Dad!" Rachael's voice was incredulous. "You ..."

"Well, maybe it was not entirely by mistake but I didn't mean to ..."

To mark her, I thought.

Esther muttered, "Imagine hitting a kid. It's the pits. I should tell teacher."

"Dad's under a lot of stress, Esther."

"So! That doesn't mean I should have to suffer."

"Essie. You know how Dad liked Noel and Rita. You can't blame him too much. What would you do if, if ... someone died belonging to you."

"See. You can't think of one friend." Esther massaged the bruise, making it more garish. "And I *am* going to tell teacher. She said there should be a helpline set up for battered children."

When he heard this, David took his hands from the steering wheel, lifted them up and banged them down again. "The corpse is coffined?" His voice was fragile.

"Yes."

He looked at Esther. "I'm sorry. I will never do that again." He winked at her.

Her petulant face wavered into a thin smile.

"I forgive you, Dad." She cocked her head in imitation of her old spirit. "And I *won't* tell teacher."

Who would *I* confide in if it ever happened to me again, I

wondered, as we prepared to drive to the church.

Next morning, most people had arrived by the time we had reached the church. A Solemn Novena was due to start on Monday. To maximise the numbers attending, the authorities had come up with a marketing ploy – stickers bearing the words 'Are you one of the 20,000?' (attending the Novena was implied but not stated). Ardent churchgoers were still distributing them to the faithful, who wore them on their lapels. A funeral was an unexpected opportunity to advertise it further.

"It's not fair. We never get anything," Esther complained when I refused to accept one.

Hawkers of religious paraphernalia had erected a grey galvanised white-roofed hut, where they sold crucifixes, holy medals, scapulars and other Solemn Novena memorabilia outside the gate.

Noel's coffin was in front of the main altar. Rita was sitting with Noel's and her own family in the top seat. Pupils, well groomed and subdued, who had Rita as their class tutor, were also there.

"Mom, there are five priests on the altar. Wow." Rachael, through her tears, revelled in the drama.

"I wish Dad would kneel like everybody else." Esther, who seconds before had been sobbing, decided to make David pay for her misery. "Why does he have to be Jewish? It's so embarrassing."

I was relieved that David, who had his head in his hands, hadn't heard.

"Shut up, Essie." I felt like kissing Rachael when she voiced what I was thinking. In the eulogy, Rita's parish priest said that Noel had been a weekly communicant, was great for collecting the yearly dues and never refused to give a hand at the bingo in the church hall. He loved his parish. Noel was a family man who was not afraid of hard work.

He asked God, on behalf of Rita and the children, for the wisdom to understand why He had taken such a good man from them. He gave a recipe for such disasters. "Put your faith in the Blessed Virgin."

After the ceremony of the incense was over, the men of the family carried the coffin down the aisle. Then a parade of priests in frocks with Rita and other close relations following. The coffin was awash with floral tributes. Rachael, Esther, David and I stayed seated.

"Thank God his parents are not alive to see him dead," a woman said, as she passed by our seat. "God's ways are a mystery."

"I never heard of God's mysteries. Only Enid Blyton's, and hers don't make me sad." Rachael, always helpful, started to get up. "Will I tell her, Mom?"

"Don't be daft, Rachael. She's talking about how stupid it is that Noel is dead when old sick people like Nana are alive."

David said, "Esther, that's not a nice thing to say."

"But that's what she meant. Isn't it, Mom?"

My rib cage contracted at the mention of my mother. I said, "Yes, Esther. That's what she meant."

David reached over and squeezed my hand and I felt, for an instant, comforted.

We walked behind the coffin to the cemetery. When the graveside prayers were over, the queues began. People there out of duty, unmoved by the tragedy, went to shake hands with the family. They sympathised with Rita, tears streaming down her cheeks, incoherent in her grief. Next they sympathised with her sons, dressed in their best clothes, clean faced and desolate. Their demeanour changed to one of bowed heads, slumped shoulders and sorrowful expressions.

I knew even before the meal began in the local restaurant that I would have to struggle through it. The turkey and ham made me feel sick. Drink flowed. If Esther and Rachael hadn't been sitting with Rita's kids, we could have left sooner. Rita had no need of me now. There were plenty around to console her.

David had paid her mortgage without consulting me. The debacle in the hospital resurfaced. One quarter of me was torn asunder with sadness and pity for Rita; a second quarter resented David's devotion to her; a third felt riven by guilt for my ill will, and the part, that completed the whole was simply addled.

I remembered the letter from Granny Goldstein. In a week she would be here. David would want to entertain her. He would have little time to comfort Rita. Possessiveness as old as time twisted in my entrails.

All the privilege I claim for my own sex ... is that of loving longest, when existence or when hope is gone. Jane Austen had written this in the nineteenth century. I put down my copy of *Persuasion* and surveyed my English class. I wondered whether it was true of my pupils. Whether it was true of me.

Had hope gone? It was because I had known such happiness with David in the past that I felt unable to cope with the present. He used to be my best friend as well as my husband.

I let my eyes linger on Jacinta Broderick who, at my insistence, was sitting in the front seat. Since our meeting in the principal's office, her attendance had been poor but, despite her absences, she persisted in doing higher-level English. The last time she was absent a virus had been her excuse for her staying at home. Despite my scepticism, I noticed that though she was usually pale, Jacinta now burned with a strange reddish pallor. My pulse raced. This hadn't happened because she was ignorant of the 'facts of life', was my first defensive thought.

In my Health Education classes, I taught Catholic doctrine on pre-marital sex and contraception but I spent the bulk of the time hammering home to them that if they were sexually active they could conceive; I outlined artificial means to prevent having a baby.

I tried not to stare at Jacinta. The severe school uniform, a gymslip of an oatmeal mix with a brown cardigan and beige blouse, looked incongruous on her pregnant frame. It wasn't necessary to look at her swollen ankles to confirm what I already suspected.

Her cardigan was buttoned to the top and she was naturally

buxom so it was easier to hide her condition. However, since the media had begun to highlight an increased frequency in teenage pregnancies, I had become more alert to signs of approaching motherhood.

Jacinta's swollen ankles could be a sign of threatened toxaemia. I felt a wave of sympathy for the poor girl. When I was carrying Esther, I had the same symptoms. My blood pressure used to soar without any warning, so I had to attend my GP three times a week to have it monitored. I had spent the last couple of weeks in hospital having complete rest.

"What are you looking at?"

Jacinta's strident tone shocked the class. You couldn't talk to Mrs. Goldstein like that and get away with it. Two pupils at the back of the class nudged each other. Bit of excitement! Better than reading about that wimp Captain Wentworth.

But behind Jacinta's aggression and bravado, I knew there lurked a frightened teenager. Faces collapsed in disappointment when I said in an even tone, "I have a message for your mother, Jacinta. Please stay after class."

Jacinta's eyes widened. She shrugged her shoulders as far as her ears and donned a brazen expression. Her eyebrows came together and her lips were a lank line. "Who does she think she is? Bloody hymie." The loud whisper sailed from the front desk to my ears.

I recalled the testimony on the wall in the staff room. *If children live with criticism they will ...* If the interview in the principal's office was anything to go by, Mrs. Broderick was a less than kind parent.

I longed to answer the bratty comment, but steeled myself. An effective teacher knows when to let indiscipline go and when to confront. Although I felt hot under my cool cotton jumper, I decided this was a time to retreat.

The bell, marking the end of class, dinned off the chinked ceiling and buffeted lockers. The usual shuffle erupted. I said, "Finish the chapter tonight and I'll question you on it tomorrow."

"Yes, Miss." The murmur, although a mixture of individual

voices, merged.

"You may leave," I said. It was a gratuitous comment as they had bolted as soon as the bell rang anyway. Jacinta dawdled. I heard her say to her friend that she'd better wait and talk to 'this wan'.

Suddenly doubt assailed me. Rita was still on compassionate leave so my main source of information wasn't there. I would have got a hint of Jacinta's pregnancy in the staff room if any of the teachers had known about it. What if I were wrong? The easiest thing would be to give her a message for her mother about the parents' committee and let her go. Neither Jacinta nor her parent had any regard for me. Why should I look for trouble? There were enough traumas in my life.

You're a teacher, Teresa, I reminded myself. You have written a book to help teenagers wade through the sexual quagmire of adolescence. You are in the throes of a follow-up. You boast of expertise in the area. You taught her Health Education in the Junior Cycle.

I had omitted the most important reason of all. Jacinta was a first cousin of the girl I had knocked off the motorbike. I was appeasing my conscience.

Another thought, too horrific to contemplate, pushed my selfish ones aside. Did she know of the pregnancy herself?

Jacinta was intent on gathering her books. Her face was like a tightened string. I had suspected she was a smoker but as I got nearer to her, I also sniffed the odour of unwashed underwear. I felt as nervous as Jacinta looked. "Who's the adult around here?" I murmured to myself.

She slapped down a book on the desk. I looked into her light grey eyes and thought of ice cubes. Without thinking, I touched her hand.

A startled look, followed by a slight thaw, crept into her frostiness.

I infused as much sympathy as I could into my voice; my reservoir of emotion had dried up since Noel's death. "Jacinta, you have been absent a lot lately. Are you unwell?"

"I'm awright." Her eyes refroze. She moved her hand away from mine. "I thought you had a message for my mother." The word mother was spat.

"Actually I wanted to have a word with you."

"What about?"

I groped for the right phrase. All I could come up with was, "You have missed a lot in the past few weeks so I wondered if ..."

"If I am going to do pass. No way." Resentment dripped from every word.

"That was not what I was going to suggest. In fact what I'm going to say has nothing to do with school work."

"What then?"

You can skirt around this forever, Teresa. You will have to do a Granny Goldstein on it. Say it straight. Despite my thoughts, I prevaricated, "Have you a boyfriend?"

Jacinta's resentment smouldered. "Now I know what this is about. Sr. Pius saw me talking to a fella outside the gate last week."

I grasped the straw. "And?"

"*He* wasn't the reason I didn't come back after lunch. I felt sick. That's all."

Kick for touch, Teresa. "And do you get sick like that often?"

Jacinta's anger flared in her response. "Sr. Pius called Michael a big galoot and told me to get rid of him. She asked if I had forgotten Mary Mags. As if. She was all she talked about during religion."

My confusion must have showed on my face.

"Mary Magdalene, the pro from the bible. Imagine she said that to me. For *talking* to the guy." Her contempt was palatable.

I felt clammy under my arms. "Jacinta, please don't take this the wrong way. Are you pregnant? I'll help you if I can." The words shuddered in the air before resting on Jacinta's shoulders.

She reminded me of a bully who has received an unexpected blow in a fight she thought she'd win. Her chest expanded. She sighed and sat down heavily. I thought of a tyre with a slow puncture. "Why are you so fucking nice?" A strangled sound came form her throat. Silence hung like a dagger. "I haven't had a period for four months." She averted her eyes as she confessed this, then raised her head defiantly. "But Michael says I can't be preggers."

"What do you think?"

"He hated using those balloon things. It was me who made him." Her voice was harsh. "It was the one thing we fought about. He said it was like going for a swim with your socks on. We done it a few times without anything." She shrugged the same way as before. "I didn't want him to go off with someone else, did I? He done a bunk after I missed the bloody curse a second time. Funny that! He says I can't be pregnant but he still skiddadled." She tossed her head. "So, I've lost out big time, haven't I?"

"Yes, you have."

Jacinta seemed to have forgotten that I was there at all. Now she looked at me carefully. "I tried to get rid of it."

I concentrated on not moving a facial muscle.

"I filled the bath to the top with steaming hot water. Then I lowered a half bottle of gin I bought at the off-licence."

Silence.

"Don't worry, it didn't work. All I done was get a whopper of a headache and a telling off for wasting so much hot water."

Silence.

"I kept ballyragging my father hoping he'd beat me up but wouldn't you know it? He's going to that Solemn Novena so no chance, at least until it finishes."

I strove to maintain my composure. As a seductive gin and tonic danced in front of my eyes, I visualised Jacinta's bespectacled crop-haired mother instead of booze. "Have you told your mother?"

"No."

"Are you going to?"

"I have to make sure if I am or not first."

"When?"

"I don't have a doctor."

I said, "I'll take you to Dr. Feerick in Claremorris. There will be less chance of you meeting someone you know." As soon as I had made the offer, I regretted it. "If that's what you want."

Jacinta pulled at a string of her hair. "Awright."

"Meet me after school this evening. We'll go then."

"Can't. I have to catch the school bus. I'm on the early one this week."

"I will need to re-arrange my schedule anyway. We'll go after school tomorrow evening. I will make the appointment for five o'clock. We'll be lucky if the doctor can squeeze us in at such short notice."

Jacinta mumbled something about not being able to get home.

"I can drop you off."

"Fine." She left without a word of gratitude.

It was a quarter past four on the following day and Jacinta and I had met as previously arranged.

"This is stupid," she said. "I'm sorry I ever said I'd go to the bloody doctor. I must be mad." There was a spot of tomato ketchup on the front of Jacinta's gym and its hem was down.

My sentiments exactly, I thought, biting my lip in frustration. I wished I had never got into this. Esther was in a sulk this morning because I was unable to take her to the only birthday party she had been invited to for ages. My "Cora will take you" had been met with "Who's the mother around here?"

It was so unfair. David was off on his Jewish odyssey while I was doing my best to remain temperate, be there for our kids, do my writing and teach. Granny Goldstein, much as I liked her, would be an extra stress when she came.

We never went out as a family anymore. It was at least six months since we'd gone to the cinema. I felt a pain between my lungs and my heart. David and I lived in the same house but he might as well be in Israel for all we saw of each other.

We got to the doctor's at five minutes to five. It was a tall, sober house; six steep steps led to blue double doors. The name Dr. Vincent Feerick was barely visible above the brass nameplate of Dr. Constance Feerick. Dr. Constance had employed a professional polisher to erase it when her husband had left the practice and the marriage to live with a woman half his age in a cottage near the town.

The waiting room was through the door on the left. It had a high ceiling and deep leather chairs. Two long tables were strewn with women's magazines.

There was a type of desk-cum-counter at the opposite end of the room from the door. A henna-haired woman, whom I didn't know, sat behind it. After we checked in, she ticked off the name in her appointments book. We sat down.

Jacinta's eyes darted along the wall to the large printed sign for *Cura*, to *The Samaritans* back to details of a shelter for battered women. She stood up suddenly and made for the door.

"Jacinta!"

"I'm just going for some fags. Won't be a sec."

It was a very long five minutes for me, before Jacinta come back with a cigarette dangling from her lips and a nervous air.

"I feel like puking," she said.

Her pasty pallor showed that she was telling the truth. At five, a patient left.

The secretary called Jacinta's name and she walked to the door of the surgery, her head lifted like a hunting dog.

"I'll wait here," I told her. I began to flick through a magazine. After five minutes I went up to the secretary, paid the consultation fee, and regained my seat. I was halfway through the problem page when Jacinta returned.

We were silent until we reached the car.

"You're not, are you?" I asked.

"Yes."

"Yes, you're not?" Drop the teacher bit, Teresa, I admonished myself. Jacinta is not skilled in the use of positives and negatives. She means she is.

"Yes, I am!" She emphasised the first word and stopped. Then banged down the second two like a hammer.

Her confirmation clung to me like a mist that wouldn't clear.

She stared at the rows of palm trees lining the doctor's garden.

"I'll drive you home."

"I'm going to tell them. My mother and father. What difference does it make now? I'm leaving so they can't do anything about it."

She kept her eyes on me but I kept mine pinned on the road.

Her voice was cold. "I'll have to leave school. Imagine Pius and that science teacher Mrs. Martin if I were to go in with a baby bulge." Her voice froze. "It's different for Michael. He'll be let do his Leaving Cert, no problem."

"What are you going to do?"

"Have the baby. What do you think I'm going to do? Bloody hell."

Silence.

Jacinta stole a glance at me. "Would you come in with me? I know what I'm going to say. I planned for this. I have enough money to take the boat." She rummaged in her pocket. "I cut this address out of an *Irish Post*, my cousin left when he was home from England."

I looked into the rear-view mirror and signalled that I was stopping before I took the piece of screwed up paper. It described the 'Irish Centre' in Camden Town and the help they gave to Irish nationals. Bishop Éamon Casey had been active in that before he became Bishop of Kerry so it was bound to be dynamic.

"They'll find me somewhere to stay until I have the baby."

"And then?"

"I'll take care of it. Don't worry." She thought for a minute. "My mother and father will be only too glad to get rid of me. They will have less hassle with me gone."

I hesitated.

"Please. Come in with me while I tell them."

After an hour, the irrefutable fact that Jacinta wanted to keep her baby wore my arguments lean. In an idealistic way, she treasured the thought of the baby as being hers exclusively, a doll of her very own to play with.

"How come you didn't suggest I make him marry me? Want to bet that's the first thing my mother and father are going to say?"

I didn't answer. My reasons for not doling out that advice were my own. I was not going to reveal that I had deliberately become pregnant to *persuade* David to marry me. I turned the key in the ignition and restarted the car, full of grief for my own predicament and Jacinta's.

A discarded washing machine, the door hanging from its front, stood outside the back door of Jacinta's house.

"Wait here," she ordered. She plodded through the open doorway before I could gather my wits. The words she threw over her shoulder were, "I won't be long."

Slightly faint, I leant on the side of the washer. The cold from the aluminium seeped through my jumper. I wanted to flee. "I think I'll go and ..."

"Bring her in," I heard Mrs. Broderick command.

Jacinta reappeared waving an impatient hand. "You heard what she said."

My feet stuck to the ground.

"Move, will you."

The whole thing felt surreal. I was conscious of the absurdity of being ordered around by an uppity pregnant schoolgirl but I still did what I was told and slunk after her. My anxiety was so severe that all I noticed, as we passed through the pantry, were dirty Wellingtons and socks in the middle of the floor. The room led into a kitchen that was also dark and cloudy, and smelled of Lifebuoy soap. It took a while for my eyes to adjust to the dimness.

Mrs. Broderick was poised over a sink wringing the soap out of a wet shirt. Through rising steam, she looked at me. Sweat or water ran down her face.

"Yes?" Her tone was impatient. "Jacinta is not giving up honour ..."

"Up on her. Up on her." Jacinta said she wished Michael had

given up getting up on her before he put her up shit creek. Her face puckered with distress. She sounded hysterical. Despite the circumstances, I was mesmerised by the word play.

She ranted to her mother that Michael had been 'on her' and 'off her' like a jockey's bollix. "Until I became pregnant. Then he didn't want to know."

"Pregnant. You? Pregnant. I don't believe it. You can't be." Mrs. Broderick whinged like a peevish child. Her face became as mottled and red as her wet hands.

"But I am." Jacinta's face stiffened but her voice became more even.

Her mother gasped and before she had let out the breath, she grabbed a wooden spoon from the draining board. Unheeded, the shirt dropped back into the suds. "Over my dead body, you are."

"No, Mammy. We spread Michael's thick coat on the ground and did the business. At least that's where we did it once."

"What? Did I ever think I'd see the day when a daughter of mine would talk to me like this?"

The climbing steam gave events the aura of a Hitchcock film. "You're having me on. You have to be." Mrs Broderick's voice had grown high-pitched with indignation.

"Mammy. I'm pregnant. Period." A demented grin sprawled across Jacinta's mouth. "I mean no period. That's the problem."

"You think this is funny?" Mrs. Broderick lunged at Jacinta.

"Oh, Mammy, don't!" As a maniac jab smashed into her pregnant belly, Jacinta lost her bold look and doubled with pain.

I ran to her side but all I could do was whisper consoling banalities.

As the sight of her daughter's agony, Mrs. Broderick's eyes refocused. She dropped the wooden spoon and wiped her brow with her rolled sleeve. "I had such high hopes for you. I was getting around your father to let you go to university like they're all startin' to do round here." Her tone was bitter. "God knows, it doesn't take much intelligence to make a baby."

Jacinta was bent in two with pain. Mrs. Broderick went over

to her daughter and put her arms around her. "Come on. You should be lying down."

Jacinta refused to look up, yet I sensed her hopelessness.

She burrowed her head into her mother's shoulder. Half bent, she left the room enveloped in Mrs. Broderick's arms.

I looked around the kitchen, its clutter still indistinct in the steam. A sleeve from the abandoned wet shirt hung out of the sink. A porcelain figure of a black cat stared at me from a shelf over the Stanley range. What looked like soup simmered on a ring. As the room's warmth muffled me, I tugged at my high-necked blouse.

A memory, constricted in my mind since I was twenty nine, dilated; my mother ironing on a doubled sheet on the kitchen table, her tongue between her teeth using the steam iron on a stubborn pleat; my father sitting on his armchair with the paper; David in the sitting room, as jumpy as if he were back barefoot on the blistering sands in Israel. Me, too apprehensive to concoct a story or make an excuse. "Mammy, Daddy, I'm going to get married."

My mother making the sign of the cross. "How on earth?" Her voice unsteady.

My father squirming on his chair. "If it's that David fellow you think you're marrying, you can forget it.

"I'm pregnant."

"Jesus, not by the Jew?" My father's tone had rivalled that of Heinrich Himmler.

Horrified by their bigotry, I hadn't empathised with what they must have felt. I was the only fruit of their loins, their bookish daughter, the one with grandiose ideas, the one who questioned everything, who refused to take advice, who enjoyed doing the unorthodox, who had gone to America on holidays and come back with a Jew in tow and was now announcing she was pregnant.

In my mother's eyes was a look of distaste stemming from her revulsion at the thought of the sex involved in making a baby. In my father's, there was distress that I was not marrying a good

Catholic west of Ireland man.

Despite their reaction, I had remained euphoric. I had achieved my goal. I was marrying the man I loved. The blood that gushed from me two hours after we had taken our wedding vows in front of my family and friends was a condemnation of my manoeuvre.

Granny Goldstein had sent money, which David used for further studies and to set up his legal practice. Because my pregnancy hadn't been public, I continued with my teaching job in the local convent. We settled to being married.

Interrupting my reverie, Mrs Broderick came back into the kitchen and catapulted past me towards the door. "Holy God. She's bleedin'. I think she's losing the blasted baby."

It was after eight o'clock when I arrived home from Jacinta's, too late to eat with Rachael. We had planned to share a bag of popcorn after relishing a deliciously fattening pizza, the kind of food that was being served at the birthday party Esther was attending. The treat would minimise Esther's chance to tease her sister about all the lovely food she'd missed.

Cora would, I knew, have left a note if she were leaving the house empty.

Walking through the downstairs rooms, I expected to hear voices. But there was no sign of life until I came to David's study. And then I could only hear a faint shuffle. I turned the handle on the door.

David was sitting with his earphones on, listening to music. When he saw me, he took off the phones and stood up. A blue haze of smoke hovered over his head. The remains of a duty free cigar lay on the pottery ashtray Esther had thrown when she was at Montessori school in America.

I felt wobbly, like a bald tyre fighting for traction on a slippery road. Tentatively, I put my hand on his.

"Cora and Rach went to collect Esther from the party," David said. "I offered to go but Cora knows Mrs. Black from bingo. When you were late, she said she'd get some food there for Rachael."

"I had to leave a pupil home. I didn't feel the time."

He looked down at me and squeezed my hand. "Is everything alright?" His kiss was weightless on my surprised lips. "Have you forgiven me for spending our money without telling you?"

My blood rose. Thoughts of Rita's mortgage, and Jacinta and

166

her unwanted, wanted baby were the last things on my mind. I pressed myself close to him.

After a few seconds, his hands searched beneath my clothes. I felt full of regret and need. We kissed deeply and as he slipped his hand through the fastening at the back of my skirt, I closed my eyes and moaned softly.

He pulled himself back. "I should stop."

"Cora and the kids will be back."

"Yes." He kissed me.

I began to sigh and rub myself against him.

"You're lovely," he whispered, his breath wet in my ear.

Though I didn't much enjoy all the huffing and puffing involved in sex, it did elicit compliments and closeness. Reluctantly, I removed his hand from my buttocks and freed myself. We weren't prepared. I could conceive. The thought both frightened and tantalised me. "We can't, David." The prospect of what this could lead to steadied me.

In the beginning, David married me because I was pregnant. I could force him to stay with me for the same reason. He was that type of guy. He hadn't changed that much in the intervening years. I wouldn't take the chance of doing it to him a second time.

"You're right." He held my gaze for a moment and touched the back of his hand to my cheek.

I nodded without speaking.

A pink glow diffused his face. His breathing was still quick. For a long moment, we stood in an uncertain and astonished silence. Tears were beginning in the corners of my eyes when I heard Cora's key in the lock.

Rachael and Esther chorused, "Goodbye, Cora."

Then Rachael shouted, "Anyone for popcorn?"

"Good old Rachael. Generous as usual." David fingered his beard and went out into the hall. "I'll have some."

"No you won't." Esther looked so coldly at David that he pulled back his hand in mid grab. "That's mine. She stole it off me. It isn't fair. She wasn't even invited to the party."

"You're just mad because I won the two-legged race."

"Only because I wasn't in it." Esther tossed her head.

Rachael's eyes were small with tiredness. She smirked. "Because nobody would run with you."

I had evaded David's eyes since our sensuous scuffle. In return, he was avoiding mine. It was as though he was waiting for me to initiate our next move. I said, "You're both tired. Time for bed."

"Before we go," said Esther, holding up her slim hand, "I have something to tell you." Her eyes slitted as she looked at Rachael. "Teacher found Mary Harvey's gloves in Rachael's bag." Her voice lowered. "I don't like telling tales but," she looked defiantly at both of us, "you always say we should tell when something bad happens."

"It was by mistake. I didn't know they were there."

David said, "It's alright, Rach. Go to bed and forget about it for tonight."

"I'm off too. See you in the morning." Esther, having had her moment of triumph, showed no further interest in the subject.

David threw me a complicit glance. His tone was soft and sexy. "Why don't we all go to bed?"

I didn't have the will to resist the intimacy of the suggestion or his appreciative gaze.

He followed me up to the room that was once ours, but was now mostly mine.

I let him undress me, passively standing by as he took off my clothes and threw them on the bed. I had to make a conscious effort not to move to fold them while he rummaged in the drawer for protection. Safely in bed wrapped in David's arms, the place I most wanted to be, I was unable to turn off my thoughts; I was dry and unaroused when he entered me. Afraid of rebuffing him, I feigned an orgasm and moaned with him as he came.

In the morning I rested my head on his chest; it was good to have him beside me. I remembered how I used to jokingly count the hairs on his chest and tell him he had seven aside. Breathing in the smell of his skin, I felt the yielding underline of his hairy jaw with my fingertips.

I was irrationally happy. It had been so long since we had experienced such closeness, I cherished each second of our togetherness. His body next to mine was a balm for my hurts. For the first time in ages I felt strong enough to conquer my ghouls.

David and I were loitering on the passenger side of the doors waiting for the Boston and New York flight to disembark when we heard Granny Goldstein's voice.

"I feel I have lugged this single-handedly all the way from Logan."

"She has arrived safely." David took me by the elbow like a loving spouse. His tone was confiding. "To tell you the truth I thought she would change her mind and not come at all." His eyes gleamed with excitement. "But I'm glad she did."

"Me too." Rachael hopped from foot to foot.

"I hope she brings me something nice." Esther stretched her neck in an effort to catch a glimpse of her.

I was the only one not part of the anticipation. I still felt exposed. It was two weeks since David and I had intercourse (I had stopped conning myself that we had made love). The following morning I had left him asleep and gone to school elated. There, Rita had gushed that David had called the previous evening but she was out. He had pushed a note in the letterbox. This depressed me. Rita was not there, so he drifted back to me.

I felt less surprised than wronged when he came home late the next night and slept in the office. For a few hours, he had given me what I yearned for – hope, love, respect, friendship – then nothing. He went back to being a lodger and me the cranky landlady.

What amazed me was that he didn't see anything wrong with what he was doing. His answer, when I told him of my hurt, was, "We took precautions, didn't we?"

Now here he was again acting as if we were Tristan and Isolde.

170

Disorientated by the strength of the recollection, I was unsure which exit Granny Goldstein would use. When David tugged at my elbow, I was looking in the wrong direction.

"Hi, hon." Granny Goldstein embraced David with enthusiasm, pulling him to her.

He in turn put her at arm's length as he scrutinised her face. "Good to see you, Goldfinger. Welcome to the auld sod."

"Hi, Tess." She held out her arms and before I went into them, she examined me, as David had done to her. The sincerity of the embrace showed me that I was much loved. "Where are my two cuties?"

For a moment, neither David nor I responded.

"The next generation, darlings. The next generation. Where are they?"

A man said in a low tone, loud enough for people close by to hear, "Typical yank." He fixed a humourless stare on Granny Goldstein's ample buttocks clad in forsythia yellow plaid trousers and added, "Yankee dresser, too."

A woman dressed in a respectable two-piece sniggered. Granny Goldstein was drowning a willing Rachael and a more self-conscious Esther with kisses and seemed not to hear the barb.

"She wouldn't care even if she did hear the schmuck," David whispered to me. Touched by the harmonisation of our thoughts, I could only nod.

Granny Goldstein let go of Esther, threw a large purple hat on top of a suitcase, looked at the critic witheringly, turned towards his tweedy wife and hollered, "Gee, hon. You must be hard up." To her grandchildren's delight, she pirouetted in the middle of astonished Clare taxi men waiting for fares, plucked her gaudy trousers with the tips of her fingers and added, "Me, I wouldn't use that Philistine for practise, wouldn't use him for practice."

I said a silent thank you that my mother was not there to witness what she would regard as Granny Goldstein 'making a show of herself.' She had never met Granny but such an introduction would have been her death knell.

I kissed her soundly on the cheek. "Good to have you here, Gran."

David stacked the last of the cases on the trolley. "Let's go, Goldie. Time to see the sights of the most Christian country in Europe."

As I manoeuvred a trolley through the front entrance, a pregnant woman squeezed past, reminding me of Jacinta. Jacinta had been absent from school since I had gone to her home and she had revealed her condition. A few days later, when I phoned her mother, she told me that she had moved out. She had ended the conversation quickly by saying that she 'couldn't talk.' I had taken this to mean that Jacinta's father was within hearing range. Before I had a chance to ask anything further, Mrs. Broderick put down the receiver.

Granny Goldstein's exclamation, when we reached the car park, about the smallness of the 'automobiles' brought me back to the present. We all got into the car; Granny Goldstein, at my insistence, sat beside David in the front. It didn't take long to reach Ennis.

"Gee this is something else," Granny Goldstein said, turning back to me. "The streets are so narrow. Hon, this is some country you have here."

"I know. It's a standing joke in Ennis that two people could shake hands from opposite sides of the road."

Granny Goldstein's head tilted as she laughed.

Esther, beside me, said, "I'm glad you're here, Gran."

Rachael, who was sitting on the left, bowed her head in agreement and moved directly behind her so she could put her arms around her neck and give her a strangulation hug.

David, who had driven to the airport in silence, began to talk animatedly about people they knew in Boston. Listening carefully, I picked up threads of longing in his reminiscences.

As it was Sunday, many people were going to Mass. In a few towns, we had to wait while a guard stood at the entrance to church grounds regulating traffic, allowing right of way, with a wave of his hand, to cars exiting Mass.

"Hon, are church and state separate here?"

"Why do you ask?" David's tone was sardonic.

"Those guys in the navy uniforms. Are they police?"

"Suah."

"The church must have plenty of loot. Plenty of loot."

"The state pays them. It's not like America, Mom. Here they close the streets on, what is the name of the day again?" he raised enquiring eyes at me in the overhead mirror.

I was quiet for a moment. "*Corpus Christi.*"

"That's it. They parade through the streets carrying an umbrella over a piece of bread."

Esther interrupted. "Rachael nearly got pneumonia walking in the procession in her communion dress. I knew it would be cold so I didn't go. I pretended I had a pain in my stomach."

I became aware of an intense irritation. "David and Esther," I kept my voice light, "between the pair of you Granny Goldstein will get a terrible impression of Ireland."

David eyed me again through the mirror. "She won't be here long before she sees it for herself."

"Dad, you sound awful cross." Rachael tightened her grip on her grandmother's neck. "Gran was only asking."

"Yes, David, I was only asking." Granny Goldstein's jocose tone dissolved the tension.

When we arrived at the house, Granny Goldstein shouted with exaggerated glee. "It's lovely to see for real what you told me about at Halloween, Tess. That developer sure didn't finish his job." She eyed a hole in the ground full of water and almost tripped over a mound of sand Roamy had made into his lookout tower. "Rachael, where is the famous Roamy?"

"Shush, Gran. He's not allowed out through the hall. If he hears his name, he'll break the door down."

It felt good to hear laughter again.

"Wait until you see what we've ready for you! You won't believe it." Esther looked from her father to me.

"I hardly believe it myself." My voice was dry.

"Come and see, Gran." Rachael ushered her into the dining

room that had been in a state of preparation for a week.

"We all helped," Rachael said.

"Mom didn't."

"Oh! Essie."

David motioned towards the white linen tablecloth and the serviettes. His smile was strained. "It was your mother who found the Red Devil that cleaned the stains on the cloth. And who went into the supermarket for napkins?" He tweaked Esther's nose. "Missy Esther!"

"You're right. I forgot. Sorry, Mom."

Granny Goldstein, during this exchange, rubbed the curve of her lips with her thumb and forefinger. The creviced fans at the corners of her eyes became more obvious as she listened. When silence took hold, she took Esther and Rachael by each hand and brought them to the table they had pushed against the wall. "Now, explain what we have here. It looks sumptuous."

"I know. I know."

"Shoot." Gran winked at Rachael as she encouraged Esther.

Esther waved her hand over an array of bread and pastries. "Almond tishpishti and baklava."

"Essie, she knows what they are."

"Goldfinger knows what they all are." David put each of his arms around his children's shoulders. "The food is only new to you." He looked towards his mother. "It's not kosher but it *is* Jewish."

"Daad, I'm supposed to be telling."

"Okay, Esther. Sorry."

"Borekes." She pointed to a Sephardic delicacy. "It's filled with potato and cheese and am ..."

"Popeye the sailor man," Rachael sang merrily

Esther threw her a grateful look. "And spinach." She continued her demonstration. "Lox." She gestured to slices so thin they were semi-transparent.

"My turn." Rachael took a basket full of bagels in her hand and pointed to the mound of cream cheese, "These are my favourites."

Esther, not to be outdone, said, "I like the white fish. Their eyes are cool."

Rachael said, "We're not going to eat pork anymore, Gran." She looked an apology at me. "We didn't eat it much anyway, except when Cora stuffed it for us."

"Mom gave us pork chops when Dad wasn't here." Esther followed her interruption by sanctimoniously adding, "We're not going to do that anymore either. Sure we're not, Rach. Dad says ..."

Granny Goldstein turned towards me, shaking her head. "I don't know what has happened to this son of mine. He sure as hell wasn't interested in Jewish food in the States."

"I think we should eat and you should go for a lie down," I said.

"Yes. I think I will. I suddenly feel dog tired." She patted Roamy, who had plodded into the dining room. "No offence."

Esther said, "Gran, Mom will kill you for petting him. He's not supposed to be in here."

"Bold dog." Rachael's further admonition caused the repentant animal to sit back on his hind legs and look imploringly at her.

Granny Goldstein patted his head. "That dog's been to a training school I can tell."

Rachael pulled out five chairs and motioned to each of us to sit. When Gran sat at the top of the table, she answered, "Gran, schools here teach kids, not dogs."

Esther said, "That's not true. I read in a book that in Dublin ..."

Gran said quickly, "Tell me about your school, Rachael. What grade are you in?"

David and I ate the delicacies as we listened to our daughters tell Granny Goldstein about school.

"Why do you call your teacher your sister?" Granny Goldstein asked.

"Because she's a nun," Esther answered. "They call the head of the convent mother."

Rachael said, "We call our chaplain Father. In the boys' school they call teacher Brother."

David was slicing a portion of fish. "Sister, Mother, Father, Brother. One big happy family."

Granny Goldstein said, "You go to a private school?"

Esther shrugged and Rachael, who was dragging Roamy out of the room by the collar, had lost interest.

David said, "No, they go to public school."

"But they're taught by religious. In America that would be a fee-paying Catholic school." She looked at David and me. "Sorry, hon. I'm forgetting that you know this already."

My voice was teacherish. "Catholic schools are state schools."

"Oh! The church finances the schools. That's neat. Saves on the tax bill."

"Mom, don't kid yourself. The church doesn't pay for the schools. The state does."

Granny, confronted with these new details, was even more confused. "You mean he who pays the trumpeter doesn't call the tune? Wow."

I felt my body tense, ready to defend. Everything they said I agreed with, but I felt excluded. "A Catholic education for a Catholic people. I don't see anything wrong with that." My tone was severe as I looked at my kids' Jewish father and grandmother. "Conservative synagogues in America would love to have full-time day schools. It's opportunity they lack."

Granny Goldstein smiled in a surprised way that forgave my accusing pitch. She kissed David and leaned towards me. "I'll hit the hay. Where am I sleeping?"

"Esther," I said, "take Granny into Dad's office and show her her bed."

"Suah." Esther loved to imitate her father.

As their footsteps receded, I stole a look at David. His lips were tight. He was drumming on the table. "I may as well set up my bed. I'll throw the fold-up in Rachael or Esther's room. Save me disturbing you when I come in."

"Why? Are you going somewhere?"

"Yes."

"Your mother has come from Boston to see you and you're

176

leaving."

"For Godsakes, I'm going out for a while. Now that Goldfinger is in bed, there should be no sweat. Surely you will be able to manage without me for a couple of hours."

I thought I heard him mutter, "You're so goddamn needy," but I wasn't sure and I was reluctant to find out.

"Who pray tell is going to have the pleasure of your company if not your family?"

"Rita." His eyes on mine were appraising. "Her husband died. She has been left with five kids; you're her friend. I don't see you giving her much support."

"You seem to be giving her enough for both of us. You ..."

Esther arrived to show off the books Granny brought her from America and cut the exchange short.

David said, "I'll go now. The sooner I get there the sooner I'll be back."

"You don't *have* to go." Even as I repeated what I said earlier, I felt humiliated. I waved my hand as if pushing the suggestion aside. "Forget it."

When he moved towards me, I recoiled. He turned away.

I was sitting in the staff room mulling over my husband's concern for the widowed Rita when a friend of Jacinta Broderick knocked on the door and told me Jacinta wanted to see me. The friend had checked the timetable and told Jacinta that I was free after the eleven o'clock break on a Tuesday.

"Hello, Miss."

"Jacinta." I was breathless after rushing from the other end of the building to the front gate. I wanted to minimise the time Jacinta would have to hang around publicly so I hadn't stopped to retrieve my coat from its hanger outside the staff room. Now the cold seeped through my cotton blouse to freeze my bones.

That she was still carrying a child was my first surprise. My second was that she was smartly dressed. The purple tent dress and the wool cape over it covered her condition delicately. Her skin was still mottled and she stank of cigarettes.

"Ta for coming to the house with me, Miss."

"You're welcome." I wasn't sure what she expected of me so I decided to let her take the initiative.

She tossed her mane of greasy hair. "See how my mother assaulted me? She's worse than my father."

I said, "She got a shock. It wasn't thought out."

"I don't believe this. You're defending her! Typical."
Silence.

I clenched my teeth to stop them from chattering. To hell with this, I thought, if one of us doesn't say something, we'll be here all day. "Who are you staying with? What happened to the idea of London?"

"None of your business!"

"Sorry, you're right, it isn't." Why was I standing there freezing with the cold when I could be inside in a warm staff room? Something of my thinking must have shown in my expression because Jacinta's face crumbled as if she were going to cry.

"I'm staying with Junie until the baby comes. I'll get it fostered and then go to London, make a bit of money and come home and get it."

Jacinta watched me closely. Junie. She expected a reaction.

"He lives in one of the Lara road houses." Staring at me defiantly, she added, "His girlfriend is there, too, so it's not what you think. I'm not having sex or anything."

Junie Lawless had spent time in Loughlan House for raiding the collection boxes in the church. It was his third offence. "Why is he befriending you?" I asked.

Jacinta said, "Mona Corless is his bird. She's a friend of mine. You might remember her. Left school as soon as she could. Dying to get out of the place, she was."

"Yes, I remember her." Hearing the scorn in my tone, I balanced it by saying, "She was good to offer you a place to stay."

"Junie made her."

"I see."

"Mona does what Junie says."

"Why?"

Jacinta's face closed like a fist. "Got to go now." She looked like a lost kid. "I might call to see you again before I have the baby. I can't go home. They'd have a fit."

I proffered my hand and said, "I know where you're staying so I'll keep in touch."

"Don't think of calling to the house or anythin' stupid like that."

Until I assured her that I wouldn't, she fiddled with her hair, reminding me again of a worried child.

"Ta again."

Jacinta was not one for thanking people. That she had come to the school was a cry for help. The principal was away at a management meeting and the guidance teacher had taken students to a career seminar. The vice principal would have told me I was mad to be getting involved. The need to maintain Jacinta's trust and yet do something constructive were the twin concerns in my head all day.

By evening, I had decided to contact the Social Services Centre and tell Sr. Nuala, the Social Services nun, my story. Ordinarily, I would have spoken to Rita about my predicament. For reasons I didn't analyse, I felt uncomfortable doing that anymore.

When I had explained the circumstances to Sr. Nuala, she agreed to investigate but admitted there was little she could do without Jacinta's co-operation. I felt slightly relieved that I had told someone about the situation.

A thought struck me. David was unaware of Jacinta's existence. A year ago if a predicament like this had occurred, I would have confided in him and valued his opinion. Now I was afraid that if I told him anything, it would result in another disagreement. Our marriage had become like one of Rita's half-ripped pieces of knitting: a tug on a strategic thread and the rest would unravel.

The domestic thought reminded me that Granny Goldstein was at home and chomping at the bit to talk to me. I smiled at my horsey imagery due, no doubt, to Rachael's re-awakened interest in horse riding. The smile still on my lips, I turned the handle of the door into the staff room. It squeaked. Rita was standing at the notice board. "Needs oil," I remarked. Sometimes I say silly things when I'm taken by surprise.

"Sorry, can't help you there." Rita, equally abashed, looked at her shoes.

Oil. Rigs. The job that had contributed to Noel's death. Because of a rush of sympathy and because I had been finding excuses not to do it, I asked her to come to dinner the following weekend.

She gathered her hair off her face to deposit it into a lump at the nape of her neck, showing her chipped nail varnish. Her relief that we were being somewhat reconciled showed in her words. "I'd love to, Teresa. Maura, next door, will babysit for me."

Good, I thought. David, much as he treasured her five boys, would be unable to take care of them on this occasion. I would be insisting that he be at the dinner party. No hardship for him of course. He would be reluctant to miss a night in Rita's company. In an exaggerated friendly tone I added, "You'll meet Granny Goldstein. David's Mom."

"I love dinner parties, hon. Been friends with Rita for a long time, have you?" Granny Goldstein pulled thick socks on over pink heavy tights and put her feet into her well-worn sneakers. When she straightened, she asked, "Who knew her first? You or David?"

I was tying Esther's hair into a ponytail. My instincts told me that I should wait to answer the question until she had left the room. But despite my reservations, I responded, "Me. Why do you ask?"

"No reason, hon."

"She lived near me all my life. We've always been friends *and* enemies. But more so since we became colleagues, I suppose."

"Granny Goldstein."

"Yes, Esther."

"You *never* say anything without a reason."

"From the mouth of babes," I pretended to banter. "Come on Granny Goldstein, out with it."

"Gee, hon, it's not for me to say. It's not for me to say at all."

I forced a smile. "Say."

"Friends and enemies. That's an interesting concept. I prefer to keep friends and enemies separate."

"I should have said friends."

"Well, David is *ve...ry* friendly with her. Where was he the other night when jet lag woke me at six a.m.?"

"He was in Rita's. I thought he already explained about the power cut in Tuam. Andy needs a nebuliser for his asthma. Rita was afraid he would get another attack. She has just lost her husband. He couldn't walk out."

"We *are* a trusting soul."

"You're falling for the oldest trick in the oldest book," I said. "Eve tempted Adam. *Ergo* Rita is tempting David. Goddammit, listen to yourself."

"Touched a nerve?" Granny Goldstein's teasing tone belied the high colour flooding her cheeks.

"No need to pull the head off *me* just because you're fighting with Granny." Esther snapped the ribbon out of my hand. "I'll do it myself. While I have *some* hair left."

"What about those calendars you mentioned? What was that all about?" Granny Goldstein asked.

"In a moment of weakness I'd started to tell her about my unwanted post but then stopped. "That was ages ago. I was just talking *ráiméis*.

"That means Mom was talking rubbish," Esther offered. "Garbage to you, nana." gran

"Whatever. I'm on your side, hon. I'm on your side. David may be my son but I can see that he's going through a crisis."

"You sound like Dad's football team. Why are you taking sides?"

"Esther, I thought you were doing your hair." Even to my own ears, I sounded unduly harsh. Of late, I had begun to take my uncertainties and stress at being abstemious out on the kids.

"Mom. It's not fair. You never tell me anything. But I bet I can guess what you're talking about."

"I wouldn't bet if I were you, Essie." Rachael, fresh from her riding lesson, came in the back door wearing her jodhpurs, black riding hat, and swinging her whip. "Last time you bet with Dad that he wouldn't be there for your fifth class concert, you lost 20p."

"Yes. Well. That wasn't my fault. He'd missed the Christmas one and the parent teacher meeting. So you can't blame me for thinking he wouldn't show up."

Granny Goldstein said, "From the mouth of babes, Tess, as you so aptly put it. From the mouth of babes. I think I should have a chat with that son of mine."

"Please don't." I felt my voice rise. "Granny Goldstein, you're supposed to be here on holidays, not solving marital problems."

"I don't go to *schul* anymore. This can be my good deed for the year." She looked at me. "I suspected something was wrong when you were over on your book tour. Tess, I love you dearly but you are too independent. You can't battle everything on your own."

I thought of the way I sometimes shook with longing to have an alcoholic drink and yet managed to deal with it on my own. My father had got off cigarettes through sheer act of will. I had come from the brink of anorexia without resorting to professional help. We were proud of our independence. The much-repeated argument sounded suddenly trite.

"You look as if you're going into battle yourself, Gran," Rachael said. You're like Brian What's His Name with his helmet on."

"Brian Boru wouldn't wear a red tea cosy on his head," Esther said.

She laughed when Granny Goldstein lunged and tickled her. "My brains may be liquid but my head is not a teapot. And listen here, young ladies, since I'm about to take my constitutional, the Mayo wind would freeze my balls off if I were not dressed warmly."

Rachael said, "Balls?"

"Okay, Okay. If I had them. Since I don't, I have to take care of what I do have." She pointed gold fingers towards her head.

"Granny Goldstein!" my tone was a mixture of censure and laughter.

"Don't worry, Tess. Well brought up children like yours won't know what I'm talking about."

"I know." Esther's eyes glittered, "You're talking about the scrotum. Balls. I can even tell you where they are. Right behind the penis." In an informative voice she continued. "That's where sperm lodges. Mom told me. She wrote a book about that stuff, you know."

"Yes, I do know."

Rachael looked pensive. "They do look like balls. I used to see Dad's."

"What?"

"When I went in to Mom and Dad's bedroom. He always got out and put on his underpants. Mom always wears pyjamas in bed."

Esther put in her speak. "Yea, Mom. How come? Dad goes to bed in the nip and you look like you're going to the North Pole."

"Because I'm a cold creature, that's why." A voice nagged in my head. Frigid, dispassionate, unresponsive; cold takes in a lot.

"You must be freezing these nights."

Trust Esther not to let it go.

"Why?" Granny Goldstein asked. "If I knew you needed pyjamas, I could have brought you a pair from Filenes instead of that chiffon scarf."

"Gran. You're a daftie sometimes." Rachael patted her on the shoulder. "Esther means, Dad isn't there to keep Mom warm."

I felt the blood rush to my cheeks. David took turns to stay in Esther's room one night and Rachael's the next. He always put away the foldup in the morning and was discreet when he carried it from room to room.

Granny continued zipping her jacket.

A knock at the door sliced the tension between us. We all heard the sound of the postman throwing in what sounded like a bulky letter. I thought of calendars.

"Esther. Get the post, please."

"It's 'Ranger Rick', Mom. Remember Dad ordered it for me from America."

The knot in my stomach disappeared.

"Hang on a sec," Esther's voice sang through to us. "There's one for you too, Mom. It's nearly as big as my one."

The knot returned.

"Hon, you cannot just stand there gaping. Open it." The bracelets on Granny Goldstein's arms jangled as she motioned towards the envelope in my hand.

"Mom, you look like death warmed up." This was Rachael's phrase of the moment.

"Why don't you do as Gran says?" Esther held up her torn envelope. "See, I've opened mine."

"Right." I ripped through the paper.

"What is it?" Rachael ran over to see what all the excitement was about.

Granny Goldstein eyed the envelope. "They don't send bombs through the mail, here do they?" Her voice held a hint of seriousness.

Rachael said, "Gran, this is Ireland."

"I know, I know. The island of saints and scholars. It says so in the brochures. Stupid of me."

I felt the breeze, before I saw David come through the back door. His face was drawn, his expression stiff and anxious.

"You're up early, Goldfinger."

"Not really, hon. You only think that because these two lazy devils are not even dressed yet."

"You must have first class, Tess. Are Transition Year back from work experience?"

I felt a glow. Despite having distanced himself from me, David still remembered my schedule.

Esther said, "Mom won't open her letter, Dad. You'd think she'd be dying to see what's inside."

"Tess, I wanted to talk to you before this happened." David wiped his forehead with the back of his hand as if warding off a blow. "I've been expecting something like this."

"Like what? You haven't seen anything yet." Granny Goldstein's eyes were riveted on her son. Her body had tensed and her impressive bosom was almost upright. While continuing to look at David, she said, "Tess, why don't you open the envelope? Just open it. I think David knows what's in it."

"Every lawyer has clients who are displeased with his work. I bet there are pupils who find fault with you, Tess."

"Hon, quit the editorials and spit it out. Just spit it out."

David's tone was resigned. "Open it and see."

As I slit the envelope, a sheet of notepaper and a black and white photograph of a two-storey house spilled upside down to the floor. Righting it with my foot, I stooped to pick it up. Esther got there before me.

Granny Goldstein said to her, "Go up and get dressed, Esther, or you'll be late for school."

Esther turned a brazen face towards her, but one look at me and she scampered, still clutching the photograph.

Granny Goldstein said, "Esther, the photograph. Give it to your mother. Rachael, go with your sister."

The house, which stared at me from the snap, had an unkempt look. The background appeared marshy, like a building site on a wet day. On the back were the words, *If your husband hadn't fucked up, this house would be ours.*

David opened his briefcase. "I got a copy." He held up an identical slip of paper and an identical photograph.

Granny Goldstein said, "There's something strange going on here."

David straightened his shoulders. "I know where *this* came from." He waved the letter, similar to mine. "I have a client, Paddy Joe Gilmore, who claims I made a mess of his house contract. The builder, Fonsey Moran, you teach his daughter, Tess, agreed to rent him the house at seventy pounds a week for two years and then sell it to him for forty thousand." He rubbed the corner of his eye nervously. "In the meantime a new industry started down the road and the house prices shot through the roof."

"So tough titty." Granny Goldstein played with her rings. "Poor Fonsey. Nice to see someone can get the jump on a builder the odd time. They usually make a killing."

"That's the problem. The agreement binding him to the fixed price had only one witness."

"You're joking. How could you have been so careless? No wonder he's raising a stink. So would I, if I were in his shoes."

At that moment, Cora arrived for work. "Bloody bad day out. Raining cats and dogs. This must be the mother, Teresa." She put out her hand to Granny Goldstein and defrosted the air with her warmth. "Where are the *maistíns*?" She looked at me. "Aren't you going to be late for school?" To David she said, "My young one is always late for school. Says she's still in before the teacher."

I said, "I'll take your advice, Cora. It's time I was leaving." Trying to keep the conversation normal, I turned to Granny Goldstein. "Will you be ready when I get back to go to visit my father? He is dying to meet you." I omitted to say that he thought of her as a *kike* but he was so lost for someone to talk to since my mother had become almost incoherent, he was prepared to tolerate her.

David surprised my by accompanying me to the car. "Tess, you'll not get another letter or photograph like this. Trust me."

Mrs. Broderick's mention of Paddy Joe Gilmore's dissatisfaction with David now made sense. The relief of knowing the reason for Paddy Joe's unhappiness was tinged with gloom. No letters would arrive concerning David, but what about those calendars, dreaded and mysterious, that continued to haunt me.

Later when Granny Goldstein met my father, she was most pleasant. "I've heard so much about you from Tess," she said.

"Tess! Oh! you mean Teresa." My father walked across the sitting room, his hand outstretched, his expression sullen.

I was taken aback by his appearance; his eyes were red-rimmed and there was a flustered air about him, reminding me of an overworked waiter, trying to hold on to ten plates with two hands.

"You have a wonderful daughter," Granny Goldstein said, shaking his hand.

"Americans stayed here once. They put Teresa up when she was in California." He cast a complicit eye towards me. "Remember, Teresa. We took them to a local festival. Mr. Cole slugged pints all night and didn't put his hand into his pocket once."

This was very out of character for my father. Agitated or not, I couldn't believe he was being so rude. He was usually charming, especially to women.

Granny Goldstein said, "Some Americans are as tight as a duck's arse." She ignored the shock on his face. "But then there are Irish people who sure as hell wouldn't give you the steam from their piss either." She smiled graciously. "Sure glad to meet you, Teresa's father. Now, can I meet Teresa's mother? I hear tell *she's* a lady."

For a moment, nothing moved but the hands of the clock. My father's bulldog expression changed to one of a Labrador. A moistness entered his eyes. I noticed that squirts of tomato sauce had congealed on the sleeve of his usually spotless jacket. Neither did his hair look as pristine clean as usual.

"I think we will leave it for today, Teresa," my father said softly to me, "Lil is not herself." Then he turned again to Granny Goldstein with a shamed look. "I find it difficult to apologise."

"Big deal."

My father, expecting sympathy, regained his belligerent expression. He said with asperity, "And I certainly will not start with you."

"Good. That saves me feeling guilty. If you had any manners, I might have said I was sorry also."

I wondered why they disliked each other so intensely after such a short meeting. "I'll go in to see Mammy on my own. Would you mind, Granny Goldstein? You can meet her another time when she's feeling better."

Their bedroom was as I remembered it all my life. Peeling onions was the likely cause of my father's red eyes, I realised, as I whiffed the air. My father ate raw onions as I ate apples. On occasion, he used to get my mother to fry chunks of them in lard, heap them on brown bread and gorge. The smell used to linger in the house, not least in the bedroom. It was his tendency to indulge at teatime so the perfume was strong on his breath all night. He was evidently frying them himself now.

On a shelf in the corner stood a six-foot statue of the sacred heart, its insides showing in glaring red. Esther had been fascinated when she saw one like it at a house in a folk park. "Nana has one wearing his heart on his chest as well," she told everyone.

Souvenirs from Knock yellowed with age, which I had brought home from a school tour when I was in First Year, vied for space with cleansing cream on the dressing table. My father's jackets hung haphazardly on wire hangers from a knob on the narrow built-in wardrobe. Two pairs of underpants and a hair net peeped from under the bed. A radio on the bedside locker hummed without sound – the transformer was banjaxed, according to Esther. Sadly, I saw that the paint, usually maintained in an immaculate condition by my mother, was peeling. The last coat, a putty colour, toned with her complexion.

Mammy was lying on her left side with her face to the wall, watched over by a picture of St. Marie Goretti. The doctor told us that she had had a series of minor strokes. Her mouth was a bit twisted; her right hand, prone on the pillow, looked lifeless. She turned her head when I opened the door but then looked away.

I wanted to be somewhere else. Was this all there was? A mediocre life and at the end merely 'Waiting for Godot.' Then my old friend guilt took over. I was a nasty person. This was my mother. I was jealous of Rita and now I was begrudging time spent with the one who should be the dearest in the world to me. I took two deep breaths to stop myself from crying aloud. "Mammy?" I whispered.

"He's still out there, isn't he?" I could hear the uneven gasp of her breathing. "He won't leave me alone, you know. Keeps pestering me."

Here we go again, I thought. Since I was a child, my mother had talked to me about her abhorrence of sex. That information had dogged my footsteps, dimmed my idealism, and gnawed at me since I was old enough to understand what she was saying. Saturday afternoons my parents went into their room; afterwards, my mother, her smile bitter as she left the 'torture chamber,' threw out crumbled sheets to be washed. This memory, unsolicited, upset me more than her agitation.

I put my hand to my mouth when I saw a holy water font sticking out from under my mother's pillow. Transported back to another time, I heard the knob of my bedroom door turn, the light tread of footsteps on the carpet. I must pretend to be asleep; I must turn out the light.

Each Saturday night, whether she knew I was awake or thought I was asleep, I endured my mother putting holy water on my forehead, sprinkling my pyjamas at the place where my breasts would later sprout, and blessing my pyjama bottoms, praying that I would not have to succumb to men's lust as she had.

I looked at my arms, subconsciously expecting to see the

pustules, later identified as psoriasis, that used erupt on my skin when my mother was particularly troubled about my nascent sexuality.

When I was ten, the weekly daytime visits to the bedroom stopped and my anointing stopped with it.

"You will have to tell him. I don't want another child. He will not leave me alone." Her voice trailed away. "All my life he's dogged me."

"Mammy." I had never seen her this bad. "Mammy. Turn around and look at me."

"Teresa!"

Lucidity came slowly into her eyes. She said she had been dreaming when I came in, but she still looked restless, distracted.

"I don't believe a wife should leave her husband," she said. "Marriage is forever. You should stick it out. Always stick it out. I nearly killed Pat with a bread knife once. That was the time he was drinking like a flounder. I'm glad I put up with him now. Sure he was doing his best. And I can face my maker with a clear conscience."

Mesmerised by all this new information, I didn't move.

"He was always pawing me. When I was having none of it, he took to the drink." Her gaze on me was pitiful. "Thank God that Mr. Goody at the cement factory threatened to sack him otherwise he would never have gone for help. Those twelve steps things he follows are a great job."

Twelve steps. That meant AA. There is a five times greater chance that a child of an alcoholic will become one. Being reminded of that bald fact upset me as much as my childhood memories had.

My mother turned eyes, compelling and regretful, towards me. "Even when he went off the drink, he wanted sex once a month." She added, "I think I had a vocation. My mother always told me I should have been a nun. God punished me for not following my calling."

I wanted my mother to stop talking. Always, I had chosen to think that my mother's life had been curtailed by my father, that she had been his victim. Now I was not sure which of them was the greater casualty.

I went over to the bed, sat on the side of it, and took her white hand. "I don't want to tire you, Mammy."

"Should I have been a nun?"

"I wouldn't have been born then. Look what you'd have missed."

My mother rewarded me with a tired smile. "I suppose you're right."

By the time I had kissed her cheek and arranged her covers, she was asleep. Re-entering the sitting room, I felt again the charged atmosphere. Initially I thought that my father and Granny Goldstein were fighting but then I realised that their chat was not full of rancour but interest. They were discussing Judaism and, horror of horrors, whether there was an afterlife.

"I don't know, hon. How could I know? How does anybody know?" Granny Goldstein winked and my austere father laughed. "What I do know is that we are here now. Of that I am certain and I sure as hell intend to enjoy it."

My mother was in the throes of dementia in the next room. My father was bantering with my mother-in-law and I was glad of it. Pity brought an ache to the back of my throat. Poor Daddy. My mother worked like a domestic for him all his life. He could have hired someone to clean the house, feed him and wash his clothes. What he needed was intimacy and love. He had been short-changed.

When Granny Goldstein excused herself and went to the bathroom, my father grasped my arm. His tone lowered. "How do you think she is?"

"I've seen her better."

"All we can do is pray." He then went to the bedroom to check on her.

Granny Goldstein whispered to me, "Why not invite your father to your dinner party, Tess? Rita and he should make an interesting combination."

"You're incorrigible." I took her by the arm. "Let's go. Before you come up with any more wild suggestions."

"I have yet to meet a man who fails to think with his dick. Why should *my* son be any different?"

Assuming her question was rhetorical, I didn't answer.

Granny Goldstein smiled an enigmatic smile. "Now let's go into the dining room and get this dinner party humming."

I followed her in, carrying a second plate of smoked salmon on brown bread.

"Looks delicious," was Rita's reaction as she held out her plate to Granny Goldstein for a helping.

The starters were turning out well. So was the conversation. David, although attentive and responsive to Rita, was taking particular care to include me.

Earlier Rita arrived in a subdued mood, carrying a 'Sweet Valley Twins' book for Esther and a 1,000 piece horsey jigsaw for Rachael.

Rachael's expression was dismal when she had finished reading on the side of the box that she was expected to put together a thousand pieces.

Rita, noticing, said, "I think it's for an older child but look it'll be nice when it's finished." She pulled Rachael down on the settee and showed her the picture on the lid of the box, displaying a completed picture of a black mare, with a white star on her forehead.

Rachael agreed that it would be nice. She pulled a face. "If I'm *able* to finish it!" She shook the box to dramatise how small the pieces were.

"Daddy can help you." Rita smiled her kittenish smile.

While I chopped carrots, and watched them, I was pleased that Rita was taking so much trouble to entertain my two.

Granny Goldstein walked back and forth bringing cutlery into the dining room. Every now and again she looked sideways at Rita, sitting the other side of David, Rachael between them. There was insignificant chatter, relaxing, reassuring. David took the jigsaw pieces from the box, put them on the coffee table, and then sat back.

Rita turned her head towards the kitchen. "Can I do anything to help?"

David answered for me, "Tess is fine. My mother will lend a hand. Just unwind while you have the chance."

I imagined that the hand he reached across to Rachael, bearing a horse's nose, didn't return. *She's a widow, Teresa. She's your friend, Teresa. You're suspicious, Teresa.* No matter how I reasoned with myself, I failed to banish what I recognised as the little green monster. Rita concluded that David and Esther would have to help Rachael with the making of the picture.

Relieved at her escape, Rachael jumped up and shouted up the stairs, "Essie, let's put on the video Dad got us." Before she left, she went into the dining room and put on *Diamonds Are Forever*.

"Especially for you, Gran," she informed us as the strains of Shirley Bassey, up at full volume, deafened us all.

"We'll move to the dining room and turn that noise down." Granny Goldstein sounded chuffed.

The change of venue forced David and Rita to sit opposite rather than beside each other. The flowers Esther had gathered, arranged and deposited on the table with the command, "Don't you dare move them, after all my trouble," obscured their view of each other. Good old Essie!

Over dinner, conversation became anecdotal. Granny Goldstein told stories heavy with Jewish humour. My attention was so riveted on the bottle of wine, they were demolishing, I missed the punch lines David and Rita found so funny. But I managed to stretch my lips in an imitation smile when one was expected.

Granny Goldstein waved her hand in the bottle's direction. "Another one, hon."

David got up, leaving the door open, and went to the kitchen for the opener. The scents of the pickled gherkins Granny Goldstein had used to complement the side salad mingled with lingering cooking whiffs of chicken supreme from the kitchen.

I was uncomfortably aware that David had had only one drink, which meant Granny Goldstein and Rita had the rest. There were only about four glasses in a bottle of wine anyway, but Granny Goldstein had three Vodka Martinis before Rita appeared at all. She was blunt enough in her sober senses so I was apprehensive as to what she might say.

My fears were realised when she asked, "Have you ever got strange *mail* through your mail box, Rita?"

Rita looked nonplussed for a moment. As usual, when she was at a loss what to say, she said nothing. She pushed her fingers through her luxurious hair and moved the chicken pieces around on the plate.

David came in with the newly opened bottle of wine.

Then she said coquettishly, "I could certainly do with a *male* these days. Wherever he comes from." She looked at Granny Goldstein. "I have a lot of work that needs to be done around the house. Noel used ..."

Granny Goldstein's voice was silky. "I thought David helped you with those." She smiled. "You can be a good handyman when you want, can't you, hon?"

I said, "We have a choice of desserts. Sherry trifle or the cheesecake Rita brought."

David said, "I'll have the sherry trifle. It'd be more than my life is worth not to sample it after all the trouble you went to making it." His eyes were on me. Beneath the assumed merriment, I discerned anxiety. He had become less proficient at hiding his feelings.

I felt the familiar tightening of my stomach that usually preceded the urge for a drink. Tonight, above any night, it would be unwise to indulge.

"Want to join me, hon?" Granny Goldstein, since her arrival, had not asked me why I had stopped drinking alcohol. Now it seemed as if her unusual restraint had fled with Bacchus.

"Tess doesn't drink alcohol anymore." David's tone was stern.

Rita and Granny Goldstein looked at him with raised eyebrows.

"Gee, hon. You sound like Solomon in all his glory." Granny Goldstein went over to the bottles on the sideboard, some of which David had taken from the drinks cabinet in the front room. She waved her hand expansively and said, "Line up for duty free, babes. There is champers here. Let's be devils and crack open a bottle."

David had included a crate of California champagne with the furniture when we were moving from Boston. He had brought it in to impress Rita. I remembered the bottle I had hidden in my slipper, the one in the washer, the one beneath my panties. My face felt hot. I couldn't go back to that again. "No, Granny Goldstein. No champers for me. Help yourself, though."

"Sure will, hon."

David let out his breath and resumed after-dinner inanity with gusto.

Granny Goldstein grabbed a tea towel she had used for carrying the hot plates from the kitchen. "Cannot have the cork going through the ceiling."

David and I laughed dutifully when the cork went pop.

Rita guffawed loudly. "Nice one, Granny Goldstein." She downed the wine in her glass quickly and when it was empty, held it out for a refill. "I'll join you."

"Good stuff."

Rita guzzled the champagne. The slight squint which appeared in her eye when she was tired showed itself. Last time I remembered Rita being any way inebriated was in her own home when she was expecting Noel's imminent return. Then she had waxed lyrical about her happy marriage. But circumstances had changed. Her partner was dead now; she was a free agent.

"A lot of females are threatened by single women." Granny

Goldstein raised her glass to Rita. "You and I are on the same raft, hon. Though you are a more acceptable commodity for the market. I'm a bit old in the tooth, as they'd say."

David pursed his lips. "Mom. Ease up on the gargle, will you? Rit doesn't need this kind of hassle."

I noticed the name abbreviation immediately.

"It's okay, David. I don't mind talking about my widowhood." Rita slugged from the champagne. "We can swap notes, your mother and me." She raised a drunken eye in my direction.

I said, "Remember you have to drive."

"Don't worry, Teresa, *I* never crash." She waved her glass about so that a dollop of champagne spilled on the tablecloth. "Sor...ry."

"Why don't we watch the *Late Late*? David looked at his mother. "Mom. You must see this. It's an Irish institution."

"Watch the box at a dinner party! Has Ireland frazzled your brain? This is supposed to be a night for convivial chatter, a time for me to get to know how Irish people tick. I don't want to watch a talk show. Not unless Tess is on it. She was brilliant on *Donoghue*. Hon, you were brilliant on *Donoghue*. She talked about ..."

"She told me." David's cauterisation was swift and sure.

"And me." Rita stifled a giggle. "Then I told the handsome Paul Walsh and Paul told Sr. Pius. The whole staff know about your success now." She shook her hair back from her face, revealing her attractive features, and pointed a finger towards herself. "Thanks to me." The sherry trifle and wine amalgamated in her stomach and rippled into a belch. "I think I'm getting a teensy weensy bit tipsy."

There was a strained silence which Granny Goldstein broke by raising her glass and lilting in a bright voice, "*L'Chayyim*."

"*L'Chayyim*." Rita's expression was confused as David and I echoed Granny Goldstein's Jewish toast.

David waved his glass in Rita's direction. "To life!"

My delight that she had been excluded was replaced by irritation at David's thoughtful explanation.

"*L'Chayyim*," Rita echoed, her glass aloft. That she had pronounced the word perfectly aggravated me further. My mouth felt sore from smiling.

"Your mother's right. We should be having a bit of fun instead of sitting around like a crowd of fuddy duddies." Rita's white teeth shone in the subdued lighting. She stood up, seductively put her palms on her hips and straightened her spine, brandishing her breasts. Her fiery hair fell forward over one eye.

For the first time I understood the meaning of blonde bombshell. Rita was a red bombshell, even more dangerous. She looked about to explode with suppressed energy.

She went over to the cassette player, silent since Rachael's tribute to Granny Goldstein had ended. There was an untidy stack of cassettes, which Esther had picked at random, lying beside it. Rita's movements were sluggish as she flipped through them. When she found one she liked she raised her head like a flamingo.

David didn't take his eyes off her as she stooped to fit Burt Bacharach's 'Greatest Hits' into the player.

Granny Goldstein sat holding her untouched champagne.

"Let's dance." Rita pressed the fast forward button with her index finger and as the tape whirred, still on her hunkers, she lazily swayed from side to side. The pose was curiously erotic, reminiscent of primitive women giving birth. When she found the song she wanted on the tape, she got up slowly, jiggled her shoulders, stroked her buttocks with the palms of her hands and slid into a dance.

I had seen Rita dance before, hundreds of times, but this was different. Her head tilted towards the ceiling leaving her neck exposed, her eyes were half closed and she hugged herself as her hips swayed to the music, slow undulations that seemed to pulsate through everyone in the room, including me.

Then she opened her eyes, turned towards David, and held out her hands to him while all the time lilting along with her chosen tune, *I long to be, Close to you ...*

As if he were the puppet and she the puppeteer, David rose to his feet. On the odd occasion that David and I did an old-time waltz together, at a school do or some other event, he would place his right hand on my shoulder, mine would be on his waist, we would join our left hands together and off we'd go. Not so with Rita.

Gently she dislodged David's hand from her shoulder and placed it on her thigh. She did the same with his other hand. Then she wound her arms around his neck as tightly as she wound the balls of wool for her closely fitted jumpers and rested her head on his chest.

Neither Granny Goldstein nor I stirred.

Music and the movement of the dancers was the only sound.

And then Esther's voice pealed through the house like thunder. "Would you turn that bloody noise down? We cannot hear a word up here."

Though I knew Esther was being a real brat, I could have kissed her. Her timing was impeccable! It wasn't that the music was loud, but she disliked Burt Bacharach's voice, hated when we listened to him.

As if her intrusion had flipped a switch, the tension in the room diffused. Rita unravelled herself from David. Granny Goldstein laughed and I joined in.

Rita regained her seat and swallowed a quarter glass of champagne in one gulp.

David said, "Rita, I'll drive you home."

"You'll what?" I asked.

"I'll drive Rita home. Surely you can see that she is not fit to drive."

"She only had a couple."

"Like you had when you crashed into the motorbike, you mean."

I felt the blood drain from my face. "That was uncalled for."

Granny Goldstein and Rita were so engrossed in conversation, neither had heard the exchange.

David gritted his teeth. "Tess, Rita has lost her husband. You don't want her to lose her licence as well."

"Talk about emotional claptrap. What has one to do with the other?"

"She needs us. We have to help as much as we can."

I remembered finding my favourite plastic doll slit from head to sandals with a bread knife. My mother blamed a tinker's child who used to come begging but I had been sceptical. Rita had envied me the doll and she was the last one I had seen with it. That was thirty years ago. For Godsakes get a grip, I told myself.

But I was afraid for David. Afraid that he was not strong enough to resist Rita, afraid that David's love for me had died and would offer no protection, afraid that Rita, as I suspected she had with the doll, would play with him and then destroy him.

Then a stream of self-knowledge flooded through me. What I was thinking was balderdash. Rita had not touched that doll. My fear was for myself. I needed the approval and participation of my husband in my life to be happy. I felt threatened. I needed a scapegoat. Rita was it.

Next I would be putting the blame on her for seducing David and absolve him from all responsibility. I constantly fought against such stereotyping in other people's relationships. It was harder when it was your own.

David's eyes melted when they rested on Rita and my introspection changed to anger. Granny Goldstein was right. Men thought with their dicks. David's face always became ruddy when he was physically aroused. And now, to my jaundiced eye he appeared to be a bright red.

David suggested to Rita that she get ready to leave. She smiled and left to retrieve her coat.

Granny Goldstein went to the bathroom. I went to the drinks cabinet.

My hand was firm on the gin bottle as I took it from the shelf. I had cherished thoughts of this moment since the day I told David I was going to stop drinking. Before and during Noel's funeral, I had been abstinent. I had mended my ways but David had not changed.

"Tess, hon, I thought you were on the dry." Granny Goldstein sounded more curious than surprised.

"I have changed," I poured myself a generous portion of gin, "my mind. I am now on the wet." I wondered why I had been denying myself for so long.

David said, "Let's go, Rita."

"Aw, David, hang on awhile. Miss Goody Two Shoes is drinking so she'll be a bit of craic. I don't feel like leaving yet."

"We should go."

Rita's eyes became dots. "Don't tell me what to do. I'll go when I feel like it." Displeasure burned in her eyes and starched her soft, sensuous mouth. She held out her glass to Granny Goldstein, who filled it without comment.

I longed for a taste of the gin I had poured. Deliberately, I brushed my elbow against the glass and sent it flying.

David glared at me then back to Rita then at the floor covered with broken glass. Annoyance replaced his sexual glow. "Are you coming, Rita?"

"No."

"I'll clean up." When I went into the kitchen, I poured myself a glass of sparkling water. My palms were sweating.

"Good decision, hon."

I was surprised by Granny Goldstein's comment from the doorway. "What do you mean?"

"David told me about your fondness for the bottle, hon. I think you're wonderful to have overcome it."

Her compliment conquered my annoyance at David having discussed my drinking habits with his mother. "Granny Goldstein, are *you* sober?"

"I've been diluting my drinks. Those two Vodka Martinis. They were just Martini, diluted with water. I thought it would be interesting to see how Rita would behave if she thought I were drunk."

"You old phoney." I was delighted by her subterfuge. "What would James Bond say if he knew you had contaminated his favourite drink?"

"Hon, let's go back in and finish the soap opera."

"What's keeping you, David? Let's go." Rita winked at Granny Goldstein. "Cannot get good chauffeurs nowadays."

"David, why not drive Rita's car? Tess, you drive your own, pick David up and drive back. Save car confusion in the morning." Gran smiled at Rita. "I'll put the kettle on, as you Irish say, and have the tea waiting."

"Good idea, Goldfinger." I imagined that David's tone was laden with sarcasm.

Rita said, "Great idea, Mrs. Goldstein."

"Okay. Let's go." David took Rita by the arm.

We were getting into our respective cars when I heard Rita slur to David, "Smart women, Jewish mothers."

"Your mother is a sick woman." My father sat at the other side of the table from me and fiddled with the pen in his pocket. I was sipping tea while simultaneously straining to hear his deliberately low tone. "The doctor says she has had another turn."

Mammy was slouched on the beloved wooden rocking chair she had inherited from her mother. Strips of bamboo peered between her legs. Because of her disability, she now pushed herself onto the chair, rather than sat into it, and so had loosened the cane of the seat. Her head was thrown back against the faded green headrest that she had spent months embroidering when I was a child. The doctor had advised getting her out of the bed every day, to prevent bedsores, a task that was proving marathon for both her and my father.

At intervals, my father pushed back his chair and manoeuvred his bulk over to where Mammy reclined. With the greatest of care, always careful to keep a hanky between his skin and hers, he wiped the spittle from her emaciated chin. She sometimes lost her balance so at intervals he had to sit her upright.

While sipping my father's weak tea, I thought of the mother I remembered as a child, her luxuriant hair curling about her ears, her eyes distant as she cleaned the spotless floor, her trendy dress covered by a stiff white apron that she put on over her head and tied in a tight knot at the small of her back. The children next door had envied me my glamorous, selfless mother. I tried to recapture the feeling of pride their envy had fanned. All I visualised was a packet of Robin starch and holy water. I picked up a teaspoon and played with it.

My father fumbled his way back to his seat. "I don't know how long more I will be able to take care of your mother. It is not, God knows, that I don't want to. You heard her yourself when she wanted to stay in bed this morning. It's the same when I try to get her out to the commode." There were dark circles under his eyes. "She hates me touching her. It's as if I have the plague."

The raw edge of my habitual dislike of my father, blunted by my mother's revelations, was whetted by his next remark. "She's my responsibility. I must find a way."

His responsibility. I felt the hard knot inside me solidify like water in a freezer. It was also his responsibility that, in his drunkenness, he had not seen anything untoward in my mother visiting my bedroom to frighten me with her bizarre behaviour.

If alcoholism were genetic, it was his responsibility that every day I gulped Soneryl and Equanil prescribed by my understanding doctor. And that, though calmed by them, I constantly craved drink.

"What do you expect *me* to do?" I put my hands to my face, but spied through my fingers his baffled expression. Though I sensed his injured thoughts and recognised the unfairness of my attack, I let the silence linger.

With jarring abruptness, my mother's accusing voice rescued me from my dilemma and fractured the stillness. "Get up and let that woman sit down."

It took me seconds to realise that my mother was referring to the formal wedding photograph standing on the top of the cabinet. Father, equally involved in his thoughts, didn't react either.

My great grandmother, in her handmade cream lace dress, and with her Scarlet O'Hara waist, looked serene and beautiful. Great grandfather sat in front of her, as moustached and handsome as any Rhett Butler, solid in his fine dark suit. They both looked directly out of the photograph, but their eyes were fixed on some distant point.

"Get up, I tell you." My mother was distraught. "Bastard."

Never in my life had I heard my mother curse.

"Typical man. Well able to get up in other areas."

Her uncharacteristic coarseness stymied me.

"He should get up and let the woman sit down." She talked to nobody in particular. "I have endured his bad manners for long enough. I'll show him."

I heard her words but they failed to register. My insides felt hollow. I was still thirsty despite the tea. The air smelled of disinfectant and stale onions.

Before either my father or I could react, Mammy pushed herself up off the chair and lurched across the room. A braided rug crumpled under her feet as she grabbed the erring photograph from the sideboard with her right hand. Her face was contorted, her eyes fierce, her hair askew where it had been lying against the back of the chair. Guttural noises sounded from deep in her throat as she lunged at the photograph of her grandfather and grandmother, took it in her hand and threw it from her. The glass shattered when it hit the floor.

"There." Spittle foamed from her mouth. "Now, neither of you are sitting." As she whirled triumphantly, her foot caught on the woven rug; she tripped and toppled heavily on the splintered glass.

Blood seeped from somewhere. When I turned her over, I saw that she had a shard of glass embedded in her abdomen. I extricated the piece and with my flattened palm put pressure on the wound. Traumatised, she lay immobile, half-conscious, unaware of her surroundings but not completely comatose.

"Daddy, get a towel from the kitchen and give it to me. Then dial 999."

"Me. Dial 999?"

"Yes and quickly."

He gave me the cloth and after some fumbling, dialled the number. There was a short exchange between him and the medics. Then he said, "They're coming." He dropped to his knees and bent over my mother, but she was unresponsive. "She'll be alright," he muttered.

The towel was red with her blood. I applied as much pressure as I could to the wound. It then came to me, with the charge of an alarm, that she was not alright at all.

Soon we heard the sound of the ambulance siren.

"I'll go out and wave them down," my father said, "they mightn't be able to find the house."

While still maintaining pressure on the gash, I managed to look out our large bay window at what was happening outside. My father flapped his arms like a scarecrow. The ambulance pulled to a stop outside the house. My father ran towards our big gate and opened it, allowing the ambulance trundle over the cement, its slow pace curiously at odds with the urgency of its blue flashing lights. It stopped at the front door and two men jumped out. Mrs. Moloney from next door came out to investigate.

Trying to understand how such a thing could have happened in front of our eyes, I focused again on my mother's skeletal face. The ambulance driver and another man came in, looked kindly at me and said, "Well done." They went on their knees on the floor beside her. I flinched as they ministered to her, knowing that if she were fully conscious and mindful, as she always was, of modesty, she would not have let them touch her. I felt childishly relieved that she was unaware of their presence.

They lifted her onto the stretcher carefully and quickly. The driver looked at his watch and murmured something about having to be somewhere else. In the ambulance, they locked the stretcher into place and we raced off. My father and I sat each side of her. When potholes jolted the ambulance, I thanked God, again, that she was unconscious.

The lump of food in my stomach churned with each bump. My father, bending over her, muttered aspirations, the cadences going up and down with the road surface. I prayed we would all reach the hospital alive. But Mammy was declared DOA.

I went through the few days, following my mother's death, in a daze. Even now, I cannot quite piece together the minutiae of that time. I just have an overall perception of events. I remember that although Granny Goldstein had never met my mother, it was to her I found myself talking. David did what he was expected to do like a robot. In the presence of Esther and Rachael, he was the supportive father, but he had nothing to say to me.

Neither he nor Granny Goldstein commented when, after leaving my mother to be laid out in the mortuary, I had my first gin. Neither did they comment when the next day I drank five more before I went to the evening ceremony in the church and endured the hugs, handshakes, expressions of sympathy and kindnesses in a state of confusion. A fog also surrounded me at the funeral mass in the cathedral the next morning but I have some memory of my mother's burial in the New Cemetery afterwards.

The graveyard stands on a hill overlooking a forest. Though called new, it is more than forty years old, having replaced the antique beside it, which had run out of space.

As the gravediggers, chosen by my father, lowered the coffin, we had a first-class view of the spruce trees that would decorate our parlours at Christmas. They reminded me of the time Santa gave me a turnip nicely wrapped in glossy paper and covered in tinsel; I was eleven and had stopped believing in him, but kept up the pretence because it suited me. My mother believed that naiveté should be nurtured and its loss punished. Since then, I have never touched turnip.

I watched the gravediggers remove the ropes as the coffin came to rest on the base of the grave. The assembled mourners stood back with their heads bowed. Fr. Pierce's surplice billowed as he intoned the funeral prayers. David motioned Esther and Rachael forward. Dutifully, to my surprise, they dropped a rose each onto the coffin and then stepped back to re-join their father.

Distressed at my exclusion, I swallowed noisily and gulped. Gin-infested mucus emerged from the back of my throat. David and my father came to stand at my side but I was disconnected from them. If I started to cry, I would be unable to stop. My hands moved convulsively back and forth over the handle of my umbrella. Rachael came to my side and tried to still my agitation by holding my hand. Though I wanted to respond to her loving gesture, I remained immobile.

The gravediggers came with their spades and began to fill in the grave. The sound of the clay striking the coffin mingled with the cacophony of hangover hammers in my head. I wasn't thinking about Rachael or even about my mother as I rushed out of the graveyard, the metalled heels of my boots beating a frantic tattoo on the tarmacadam. The taste of the gin, however convoluted, was still in my mouth, causing me to long for the bottle reclining in the dash of the car.

The funeral lunch was held in the local hotel in the town square about half a mile from where my mother and father had lived. I spied Pamela Crawley crush with Caseys and Duggans into the allotted room and crowd around the bar. I noticed her especially because of my relief that she had come alone. My colleagues had attended the removal the previous night as today was a working day so no Creepy Crawley to endure. The first drink was free. They then heaved themselves onto the bench, which ran parallel to the long table, set for lunch.

The coveted gin in my hand helped me feel more alert and confident. I nodded gravely in recognition of condolences, and made sure that I spoke to anyone whom I suspected I had missed in the church and at the grave. Once or twice, I glanced at my father, talking to a cousin who had come 'all the way from England' for the funeral and at David who was entertaining Rita's mother. Several of those I talked to insisted on buying me a drink.

The more I drank, the more morose I became. I hid it, of course. I tried to make up for the omissions of the previous few days and be the perfect bereaved daughter of a good Catholic woman. My exhibition shrouded all the anger, bewilderment and sadness that boiled inside me.

When everyone had scrambled to their seats at the tables and squeezed in to make room for each other, I focused on David and Rita, who were deep in conversation opposite me. As I played with the jelly in my dish and gulped the glasses of white wine the waitress constantly refilled, I bristled with jealousy and begrudgery.

The mention of the name *Lily* by David brought my mother into the room to sit beside me. Grief, so long denied or numbed, assailed me. Sweat seeped through my palms and I felt my back clammy. The smell of strong coffee aggravated my sudden nausea. My tongue felt like sandpaper.

As I raised yet another glass to my lips, my mother smiled and offered me tea, and abused my father for criticising David. Our last conversation came back to me about her wanting to be a nun. Tears pricked my eyes.

I heard someone across the table mention leaving. Rita was standing, getting ready to retrieve her bag from the floor. "Don't forget the rest of your baggage, will you?" I cautioned.

David's return gaze was sharp and unflinching.

"Yes, David dear. *You* are the baggage." My voice was falsetto, quite unlike its usual timbre.

"What's wrong with you, Teresa? Are you drunk?"

"Why do you always insist on asking me that question, Dave? No, I am *not* drunk. What I am is lonely. I have just buried my mother. Do you think I have a right to be lonely?" Briefly I wondered why had I said that and in such a belligerent way.

Rita said, "I'll take you home, Teresa."

"Would you? I'd appreciate it."

"I don't want the kids to see her like this," she whispered in an aside to David.

"I would have gone with her if I hadn't guessed what she'd said."

Angry, I grabbed the pint of a distant relation seated beside me. Soon it was in mid air over the table. David saw it coming before Rita. He put his hand on her shoulder and shoved her sideways. The result of his good act was that the foamy, sticky liquid spilled over both of them. It left a dark stain on David's suit and large splashes on Rita's face, neck and bosom.

The thought struck me that maybe I shouldn't have drunk so much wine, on top of the gins I had at the bar. I had been called to the bar. Like David. I giggled hysterically.

Rita's hair was lank from the porter and her expression shocked. David was palely furious.

I was beginning to feel sick. The mixture of outer heat (the central heating was up high), and inner cold had made my head light. The table swam towards me, dipping and swaying off centre. When I finally got a grip of it, I held on tightly. I took up my wine glass and took a slug. When I tried to put it back, I misjudged the edge of the table and left it to soar in mid air. It alighted to shatter on the gaily-coloured tiles.

"On your feet then, there's a good girl." Pamela, who had been sitting at the end of the table, came towards me and took charge.

As a psychiatrist, she should have known that I was a grown woman and would resent her bloody help. But, undeterred by my forbidding expression, she bent over my chair and put her hand on the small of my back. "Come on, Teresa. Help me here. That's it. Upsy-daisy."

David's expression was dark with anger and humiliation.

Rita looked ashen, upset and pretended to be concerned for me. But I was smart enough to detect her falseness.

Pamela changed her hands from my back to my arms and gripped me tightly. "Don't worry. I'll get you home."

Through cajoling and bullying, she persuaded me to struggle to my feet. Who did she think she was? She was David's shrink, not mine. Creepy Crawley's wife. Ugh. I had walked a few steps when I decided to defy her. I landed a vicious kick on her shin with my metalled heeled shoe. When she bent to rub the injury, I aimed at her posterior and sent her spinning across the room.

Stunned silence.

Then David's words, strident and unforgiving. "We're going home. Someone look after Pamela."

My legs were trembling as I tried to keep my nails from digging into David's arm. To hell with them. Mammy was dead. When we came out into the air, I relaxed my hold and felt myself totter. The small wall surrounding the hotel proved my saviour. Without ado, I grabbed on to it. It held steady, which was more than anything else seemed able to do. When I sat on it, it felt wet beneath my light dress.

"Get up off that wall or you will catch your death of cold." My mother's voice sounded very near.

"Come on," David said. "You cannot stay here all night."

The street light was behind him so I could see the worry lines on his face, more obvious than usual. I suddenly had a desire to massage them away with my fingertips. Stumbling against him, I threw my arms around his neck. It was like embracing a plastic mannequin. He stepped backwards to keep his balance.

"Poor Rita. Poor Pamela." The hurt I could still feel at his rejection was unexpected. "What about poor Teresa? I've been sitting in there at my own mother's funeral like a spare and you wonder why I had a little too much to drink. Get real." Esther's jargon had its uses.

"That's the problem. You're spoiled. Attention, attention. You love attention." His voice was devoid of feeling as he raised his head in imitation of me. "I talk to another woman and you go berserk." He stopped. "And I have not found someone else." He pronounced each word so that there would be no confusion. "I'm just tired of you." He looked at me through half closed eyes.

"David, I feel sick."

"Poor you."

Over and over I vomited on the grass verge. A mixture of gin and wine spurted from my mouth like water from a gargoyle. Followed by the Brussels sprouts, pieces of turkey and dollops of ice cream I had consumed earlier. It got on my hands, my hair, my dress.

David's arms remained rigidly by his side as he watched me puke my guts out.

When we reached the car, I felt more sober. Ensconced in his Ascona, he continued his diatribe. "Then I get all this crap about feminism. Feminist, how do. I'm not the bra burning type." This time he imitated my voice to perfection and pursed his lips as I had a habit of doing when I was in full flow.

"It's me who balances the money, brings out the garbage, makes sure your car has oil, drives when we go anywhere, makes excuses when you drink." A bead of perspiration stood on his forehead although it was cold. "We are back on the merry go round now, I guess." Silence reigned. Then his voice gentled. "This is not the time for this. Your mother has died, but I *am* going to change things around here."

My voice trembled. "What do you mean? Marriage is for life. We still love each other."

"Do we? Think about it, Tess. Anytime we talk, we fight. You don't enjoy sex. It is like you are going to the dentist when I suggest it." He tugged angrily at his beard. "What will you do when your periods go? Your excuse for avoiding it will be gone with them."

Upset as I was, I knew he had spoken the truth. I had often pretended to have my periods for over a week so that he would be less inclined to bother me.

He must have noticed how stricken I was because he put his hand on my shoulder as he stopped the car outside the house and said again, "This is not the time to decide anything. You need to sleep."

For five days after the debacle of the funeral, David, Granny Goldstein, Esther and Rachael contrived to keep me in bed, or at least insulated on the leather sofa, covered with a duvet. I felt glad of the attention if not the confinement, suspecting that they were afraid I would raid the drinks cabinet.

One of Mayo's bad spells started the day my mother was buried, and bound Claremorris fast in its charms for nearly a week. Without Esther and Rachael during the day, the house was dismal and depressing.

Granny Goldstein, in one of her heavy sweaters, put a fire in the front room each morning. At eleven o'clock she used take my Tradia and drive to my father's house. "Better than that stick shift of David's, Tess. Your dad seems glad of a bit of company." She was always back at three o'clock when she fought with Cora about who would make the children their dinner, and with the children themselves about who would feed Roamy.

Through it all, I lay on the settee taut, like an extended wire, with fatigue and sorrow and guilt that I was unworthy of being cosseted merely because I had a bad hangover. A bad hangover – yet I continually longed for a drink.

We were getting on with our lives only because we were sticking to a routine. Nobody mentioned my behaviour at the funeral. Even Esther managed to keep her mouth shut. It was as if we were following a rulebook for those who lived on after the death of a marriage, death of love, death of respect. We followed it meticulously. I closed my eyes to the anger I felt at David's championing of Rita, and to the pain and grief that devoured me following my mother's death. David, Esther and Rachael had their own pain and disillusionment to bear and we each did it silently.

On the fourth day, I forced myself to move off the settee and threw myself into my book, compiling and subtracting facts about teenage pregnancy. I figured that the pile of notes, which kept my mind diverted and my hands busy, would protect me from having a drink.

David's solution was continual absence. He escaped the need for decision-making by not being around.

On the Monday, I returned to school (Rita blamed grief for my bad behaviour at the funeral lunch and passed it off). Granny Goldstein extended her stay, ostensibly to look after Esther and Rachael while Cora had her varicose veins removed.

After a few weeks, I was sleeping fairly well again. David and I soldiered on. We didn't hold each other close, but when he was there, for the sake of his mother and the kids, we stood shoulder to shoulder.

But in quiet moments I asked myself what next? I tortured myself by examining life without David from every angle. I hated having the bed to myself; I missed the way he snorted in his sleep, the faint smell of aftershave that he rubbed on his beard because he liked the smell; the way, in repose, he threw his arms across me. I even missed the smells in our bedroom after he had eaten a spicy veggie curry.

Then the inevitable happened and Granny Goldstein spoke her mind. "Tess, hon, I was not prepared to say anything until now because, firstly, I was not sure what I wanted to say and secondly, I felt you were unwell but I cannot contain myself any longer. What you need is some reality therapy. Your marriage is crumbling around you and you're acting as if everything is kosher. Esther or Rachael have more spunk than you." She swept the tablecloth off the table with a flourish. "I cannot believe this docility."

I felt my mouth sag in shock.

"I thought it was only Jews who believed that the meek shall inherit the earth."

"Meaning? What do you expect me to do?" Resonances of what I said to my father on the morning my mother died. I put the last of the plates into the dishwasher. Then I began to wipe the worktop. My eyes were burning.

"Hon, if you think David is jerk enough to have a thing going with Rita, ask him."

"I'd only make it worse if I said anything. It's my fault. He was always too good for me. I forced him to marry me." I put my hand up to my mouth and talked through my fingers so that my voice came out in a muffled whisper. "I think I'm a bit paranoid. Rita is his friend as she is mine. Maybe other women don't enter his head. Maybe he's just tired of the one he's got." He said exactly that on the day of the funeral, I recalled.

"You could be right. He likes women, but I think he thinks one at a time is enough. Will you stop cleaning the darn worktop?" She herself started to scrub the spotless table.

The cloth twined around my fingers like a striped blue bandage. "I cannot have a heavy discussion with him every time I see him. It'll drive him away."

"It's better not knowing?" Granny Goldstein put her hand on the place where her hipbone would have protruded if it had not been protected by layers of flesh.

"As Pope said ..."

"Is there anything you Catholics don't give that fella a say in?" Granny Goldstein shook her head, making her new long earrings swing like pendulums.

I laughed humourlessly. I was about to quote Alexander Pope, not *the pope*. "A little learning is a dangerous thing?"

Granny Goldstein came closer to me. Though smaller, the high candid ground on which she stood made her appear taller.

"Did he also say that knowledge is power?" She eyed me speculatively. "You could always hire a private eye." Her tone was wry.

Taking a step backwards, I said, "Gran. As Esther would say, it's Ireland you're in now. I'd rather leave him than do that."

Her intonation changed, became more sombre. "Why should

you be the one to leave? He's the one who's acting the maggot."

"I've no intention of leaving him," I said gently. "He's my life."

Anxiety contracted to a pinpoint in Granny Goldstein's eyes. "You can find out what's going on if you ask the right questions. If this place is anything like Boston, there will be plenty of people delighted to tell you if he's having an affair."

I knew that, despite my best efforts, a frown mongrelised my deliberate expression of indifference. "I prefer not to know. I've been hoping it will pass. It's mid life crisis stuff."

Gran snorted. "It makes it easier when you label behaviour. It is only a mid-life crisis. Nothing to do with me. I have no changing to do."

The silence hung heavy.

I turned towards the sink. "What are you getting at?" I felt resentment well up in me. "Whose side are you on anyway?"

"I used to be on yours but I'm on nobody's now. He's my son." She walked to the other side of the sink so that she wouldn't be talking to my back. "You're like my daughter." Her tone lowered. "I am on nobody's side now."

I turned on the tap and water splashed over the J-cloth. "If he keeps going on like this, he'll drive me mad."

Granny Goldstein looked towards me, serious-faced. "Tess, you'll drive yourself mad. Stop blaming David for everything."

The cold water made my hands tingle. "I cannot understand why he has changed so much. I can't."

"Hon, you surprise me. You really don't think that any of this is your fault?" Granny Goldstein's face reddened. She fiddled with her rings. "For starters, you're a lush." Her tone was full of intensity. "If you don't bite the bullet and get on the wagon and stay there, there will be plenty of cowboys to take advantage."

Gran's Texas-inspired metaphors annoyed me. I turned on the hot tap as well. The cascade was a welcome distraction. As I regulated the volume of water and watched the droplets patter on the back of my hands, I had to admit to myself that she was right. I thought of my behaviour at the funeral and felt again the vultures swoop. Although what she said hurt, I knew she said it out of concern.

She continued, "You have your finances in order, I hope."

The warm kitchen felt cold. "I don't pay much attention. I presume the mortgage is in both our names. I've always left finances to David."

Granny Goldstein's voice quaked. "Tess, you'd better start paying attention. I love you dearly but it's time you stopped acting like a child. David takes care of the money." She hesitated. "I hope for your sake he has done it the way you expected. You must have made a lot of lolly out of the book. Where is it?"

Tired of the water flowing over me, I turned off the taps. "I told you. David manages our finances. After all, he *is* a lawyer."

"Even worse. He knows a million ways of swindling you – and make it look legal."

I went over to the press in search of a clean towel. Granny Goldstein was unaware that David had paid Rita's mortgage for six months without my knowledge, and she was talking like this. I went on the defensive. "How can you talk like that about your own son?"

"Easy. You open your mouth and the words flow out."

Her wisecrack answer showed how uncomfortable she was with my question. I rubbed my hands vigorously. "You know what I mean. I can't imagine him acting that way."

"Suah you can, hon. Would you have imagined when you were over with me at Halloween that we would even be having this conversation? That he would be gone so often that you would be suspecting him of two-timing you?"

"You know that I was pregnant when he married me. I'm convinced it wouldn't have happened otherwise."

"Be fruitful and multiply. David loves children but I don't think he'd have gone through the marriage ceremony with a gentile unless it was what he wanted. He could have supported the child without becoming your husband." She puckered her cherry-coloured lips and added in a softer tone, "When you lost the baby after the ceremony, he could have hightailed it off."

Whether it was true or not, I felt grateful to her for having said it.

"Talk to him," Granny Goldstein cajoled.

I agreed, relieved that I was about to do something positive about my situation.

A bark, and Roamy loped through the dog door. He padded through the utility room, and in to me in the kitchen. As he laid his head in my lap, he sensed my mood and his tail drooped.

"I'll go and pick up the kids." Granny Goldstein dug for the car keys in her tracksuit pocket. She opened her mouth to say something but then changed her mind. Instead, she threw me a kiss and bounded out.

In the still house, I sat and stared. I was being honest with myself. If *I* were indulging in self-analysis, David could be also. What a mess.

I was drinking again. From a cup Rachael had given me for mother's day. It was garish and sentimental but lifted my veil of self-pity.

I was correcting the last of a bunch of Leaving Cert comprehension tests when the staff room phone rang. The secretary told me that Jacinta Broderick was outside the main door wanting to talk to me. My hangover headache throbbed. It was a dismal day. "What does she want?"

The secretary was abrupt. "I didn't ask her."

"Is she still pregnant?"

"I didn't ask her that either."

In spite of my irritability, I felt a rebuke in the secretary's tone. I tempered my own. "I'll be out in a few minutes."

Jacinta shifted her bulk from leg to leg as she watched me approach. Standing back, she eyed the grey pebble-dashed building that had been her school. "The place is still the same." Her words sounded like an accusation.

"Yes, Jacinta. The school is surviving despite your absence."

"Did the Social Services nun tell you I told her to fuck off?"

"No. Did you?"

"She said they could fix me up with a family to live with 'till I had the baby. No chance. Don't want holy Joes looking down on me."

"Why are you here, Jacinta? You don't seem to want to accept any help?"

"Sr. Nuala's notion of staying with a family while I had the baby gave me an idea." Jacinta raised her head. "Mrs. Goldstein, I wouldn't have come if I could think of anything else. I phoned my mother but my father refused to let her talk to me. I hitched out there the other day but they kept the door closed. I saw him through the window, standing in front of the sacred heart lamp."

I felt my head spin. "How can *I* help?"

Jacinta flinched but then steadied herself. She lifted her head even higher and said, "I know this is cheeky but ..." She hesitated for a moment. "Your mother died, right?"

"Yes."

"Your father is living on his own. Nobody visits him except some dame who is as broad as she is long. American, I think. She shouts when she talks."

"How do you know all this?"

Jacinta looked sly. "I watch him."

I moved away, disgusted.

Jacinta followed. "I'm desperate. I have to think of this." She gestured towards her belly. "I need somewhere to stay. For a while."

"For Godsakes what has my father got to do with your baby?"

He needs someone to keep house for him. I could do it. I'm handy when I want to be." She looked entreatingly at me. "Honest, Miss. I would keep the house spotless. If he let me stay, and gave me a couple of quid, I'd have the baby and then he could get rid of me if he wanted. Please, Miss."

She whispered so that I had to move closer to her.

"My friend has male friends in. They pay her for ... you know." Her voice hardened. "For what I did for nothing. Junie is her pimp. He thinks he's mine too. Being pregnant turns some men on, he says. I managed to stall him 'till now but he's given me two days to make up my mind. Then I'm out on my ear. Please, Miss.

I'll do anything. Even clean floors."

Prostitution in rural Ireland. I was about to pooh-pooh it as imagination but when I looked at her pleading expression, I began to relent.

"Look, all I'm interested in is getting somewhere to stay until my baby is born. Then I'll find another place."

"Jacinta, I'm sorry. It's out of the question. My father would never agree. He condemns premarital sex."

"Better if I'd got rid of it, I suppose. How do *you* know what he agrees with?"

I was about to refuse again when I realised that, indeed, I was finding out that I was ignorant about what my father believed anymore. "I'll get Granny Goldstein to talk to him."

"Granny. Jesus."

"The woman you described so graphically as the only one who visits him."

"She's Granny?"

"Yes, she's Granny. Any objections?"

"No. She has a kind face."

"Have you the use of a phone?"

"Yea. I can manage that."

The gumption was back in Jacinta's voice but I wasn't fooled. She was frightened. "Ring me tomorrow at school. I'll give you the answer then."

"What do you think? Is there a chance he'll put me up?"

My father liked his comforts. No matter how he had changed, I knew that was still true. "I think we can rely on Granny Goldstein to convince him. She will make you out to be a regular Mrs. Beeton."

"I don't give a tinker's curse who she says I am as long as I have a roof over my head." She smiled suddenly, transforming herself into someone attractive. "I think that auld wan might be able to swing something, though. Have they a thing going or wha?"

Jacinta must have noticed the look of something akin to pain that passed over my face. "Sorry. Shouldn't have said that. With

220

your mother havin' snuffed it and all."

"I hope for your sake she *can* sway him, otherwise you're in trouble." Feeling a glow of bitchy satisfaction, I turned towards the double doors leading to the school.

"So long ,Miss. Sorry."

I went in to finish my cold tea and savour the prospect that, if Jacinta were correct, I may be on the verge of finishing a relationship with one Goldstein while my father started a relationship with another Goldstein.

Two days later, I stood by the window in a pool of jaundice yellow winter sun and agonised about my promise to Granny Goldstein that I would talk to David. Roamy was chewing what looked like the toe of one of Esther's socks. As I looked at the dog, I visualised opening him and finding a haberdashery of bras, boots, false teeth (he hadn't actually swallowed my father's but had tried), ties and tights.

Thinking of my father reminded me of my indebtedness to Granny Goldstein. Pleased that she had retained her powers of persuasion, she had organised Jacinta's move into my father's house the previous day.

My smile faded as I heard raised voices from the kitchen. I walked quietly in my stocking feet out into the hall and unashamedly listened. Even if I remained where I was, I told myself afterwards, I would have been able to hear them.

"Gee, David, you can't up and leave. What about the kids?"

"That's why I'm moving to Paddy's. For Chrissakes do you think I want to go *there*? But I have to leave here or it will do my head in."

Granny Goldstein's tone was icy. "And you think Pat won't do your head in."

"I want to stay close for the kids' sake. If I'm staying with their grandfather, the break won't be as upsetting for them."

"What's wrong, David? Is it just relations with Tess or is there something else amiss?"

"I'm going to stay in Pat's house. You visit there often enough. I'm sure we will have this discussion again."

"He has a housekeeper now. I bet she did not reckon on

having to cook for two brawny males."

"When did this happen? Pat didn't mention anything about a housekeeper to me."

From outside the door, I heard the surprise in David's voice.

"She moved in yesterday. Don't worry. I'm sure he will not go back on his word if he has already committed." She sounded angry. "He didn't mention anything to me about your plans."

"He probably gauged that you would react angrily, correctly as it turns out."

"He knows nothing about me."

"Pat has changed," David said, "become more perceptive. He's still a bigot but less so. Obvious in the way he's behaving with you."

"What do you mean, 'behaving with me'?"

I imagined Granny Goldstein's eyebrows reaching her hairline.

"I visit him because he's lonely. No other reason."

"Yes, Mom. I'm sure you do."

"You're impossible. You're the one deserting your wife and daughters and I'm the one feeling guilty. Nice one, David."

"I'm taking a sabbatical, that's all."

"Have you told Tess yet?" Granny Goldstein asked.

"No."

"You cannot put it off forever."

"I'll tell her soon."

I concentrated on controlling my voice as I entered the room. "No need. I heard. You're going to live with my father, for the sake of the children. Otherwise, you would have gone further away. Did I get it right?"

"You got it right."

There was a tremor in David's voice but his expression remained impassive. He didn't apologise when he bumped against me on the way out.

Granny Goldstein put her hand on my arm. "Sorry you had to hear it like that, hon."

"I don't mind, Gran, really." As I said it, I realised, with surprise, that I meant it. The uncertainty was over. He would not be living here. I would not have to stay awake waiting for him to come in or wonder what he would do when he was here.

A fizzy liver salts feeling welled up in my chest. I needed a vodka. Vodka didn't smell. Granny Goldstein would disapprove but to hell. I was about to give my husband an experience he would remember for a while.

"I'll be leaving in the morning." David had gathered clothes from the bedroom wardrobe and was stuffing them into his suitcase. Our suitcase. The only sign of his perturbation was the red blotches on his neck underneath his beard.

"There are some papers I need to gather from the spare room."

The three stiff vodkas I had imbibed had taken the edge off my nervousness. I felt both vulnerable and uncharacteristically sexual. As if I had flicked a switch in my mind, I turned off my current of grief and loneliness and concentrated on the present moment. I saw only him. No melody of past, no promise of future. David, as exciting as the day I had first met him in the kibbutz.

My heart hammered above my ribs. Intuitively, I knew that I looked well. David always said the classic black baggy trousers and short jacket I was wearing made me look like a matador. His back was turned to me as he put the last of his ties into the outside pocket of the bag. "David," I purred.

He turned abruptly, a navy tie still in his hand. "What?"

I moved closer to him until we were almost touching. Beard bristles scratched my fingers as I caressed his cheek. He dropped the tie, covered my hand with his and gently removed it.

Seduction I was not good at. Distracting him from thoughts of sex was my *forte*.

He had turned his attention back to the ties when I came from behind and put my arms around his waist.

"I should get rid of some of these," he said. "I haven't worn them for ages."

I put my face into his broad back and tightened my grasp.

He endured it for a minute before unwinding my hands from his midriff and turning to face me. "I like to see what I am dealing with." He looked half in earnest.

I stifled the voice telling me I could still withdraw. "I always fancied myself as an Eve," I lied.

He said nothing but opened his arms and I went into them. Holding me close, but slackly, he trailed the path of my body from my breasts to my thighs with one hand.

I tingled.

"You'll have to ask," he said. "I don't want this used against me. I'm still leaving. It changes nothing."

"I'm asking." I put my head on his chest and listened to his heart. "Show me ... that you still love me."

He hesitated.

I lifted my face up and kissed him, a long, slow, open-mouthed kiss.

"Tess. Oh! Tess." He led me over to the bed, sat me down beside the packed bag. His tongue flicked, teased and heated me from my mouth to my toes.

We undressed and rediscovered each other's bodies. When he spurted into me, and his semen mixed with my menstrual blood, I heard myself whisper, "You still love me."

He lay beside me, with my head on his shoulder. He didn't speak except to draw my attention to the blood. It was beginning to get dark so I could not see his face but I didn't sense any embarrassment at the sight of the stained sheet, reminiscent of our first coupling. In a voice that sounded in my ears, very unsure, I asked, "Was it ... okay? Was it good for you?"

He kissed me briefly on the forehead, unscrambled his legs from mine, took a deep breath and laughed, but kindly. "I don't believe that after sixteen years you have finally got around to asking me that."

He picked up his discarded clothes, showered hastily in the en suite and came out to find his errant tie and resume his packing.

Cast off, like a row of Rita's stitches, I lay in my nakedness conscious of the blood seeping into the sheets. "David."

He turned as he went out the door. "I'm going to get some of my books from the spare room," he said. "I'll be back."

"It's over. You and me. Finished. That's how you see it. We'll never get back together."

"Never say never, Tess." He pulled at an imaginary pimple on his nose. "Never say never, *libling.*"

When you've become used to loving somebody for a long time and he is not there anymore, it's like having a leg or an arm chopped off. I had often told my History classes about amputees from the Second World War who felt their lost leg or arm long after it had been severed. Phantom pains.

It takes a while for the brain to realise it has lost a part of its network. It's only after it has sent the wrong signals a few times, and the spinal cord has funnelled it through a network of nerves, in and out, to and from, nothing but a stump, that it eventually gets the message.

After my mother died, I kept asking her things I had always wanted to ask her when she was alive. Now I had spent the weekend doing the same with David, saying things I should have said when he was here.

On Monday I drove from Claremorris to school in a daze of rage and despair – I felt foul. When I went into the staff room, Rita and Sr. Pius were huddled together examining what looked to me like a greeting card.

"Teresa." Rita's eyes were luminous. "I wanted you to be the first to see this. When you weren't in, I showed it to Sr. Pius."

"You mean I *asked* you to show it to me."

"Well, whatever."

"So what is it that we should be all dying to see?" I threw myself on the seat beside them and grabbed the card. I stared at Noel without seeing him properly. *Fold him O Jesus in Thine arms and let him henceforth be a messenger of love between our human hearts and thee.*

David's words, when leaving me, went round and round in my head. The mortuary card felt alien in my hand. I threw it

226

back to a bewildered Rita. "At least *he* had no control over his going."

Sr. Pius winced, "I'll turn on the Bunsen burner and we'll have a nice cup of tea."

"No, thanks." I turned and walked quickly out of the room to search for a bolthole. Luckily, the photocopying room was open. I felt like the sheets of paper that littered the top of the machine ... a photocopy of whom I had been on Friday when I had David. The unexpected picture of Noel had panicked me, made me realise that David was as dead to me as Noel was to Rita.

I saw the gaping dark hole into which they had put Noel's body. That was what lay ahead for me too, a gaping black emptiness. No David around. *Is fearr an troid ná an t-uaigneas.* Was fighting better than loneliness?

I sat on the seat by the wall and rested my head against its coolness. One, two, three, four. Count to 200 in batches of four numbers. If I counted to 1,000, I might bore the pain out of me. I had reached 150 when Rita pushed the door open.

"What's wrong, Teresa? What has happened?" Rita regarded me with curiosity, warm, intense, and loving, the gaze of a friend.

"Nothing. I've something to photocopy. I'm busy." I had to hold my feeling in check or I would roar like a fire gone wild.

Rita looked at the dead machine. "Can I help?"

"Leave me alone. I'm not in good form and I don't want to take it out on you." I paused. "Anymore than I have done already."

"I rang your house on Saturday," Rita said. "Rachael told me you weren't feeling well. That you had gone to bed for a while."

That would have been after I had switched off the television on Esther and told Rachael that her room was like a pigsty. When both protested, I had slammed the door of the kitchen and flounced off to bed in a melodramatic drunken flurry. "I didn't get up again until ten o'clock. By that time the kids had gone to their rooms."

Rita sat on the chair beside me. Her presence was comforting as we sat in silence. Before I could stop myself, I said, "He's gone."

"Who's gone?"

"David. He's staying with my father."

"Really?"

"He has the perfect excuse. He's company for daddy and his office is very near where I used to live."

"He'll be back. You'll see. He just needs some time out." Silence. "Maybe you both need space."

"I don't want space. I want David." Though I sounded pathetic, they were the most honest words I was to utter about him for several months.

Immediately after he left, I expected him to come home. It was only a matter of time until he came to his senses. When he came back, I would stop drinking and we would go to a marriage counsellor. There was nothing seriously wrong with our relationship.

Although he had been absent from home a lot in recent months, I always knew he'd be back. I had got used to storing up confidences to tell him, or leaving things undecided until I asked his advice. I still found it hard to get it into my thick head that he was gone. And when the truth did start to seep in, I drowned it with alcohol.

Attempting to lean on an emotional prop that was no longer there led to my mental collapse. Physically the alcohol flattened me. After a few weeks, I felt confused and wearied; by the end of a month I was as psychologically sore as I was physically (I had almost tripped over a rug and fallen down the stairs). This upset me, reminding me as it did of my mother's end.

Cora, who had gone in for a simple varicose veins operation, had been held in for further tests to do with a blood disorder, diagnosed when she had her last child.

I became aware that *never* can and did indeed mean what it said. David was gone now for over three months. I scarcely saw him.

Mobile in the run-about Granny Goldstein bought from the local garage, she used to drive the children to my father's house. She was not in any hurry to go back to Boston. Her apartment was paid a year in advance so caretakers were looking after it as if she were there herself. "As long as they have the filthy lucre, hon, they don't care a toot whether I'm there on not," she assured me.

It was an irritant that she was still here. When I came home from work, I looked forward to a couple of cocktails to add to the gin I had imbibed from Esther's mug at school, but Granny Goldstein made me uncomfortable.

I knew Esther and Rachael were disgusted by my drinking. I thought it was the secretiveness of what I was doing that had frightened them. When *they* hid something, it was because it was wrong so I didn't hide my intake anymore. But it only made things worse.

Getting up in the morning for school, and everything in between that and going to bed had become an obstacle. I tottered through the days like a sack of weasels, begrudging any extra minute I worked at school, undermining anybody who put forward new ideas, harshly disciplining pupils for not having the uniform or for chewing gum. Generally, I made life unbearable for those who didn't keep out of my way.

As time went on, anger replaced denial. How could David have done this to the kids and me? We were the victims. I fuelled my animosity each time Esther and Rachael came back from seeing him, relaxed and happy. I convinced myself that they were putting on an act for my sake, that they were distraught, that their lives were ruined. Esther called my bluff.

"We're happier now than when Dad was living here. We have you and Granny Goldstein in Claremorris, Dad, Granddad, and Jacinta outside Tuam. Two homes."

"Essie." Rachael noticed my pained expression.

"Well, it's true. You said so yourself. No more shouting and roaring. And at least Dad or Granddad are not always drinking. Like Mom."

"Mom doesn't smoke cigars like Dad."

Knowing that it was the only defence Rachael could think of made me sad. I had a shot of gin. One led to two and by the time Granny Goldstein discovered me sitting on the bed in the spare room, the bottle was almost finished. I pushed my hair back from my forehead. "I drank more than I intended."

The weight of her distaste bent Granny Goldstein's face out of shape. "This can't go on, hon. I love you dearly but you've lost the plot. There are the kids to think of. You'll have to do something about your drinking."

"I liked it better when you were hiding the bottles everywhere." Esther, who had been in her room doing a project for teacher, had come in quietly behind Granny Goldstein. She waved her exercise copy for emphasis. "Now you don't give a shit whether we mind or not."

"What did you say, Miss?" I heard the slur in my voice but ignored it. "How dare you use such language in my house."

"It's Dad's house as well. I wish we were living with him instead of you." Esther's face was pale with two red spots in the centre of her cheeks. Her voice shook as she cast appealing glances at Granny Goldstein.

"Why, you little brat. After all I've done for you, you dare to talk to me like that. I've a good mind to ..."

"To what?"

"To give you a good skelping." What was I saying? I was against hitting kids. Always maintaining that might wasn't right.

"In the States it's illegal to hit children. Isn't it, Granny Goldstein?"

Somewhere in my head, I knew I should leave it for now, but alcohol had dimmed my judgement.

"I hate you, Mom."

Red hot anger suffused my brain. Months of frustration surfaced. I wanted to lash out at everybody. "I'm sorry, Esther. I'm unable to cope anymore." My whine told me that I had reached the maudlin stage of drunkenness. The look that passed between her and Granny Goldstein fuelled my anger. Esther's collusion with David's mother made me feel hurt and betrayed. I fiddled with the marble bookend, redundant since David had taken away his legal tomes.

"I want to live with Dad." Esther moved closer to Granny Goldstein.

"What did you say?" I sounded shrill.

"I want to live with Dad." Her voice was stronger the second time.

My heart collapsed like a crushed egg. Of its own volition, my hand clutched the bookend. I felt a rush of blood to my head. My stomach felt as it did before my periods, tight and tense. The marble felt cold under my sweating palm. As a flood of hurt anger flowed through me, and before I knew quite what had happened, I threw the bookend at her.

The blood that gushed from the gash on Esther's forehead was bright red. "I'm bleeding. Granny Goldstein. Look, I'm bleeding." The wail that she let rivalled the *banshees*.

Before Granny Goldstein could respond, she crumbled to the floor in a faint. The back of her head struck the ground.

"What's wrong, Esther?" Rachael put her head around the door, the jigsaw Rita had brought her clutched in her hand. "I heard you screaming like a lunatic." She stopped when she saw the figure on the floor. "Oh, God. Essie. What's wrong?" She ran into the room and stopped to crouch beside her sister. Her face was white.

Granny Goldstein said, "Teresa, go to the medicine chest and get a bandage and some antiseptic. Rachael, get a cushion and put it under her head. I'll call the doctor. Feerick, isn't it?"

When I looked towards her to nod my assent, our eyes met, admitting our fear. Don't anticipate the worst! This is not serious. Just a small gash. But you did it, Teresa. You caused it. It is *your* fault.

I was confused, guilty and afraid, as if I were watching everything in slow motion. I wanted to cradle Esther in my arms and will her to wake up, but I did as Granny Goldstein told me.

The water I poured from the tap into a bowl chilled my hands and a shiver ran through me. When I went back into the room with the bandage, antiseptic and water, my legs were shaky. As I wiped blood from the gash, my tears fell on Esther's cheeks. Initially it looked as if I had succeeded in stopping the bleeding but soon the white bandage around her forehead turned into a red bandanna.

"Doctor says that when she regains consciousness we are to bring her in," Granny Goldstein said. "She'll probably need stitches."

"What if she doesn't wake up?" Rachael voiced all our fears.

"She'll wake up." I sounded more sure than I felt. There was a pain in my chest. My breath was coming in short gasps. "Esther." I was sobbing now. Nothing beyond the figure on the ground existed.

I had no doubt in that second that she was dead. Her face had the whitish yellow glaze that I had seen on Noel and Mammy's after their deaths and she was lying inert, on her back, with her arms by her sides. Her eyes were closed, the area peeping from under her 'red bandanna' dark and sore looking.

I made a choking sound and breathed deeply. Then I looked away.

"She's moving, Mom." Rachael's tears splashed over her black eyelashes onto her cheeks. "Mom. She's okay. She's awake."

I uttered a small "Oh!" and looked; her eyes were open and she turned her head towards me. She still had no colour but the cadaverous paleness was gone.

Esther squinted up at me. "Stop blubbering, Mom." Her voice was weak but indulgent.

"You're awake. Thank God."

"What happened? Ow, my head hurts." As she looked at me, her eyes darkened and memory returned. Her little nose screwed itself into an exclamation mark and her eyebrows arched. She took Rachael's hand and squeezed it. "Mom did this to me. She threw that at me." She got up on an elbow and pointed towards the bookend. "You could have killed me."

My first reaction was to shout to Granny Goldstein. "She's alright. No concussion and it is not deep enough to stitch."

"Good. We'll take her to the doctor in case. Come on. We'll go."

"I'll drive." I helped Esther to her feet and put my arms around her.

232

"Are you mad, woman? Do you want to be stopped by the police? Your alcohol content is way up."

"You're right."

"Darn sure I'm right. I'll take her in my car. You can come if you like."

"If I like. I'm her mother, remember."

"Funny that. I thought you were the one who had forgotten."

Esther, her face stark, shrugged herself out of my embrace and gripped Rachael's arm.

Granny Goldstein walked behind them towards the car. She unlocked the back door to allow Esther and Rachael get in, and then opened the driver's door. This left me to walk around to the passenger seat if I wanted or to stay at home if I wanted.

Ensconced in the front seat, I tried not to move. I knew if I did, I was going to vomit.

The road had never seemed so windy. We came to the edge of the town.

"Keep going straight, Granny Goldstein."

When Rachael started giving directions, I remembered Granny Goldstein didn't know the way. I infused my voice with an air of authority. "Then, turn left, it is past the church."

"Clean the window there, Tess. The condensation is the pits. Rachael is a whiz at the directions. Leave it to her." With a dismissive air, Granny Goldstein handed me the chamois.

"I can't." There were black spots at the edge of my vision.

"I'll do it, Gran." Rachael reached over my shoulder from the back, and tried but failed to reach the front window.

Dimly aware that Esther was saying something, I tried my best to keep the curry, mixed with the large gins, where I had put them. The last time I had vomited from drink was the day of my mother's funeral.

I put down the window. The car jolted; I pressed my palm to my mouth to keep down a spurt of masticated spicy beef but in vain. Convulsively, I emptied the contents of my stomach onto the moving road.

I saw the doctor's sign. At the edge of her drive, I spied Kieran

Crawley wearing a blue windbreaker. With a forward motion of his hand, he guided us in. The sight of him added to the sour taste in my mouth.

Esther added to my distress when she stated, "No matter what happens about my head," in the back of the car she grasped Rachael's hand, "I'm going to live with my Dad. And Rachael is coming, too."

It was weeks since I had thrown the bookend at Esther and had abstained from alcohol. Immediately after I hit her, I became despondent. I was off the booze but I was still delirious, oblivious to my children and my surroundings, the option of taking my own life flitting through my mind.

The doctor had been severe the day we brought Esther to her. Despite my excuses, she'd insisted on documenting what had happened. Granny Goldstein had been frank. She said that I'd been drunk and injured Esther. There was no hiding the facts. I didn't know which was worse, the realisation that I had been found out, or the realisation of what I had done.

Nobody from school, except Rita, attempted to ask me how I was, what I was thinking, why I was sending in doctor's certificates. But my suspicions about a love affair between her and David re-surfaced and that precluded her as a confidant. Anytime she called, I told whoever answered to make an excuse. Granny Goldstein, I believed, was taking sides with her son. My father. I didn't know what my father was thinking. My mother would have been disappointed; she liked David. But regardless of her affection for him, it was more likely she would have said I was better off without a man to paw me.

The children and Granny Goldstein went about their daily routine while I brooded, lolled in bed or watched television. My manuscript was left untouched. I got up each day longing for alcohol. Reluctantly my doctor had given me a certificate citing fatigue and stress with, of course, a renewal of my prescription for tranquillisers.

Though David would have visited his office in Claremorris,

he hadn't called out to the house or talked to me on the phone. My hope that he would come back grew dimmer as time elapsed.

During the weeks following the accident, Esther's resolve to live with her father strengthened. In the end, I was allowing her to stay there for five days. I watched as she gathered her stuff to leave with Granny Goldstein. Rachael, initially, had decided to go also, but seeing my distress, changed her mind.

My need to see my children to the car forced me out of my dressing gown. I put on a denim skirt, with navy and red accessories. Now, as I waited for them to leave with Granny Goldstein, I understood what T.S. Eliot meant by 'putting on a face to meet the faces that we meet'. My jawbone ached from trying not to cry.

Esther's face was pale, her confident demeanour forced. Rachael had lost her jauntiness. Now she followed Esther meekly. Her decision not to remain in my father's house with Esther had been a difficult one. Rachael would always side with the underdog, in this case me.

My civilised rehearsed speech flew out the window. Stooping down, I pulled Esther to me. My shame mixed with affection. "I love you. Don't forget that." She blinked and looked away but then, to my delight, she kissed me on the side of the cheek.

"See you soon, Mom." Rachael, her face blotched with tears, hugged me quickly.

Granny Goldstein collapsed into the car and waved as she pulled away. "Back soon, Tess. Give us a couple of hours. I'll have to take it slowly. That fog is pretty damn thick."

When Esther had insisted I make a decision about her going to stay with her father, my energy returned. Foolishly, I believed that after David spent a week away from me, he would be longing to come back. Now I realised that I had played it all wrong, had condemned him for leaving rather than persuading him to return. My kids were on their way to him but all was not lost. There and then, I decided to follow them, talk to David, and re-establish something of what was lost.

Before I could change my mind, I pulled on my jacket,

grabbed my car keys from the back of the door and left the house. The fog had eased but the weather forecast said it would thicken again later in the afternoon.

Roamy escorted me down the drive. Opening the driver's window, I shouted, "Go home." He flattened his ears and retreated towards the house only to turn again and run after the car. Quickly I got out, scooped stones from the ground and threw them in his direction. His face full of disappointment, he slunk around the back – to the dog door, I guessed. I resolved to take him for a walk when I returned from my mission.

My attention was fully engaged as I drove the familiar route. Usually, I could do the journey in my sleep but a residual fog still blurred known landmarks, softening them.

The fields, which in the morning light would have been a greeny gold, were now like a grey coarse underblanket, darned with reels of trees and a narrow band of bungalows. The unfamiliarity of the countryside complemented my altered mood and, for the first time in months, I laughed and relaxed my grip on the steering wheel.

I thought of Roamy and remembered the time we chose a dog door for him. David and I had pored over details of weatherproofing, transparent vision, security-locking panels, and silent action flaps until we both agreed on the best one to buy. Then he had spent a weekend installing it.

A vision of Eskimo David rubbing noses with Rachael and coaxing Esther to join in started me humming the theme song from *Far and Away*.

I wished to re-create our lost happiness, wanted him to envelop me in his arms and ... I banished the fantasy and concentrated on getting to Tuam faster.

When I came to the level crossing, I was surprised to see the red and white wings of the barricade alight. Foolish though it was, I put my foot down and the car leapt forward. I hadn't seen David for three months, but now that I had spurred myself into action, I was testy with impatience. Closer to the crossing itself, I saw that the gates were closed and the red warning lights flashing to indicate a train coming. "This is all I need," I muttered, slowing to a stop.

I was so busy wondering what I would do when I got to my destination, I didn't notice immediately that a car had pulled up the other side of the tracks.

Though it blended perfectly with the surrounding fog, I recognised David's metallic Ascona. He was driving to his office in Claremorris, nothing curious about that. What *was* unexpected was that there was somebody with him.

I put down the window to clear the condensation. Though my eyes watered from the moistness, that wasn't what bothered me.

David's head was inclined towards the woman, the wet square of his mouth barely visible as he opened and closed it in an absorbed conversation. I clutched the seat belt. There was a rapport between them that was inappropriate for a married man with two children.

I felt like a crystalline construction that could shatter into treacherous shards. Everything I had worked to maintain in my marriage had been smashed or stolen from me. The base of my back hurt. The heat in the car was stifling. There was a rush of humiliating tears to my throat, I fumbled in the dashboard for a tissue and told myself I had no right to judge their behaviour so summarily. It was more paranoia. Then I saw that it was Rita. I was convinced I had been suckered.

By the time the goods train passed, I had beaten the panic and begun to muster my thoughts. There was a simple explanation. After all, David and Rita were good friends. Who better?

Once the train had sped by, my view was clear. The sight that met my gaze stole my breath away. David and Rita were reluctantly pulling apart; they had obviously kissed in the seconds it had taken the train to pass.

The red light at the side of the barrier stopped flashing. The railway gates mechanically swung upwards. The road was clear. I stared ahead blankly.

David and Rita saw me. They both smiled. Rita, her expression full of excitement, waved her left hand and gestured towards her ring finger. David's expression, after the initial smile, was neutral, but he hadn't seen me for three months. What did I expect?

David, Jezebel beside him, drove slowly towards me with the window down, obviously hoping for a chat. I jammed my car into gear and bumped over the railway line, speeding past them.

Vaguely, I registered that, even as she passed, Rita was still trying to draw my attention to her ring finger. She was a good actress. I had to grant her that. To be able, so quickly, to hide her feelings of alarm with smiles of friendship was the work of a consummate performer.

I pressed on the accelerator until I saw that the needle had hit seventy miles an hour. I was a little ashamed. What if I killed someone? Slowing down, I drove on.

I tried to lay straight in my mind the implications of what I had seen, did my best to dismiss the image of David and Rita, in the dining room, entwined, as they were the night of the dinner, and tried to be logical and fair. Two miles further on, while still thinking of betrayal and ruined friendship, I saw Rita's Fiat parked in a layby.

I pulled in, deadened the engine, took off my seat belt, lay my head against the backrest and tried to quell my suspicions. After all, I reasoned, there must be an ordinary explanation. Her car could have broken down. David was passing by and he gave her a lift. Her car had not broken down but he had given her a lift anyway.

Though I sought reassurance, all I found were questions. Why, on a Thursday, in the middle of the day, was Rita coming to Claremorris when she should have been at school? I recalled their closeness, his look of tenderness.

Deep down I thought it was Rita's overt sexuality that charmed David. Stupidly, despite the mortgage episode and his concern for her kids, I hadn't realised how much he cared for her. His affection for her upset me even more than the erotic dance episode had. I wished that even if he didn't want me as he once had, he might treat me with the same tenderness as he treated Rita. I longed for his head close to mine, for his voice in my ear.

"Please God," I said, to myself and anyone else up there who was listening, "let them just be friends." More at peace, I re-started the ignition. The engine jumped into life.

Optimism carried me back to the house and then deserted me. To woo it back I had a few tipples of gin. Tiredness got the better of me and I tucked myself into bed fully dressed where I dreamed, not of David, nor Rita, nor even Esther or Rachael, but of my mother.

I woke in a heavy sweat and threw off the duvet. Sitting up in the bed, I snapped on the bedside light and then lay down again. I closed my eyes, but the relentless power of memory thrust deep into my past, and goaded into life half-retained scenes from my childhood.

I was back in my bedroom with its flowery wallpaper and mahogany furniture. The door swung open before me and I stared at my mother as she bounded in with holy water. Hands fumbled at my clothes. She took off my pyjama top.

Defiantly, I opened my eyes. I had always told myself that I was fully clothed when she went about her ministrations. This was another booze-induced hallucination. Nothing more.

Two more empty hours elapsed as I reclined on the couch in the front room. It was four o'clock. Still no Granny Goldstein, no Rachael. No David. No Rita.

I had guzzled three quarters of a bottle of gin when the phone rang in the hall. I picked up the extension beside me. A long pause met my greeting.

"Hallo ... Is that Teresa?"

The voice was male, low, ingratiating, and instantly recognisable. "Who is this?" I inquired, convinced that either the alcohol or pique that nobody from school had rung me up to this had driven me to delusion.

"It's Kieran, Teresa. Kieran Crawley."

The room danced before my eyes.

"Who is it? How did you get my number?"

"It's Kieran Crawley," the voice repeated, this time in a less conciliatory tone. "You gave me the number yourself."

My mind steered away from unwanted likelihoods. I had forced myself not to think of him since I stopped going to school, had not spoken his name or Pamela's for weeks, and now here he was, the personification of my most bizarre nightmares, ringing to torment me.

"How did you get this number?" I repeated, knowing through my haze that it was a ridiculous question. Though I was ex-directory, he could have asked any of the teachers with whom I was friendly for it.

His voice became more strident. "*You* gave it to me."

"When?"

"You know when," he wheedled. "Don't pretend that you don't remember."

The room was now spinning at an alarming pace, and I grabbed at the edge of the telephone table. I stared at the phone. Whatever the reason for his ringing, I did *not* want to know. The room spun faster. My clasp on the table loosened, as did my clasp on the door I had so meticulously bolted against memories of drunken deeds.

David and Rita's betrayal and my kids' desertion had forced me back on the gargle. I was tired of being alone. Tired of constantly battling. Tired of life. I needed air.

Without uttering another syllable, I slammed the phone on Creepy Crawley, and faltered from the sitting room, through the hall to the kitchen.

Roamy looked at me expectantly, hesitantly wagging his tail, exacting my promise to take him for a walk. Rachael's skipping rope and a tennis ball belonging to Esther fell on my head when I pulled his lead from the top of the fridge.

I knew he would spend his time straining to be off because Dusky, the bitch up the road, was in heat. Though I suspected

Roamy had paid a visit to her kennel already, it had only peaked his appetite for her. Bringing him with me I knew was foolish but it was one promise I could keep.

I put on my coat and threw a scarf around my head against the swirling, freezing fog. Stepping out the front door into the density, I felt blessedly ill-defined. The light was strange, greyish-white with a bluish tinge. Dampness seeped up my nostrils, curled into my mouth and enfolded my face. I decided to walk down the private road by the river. I'd taken this walk many times before. There would be no cars. The people in the big house were not there and it was a different direction from Roamy's Dusky. The arguments were convincing.

The County Council workers, who were dredging the other side of the river, were far enough away not to disturb my half-baked plans. As everything slotted into place, I felt like an actress whose sets were ready but who was not quite sure of her role.

I remembered why the workmen were there. The river had become swollen during the bad weather following my mother's funeral, and they were still pumping water out of the low-lying houses. The ganger was collecting shovels from his near-invisible crew so it must be near knocking-off time.

Seeing the smoke screen effect of the fog on the men, and sedated by the volume of alcohol I had consumed, I fell in love with the idea of becoming invisible too. Behind me, the lights of neighbouring houses barely penetrated the gloom. In the middle of the road two men chatted, their yellow Macintoshes glittering with drops.

Roamy, as I expected he would, dragged me along, pink tongue aloll, sniffing as he went. Too late, I remembered that there was a shortcut this way towards Dusky's house. The cold aggravated the blotches on my fingers and made it painful to keep a tight lead on Roamy. A slight wind occasionally stirred the fog. I bent to stroke my Don Juan, whose hair had turned a pearly colour. He appeared fat in the fog and I could feel the humid heat of his body. I hoped someone would be kind to him, and take him home.

The trees dripped as I stood with both hands on the balustrade of the wooden bridge. The serrated wood pained my palms as I squeezed. I suppressed the compulsion to laugh. I had been brought up to pretend that everything in my life was superb.

To behave like I did then, bawling, shouting at the sky, banging my hands on the rails like a madwoman as tears ran down my face, shrieking at the unfairness of a life that took my family from me and caused obnoxious men to ring me out of the blue, was contrary to anything I had previously done.

The pattern had been set by my mother. Always keep the flag flying. Helped by my liquid crutch, I had spent years doing that, but now I was lame, drained, crippled.

I approached the barbed wire that hindered walkers from strolling abreast of the river. My inappropriate shoes slid in the wet grass. Here and there, the path was under water.

Behind the wire, the river flowed strongly. An object wrapped in a black plastic bin bag, a dead cat or maybe a dead body, bounced on its surface, catapulted onwards by the current. Not much hope of surviving if one fell into that. Drawn, as if by a sceptre, towards the wire, I cringed at its spiky coldness against my knees. Roamy licked my wet face as I bent again to hug him. I righted myself and looped the lead halfway down on a post. There would be no danger of him pulling it off and coming after me.

My mind felt as murky as the air. A half a yard separated me from the tumult. I pulled up my skirt, and stepped over the fence. A spike tore my tights and broke the skin on the side of my leg. The trickling blood failed to jolt me from my confused state.

Everybody in Claremorris knew better than to go too near the river on this side of the bank. If they fell in, they would be sucked under and drown.

I was shaking, appalled by the thought of the dirty water and the clogging death, which seemed to be my only escape from addiction, betrayal, abandonment. At the same time, I despised the idea of going back into a life which had become unbearable.

David was my *raison d'être*. If he weren't there ... Even my kids had taken sides with him. They would have Rita as their stepmother. Coquettish, kittenish Rita.

A voice said, "Good dog. There there. It's alright."

The voice sounded far away at first, then close to my ear.

A hand clasped me by the shoulders and the same accent said, "And what in the name of Jesus do you think you're doing?" The man's hard hat tilted as he looked down at me.

The question was so pertinent that my mind stood still.

"You forgot your dog, missus." The voice was kindly now. "Fancied a walk on yor own?"

Millions of thoughts spun through my head and my mouth framed an answer, but no words came. I took his outstretched hand and he helped me back onto the safe side of the fence.

He wore a contractor's waterproofs. I stared at his midriff. The silence lengthened. Roamy barked again. I forced myself to look at the ganger I had seen earlier. The roughness of his manner didn't cover the concern in his eyes.

I was at a loss what to do.

"You gave me a fright," he said without inflection, like a newsreader imparting information. "You must have got a fright too." He looked at me from questioning eyes. "The fog led you astray. It's dangerous to be out in a mist like this. 'Twas luck you had the dog with you."

When I continued to look at him as if he were a moron, he said, "You should get a hot drink inside you. You're shivering."

He supported me over to a small caravan on the other side of the river. A careworn man in grubby overalls gave me a mug of hot tea.

"You're the one who came home from America a while back. Your husband's Jewish. No offence, Missus. Just trying to place you, that's all." He looked towards my saviour. "I think you gave Jim here a fright."

I closed my eyes and took deep breaths. The red spots disappeared. I felt cold. I couldn't banish the thought of water closing over my head as I went to sleep. After a minute or two, I opened them and raised my head.

My rescuer smiled reassuringly. "Well, now, you're alright." He looked at me carefully. "And don't step over that wire again."

"I won't," I whispered, and smiled crookedly at the top of his head.

He turned to the hovering youngster holding Roamy. "If I hadn't heard your dog barking, you might easily have slipped and fallen in. What would have happened then?'" His eyes were watchful. "Go home and have a good rest. Things will look brighter in daylight."

"I will." I drank the rest of the tea appreciatively and at the urging of the second man, sat for a while to rest. Bit by bit my deadened brain became alive but I was still half-drunk and my limbs felt as if they were weighted by rocks. Slowly, with deliberate movements I got up from the chair. My eyes brimmed as I thanked them. I would do as the man said. Go home to bed. Where else was there to go?

All was still as I plunged through the fog, Roamy leading the way. No suggestion of a breeze disturbed the grass and no crows cawed. Because of the silence, the distant bark of a dog was intensified, more blatant. Roamy cocked his ears and pulled. My slack hold on the lead gave way. The dragging leather irritated my fingers as he pulled it from my grasp. I screwed my eyes shut, and roared, "Roam...eeee. Come back." My voice had no inflection, no capacity.

Mist hovered between the tree trunks and clung to the leaves; I lifted the hem of my skirt, gulped air and ran. As I slithered on a circle of *cac bó*, a thin, screaming sound set my heart crossways.

I thought at first that it was a car braking suddenly, so I ran towards the road, expecting to be castigated by an irate driver for letting a dog off by himself. Then, as the screams scaled higher, I realised that it was a living being in pain. Roamy? The sound rose and fell; brambles scratched my skin as I broke through onto the road.

Then I saw him, flat on his stomach, paws outstretched, and his tongue protruding between his teeth. Although the cries of pain had lowered to whimpers, the sight of his convulsing body was hard to bear.

Fog, inside and outside my brain, threatened to engulf me. Sickened, I dropped to my knees and reached out to touch him. I put my arms under him and lifted him from the dirt. A twig, shaped like a rude cross, was matted in his underbelly hair. I pressed him to me, the dampness of his coat seeping into mine. Blood dripped from his mouth onto my denim skirt.

His body lay limp in my arms, the hindquarters jerking and

quivering as I tottered along the grass margin, vaguely conscious of the reassuring sight of the sun, penetrating the mist. His moans were quieter now. I didn't look at him, just stared ahead like a sleepwalker. I felt him twist his head to one side, quiver and be still.

"I'll take him from you, Missus." It was the man who had given me the tea in the caravan earlier.

"The driver didn't stop," I said.

"Grateful you should be that he didn't. He's a strong dog. Would have dented the car if he was running. Be thankful for the fog. He probably didn't realise there would be damage. Could have taken you to the cleaners. Wouldn't that be a nice state of affairs? A dead dog as well as a fat bill."

That is disgusting, disgusting, I thought. Tears were in my eyes and I couldn't brush them away.

"Here. Give him to me. I'll carry him."

"No," I said. Bet the man was, despite what he'd said earlier, anti-Semitic. Burdened by disillusionment, sadness and self-loathing, I persevered with the dead weight as far as the front door and then lay him beside his kennel.

Granny Goldstein and Rachael were back from depositing Esther and ensconced at the kitchen table finishing some left-over pizza.

"Where were you, hon?" Granny Goldstein asked.

Before I had a chance to answer, Rachael intervened, "Jacinta thought she was going to have the baby, Mom. She didn't, though. It was just that she had eaten some of Granddad's fried onions."

"And boy did they give her indigestion." Even in my perturbed state, I detected a note of satisfaction in Granny Goldstein's tone. This morning seemed aeons away.

I became conscious of my bloodied clothes the same time as Rachael did.

"What happened to you, Mom? You look as if you've been through the wars. Poor Roamy. He must be up to his ears in muck too. Where did you go?"

My voice faltered. "Down by the river. It was very foggy. Roamy broke away." My heart hurled itself at my ribs. "Rach. Roamy is ..."

Coldly, she cut me short. "What's wrong with him. Has he hurt his paw or something?" Though now sitting ramrod-straight, she looked very small.

I caught hold of her hand but she recoiled so violently she fell backwards before scrambling to her feet. "Where is he?"

"Outside his kennel. Rach, he has done more than hurt his paw." My expression alarmed them both.

"What's happened, hon?"

Rachael stared at me, her expression a mixture of hope and dread, her voice toneless. "He'll get better." With typical Rachael brightness, she straightened her shoulders, tilted her chin and forced a smile. "He's hurt but I'll take care of him and he'll get better."

"He won't, darling. He was knocked down by a car."

She cried then and her face turned inside out like a flimsy umbrella, caught by an unexpected wind. The strength of her feelings echoed in her scream. "Why did you let him go? Bet you were drunk."

'Mom did this to me. She threw that at me.' Esther's voice. A feeling of despair, and then a roaring in my head.

I sprint towards the open road while like a ribbon of mist after me comes the voice in my head, 'Roam...eeee...'

In the kitchen, I am on my hunkers, looking into the press, underneath the sink, where I had hidden a bottle of gin. There it is in a saucepan, the frying pan covering it.

I unscrew the cap and put the bottle to my nose. The sharpness of the smell makes my head reel.

As I watch myself rise from my squatting position to reach for a glass, Esther grabs the bottle from me and dashes it against the sink.

A familiar look of desperation, love and fear conflict on her face.

Roamy comes to lick the spill and howls piteously when he gets a splinter in his paw. Esther, with the gentleness of a nursing mother, extricates it. With the ferocity of a tiger, she sticks the piece of glass into my side. Blood and alcohol flow out.

Involuntarily flinching, I awoke in the addiction centre to the sound of morning traffic and an ambulance siren. Huddled on the bed, I felt burdened by an accumulation of earlier hassles, judgements, expectations. David had left me no option but to come to this place. He would have had me declared an unfit mother and applied for custody of Esther and Rachael if I had refused to check myself into a centre. "You're not doing a snow job on me this time, that's for certain. I mean what I say, Tess. The kids come first," he'd said.

Though I had managed to drag out my leaving for two weeks, in the end even I saw that he was determined I receive treatment.

Esther and Rachael had come 'home' to say goodbye on the day I left. As I walked out to the car, their hostile gazes troubled me. It was as if a Kieran Crawley caterpillar were crawling across my back.

I hear the voices in my head again, feel my heart race, taste the smell of fear, and thirst for the gin lost in my dream. My mind feels like a failing car engine, a few revs too slow. Memory returns sluggishly at first, then clearly.

It had been eight weeks since a car killed Roamy and Rachael had blamed me for being drunk and letting him off the lead.

I recall going through the drinks cabinet and drinking bottle after bottle. I remember puking brandy into the toilet and then gulping more after each bout of vomiting. Drinking, getting sick, drinking, and getting sick. Drinking . . . I must have eventually passed out because when I woke, David was there. The sight of him had been less than the blessing I expected when I yearned for him during the past months.

They got inside your head in this place. I had heard of brainwashing but that was brain stripping. What had they in mind? Replastering? I didn't want a new mind. My own was fine, thank you very much. I pulled the bedclothes round me and shuddered.

At a group meeting, I had almost told them about how I had come to marry David. Goddammit, wouldn't I have looked a right fool if I had. Bet they would have been judgemental. Okay, they would have pretended otherwise but I know what they'd be thinking. They'd have reached all kinds of conclusions about me. I would have reached all kinds of conclusions about myself.

Where would I have begun? Twenty years ago when I was twenty and in love with a law student on a kibbutz? My beloved David – eager to make love but not pushy, which made me love him more.

Would I have started with my most vivid memory – the end of our stint in Israel when I was prepared to make the sacrifice and sleep with him and his honesty stopped him? "You are a one man, one woman person. I don't need the responsibility, *libling*," he'd said.

Sweat trickled down my face. If I couldn't have alcohol, for fuck's sake couldn't they give me Librium? I looked over the duvet at the carpet. It was a wonder there was not a path worn in it with all the pacing I'd done since I'd come. Over, back. Over, back. Over, back.

My sleeping cellmate was here for four weeks. They always lumped a veteran and a newcomer together. She was as dumb and as still as a cow. She watched me with her eyes closed.

The words of that blasted counsellor kept returning. "You are not in the group to make friends but to learn to interact with others. Learn new skills." Why had she said that to me? I was able to communicate. David always maintained that I was good with people.

David. I could have told the group about my return to Ireland to resume my studies at university and about my hope that I would meet someone more suitable whom I wished to marry. I would have had to reveal that I didn't say "yes" to anyone. The men I met wanted, understandably, more than a shallow kiss.

I was not entirely without emotional entanglements during those years; sometime I fooled myself into believing I loved someone, but when it came to any physical commitment, there was always the sound of my mother's voice reprimanding me: "Without marriage? You're going to go through all that pawing for nothing. Are you crazy?"

After David, I never again experienced love's magic. The magic that converted differences of opinion into the attraction of opposites. If they were nice, I went out with them a few times, until they demanded more than I was able to give. My relationships never overwhelmed me to the extent that I forgot my fears about sex.

I was twenty-five when my inner voice stopped critiquing every man I met and started to protest and complain, "Do you want to spend your life alone? You want to have children. Remember your history. Think of Machiavelli. The end justifies the means."

252

My stomach rumbled, reminding me that I was hungry; they insisted that you ate substantially during the thirty days you were there. I had got used to eating like a sparrow for the last couple of months. An emaciated fellow in the group had said that drink has a quicker effect if you have nothing else in your stomach so he used to starve himself. But he was definitely an alcoholic. Nothing like me.

I wondered what would have happened if I had shared with the group how I had begun to get nostalgic about David, with whom I'd kept in touch. He had graduated from Harvard Law School and was an attorney in Cambridge. His liaison with a journalist from Winthrop had just ended.

Once when I had a half day from school, I took out my letters from Kibbutniks. After reading David's letters, I envisaged his serious dark eyes and realised that I'd never met anyone as wonderful. At last, I understood why I hadn't fallen for a man in ten years.

I screwed up my face to try to recall the happiest time of my life, something to carry me beyond this hellhole.

I remembered how the summer holidays had been coming up. It was time to act. There was no use pretending any longer that I chose Boston for a holiday for any other reason than because David worked there. Nor was it coincidental that I arranged my holiday to correspond with the Fourth of July celebrations, when he would be free.

At the time, I fooled myself that I would take a car from Logan airport, drive to Plymouth and get the ferry to Nantucket. From there I would go to Martha's Vineyard and visit the Kennedy compound. I'd cross the bridge where Mary Jo Kopechne met her Waterloo, and buy some trinkets to bring back. Then, when I'd had my fill of exploring, I'd call David and tell him where I was and that I was thinking of staying in Boston for a few days.

The day I landed in Logan, I disembarked, reclaimed my luggage, hopped aboard the T and zoomed downtown.

I checked into The Boston Park Plaza, slept for a couple of

hours and then went on the prowl. David had told me the name of his law firm in one of his letters and I'd purchased a street map to find its location. After three days of reconnoitring, I was glad I had the foresight to book an open ticket. It looked as if David wasn't going to be as available as I expected.

Why hadn't I called him, as any sensible woman would have done? Was it because I felt guilty about the way I was behaving and I wanted one of us, at least, to think we'd met by accident?

On the evening of the third day, I sat by a window in a pizzeria opposite his office and re-arranged olives on the top of my pizza with my fork – olives so black they reminded me of David's eyes. I was drinking the dregs of a carafe of wine when I saw him.

The angle of the head was the same. The beard was more lush, the girth broader, but the face was David's. He walked briskly from the office building, clutching a leather briefcase. His shirt and tie blended with his grey suit, he was proper and urban, very different from the kibbutz David.

As he started to cross the road, I called for the check and quickly paid. If I had planned this, it couldn't have been more to my liking. I had a few days in my hotel opposite Boston Common from which to explore the bookshops, to relax and think about my future – a few days to prepare myself for this meeting.

I imagined the long lean legs those dreary trousers were covering, and ignored the paunch that peeped over his waistband. In the evening light the tiny lines on his face didn't show; I would recognise him anywhere.

He saw me looking at him expectantly as I stood under the awning of the Pizza Hut. His expression was blank.

"David." My voice was soft, almost inaudible.

He hesitated, walked on a few steps, then stopped to look back.

"You don't recognise me, David Goldstein. You used to say you would never forget me." The wine was making all this very easy.

254

We stood looking at each other for a long moment; then he sauntered towards me.

"Teresa," he said. "Tess from the kibbutz. English major Teresa." Surprised delight resonated in his voice. His ebony eyes could still bewitch.

"Why didn't you let me know you were coming?"

Though I hoped my smile masked it, I felt anxious. Was he genuinely glad to see me? Was there any of the old spark left? As if in answer to my question, my instincts told me yes. His face, with its sharp nose, high forehead and voluptuous mouth, though less than handsome, held the same special affection for me.

While I examined him, he did the same to me. In the kibbutz we had often talked about our degree courses. I had been on my poetic binge. I used to quote Shakespeare and Keats to him and we would philosophise, as only 'immortal' students do, of decaying beauty and the ravages wrought by time.

I blushed, for it seemed to me he must be remembering this too.

"Shall I compare thee to a summer's day?" His spontaneity made him blush.

His embarrassment embarrassed me.

"Did you know I worked across the road or is this a coincidence?"

I had practised this a dozen times, had planned to be learned and quote Einstein, 'coincidence is god's way of remaining anonymous.' But all I said was, "I knew."

He laughed a laugh of satisfaction and of male complacency.

"Great, Tess! Great." He took me by the arm and said, "Let's go for a coffee. Can you bear the pizzeria again or will we go somewhere else?"

When David hugged me as we left the pizzeria, I knew I was going to make the most of this opportunity...

For the following couple of weeks I had been happy to walk the Freedom Trail, explore the Boston Tea Party ship, and just sit by the river Charles and languish in the sun. Now I had someone to date, someone I trusted, with whom I didn't have to watch every word and action. Usually with male friends I was so nervous, I couldn't sustain any kind of decent conversation.

I felt I had reached a turning point in my life. Sometimes at night as I lay in my hotel, I reflected on my future with David. I didn't, for a minute, consider it didn't lie with him, or that he might have anything to say to the contrary. I took it as given that we both felt the same and that it was only a matter of time before he would declare himself.

We went to Bennington and visited Robert Frost's grave. I had mentioned that I had done 'The Road Not Taken' with a junior stream at school. Had I been trying to get him around to making a decision, even then, I wondered now from the depths of my bedclothes.

We had gone sailing and swimming in Kennebunkport. Often we would rest together in the sun after a swim, and kiss and caress each other, and it was a precious, easy pleasure, associated in my mind and body with sanctuary and shared enjoyment and no demands with which I couldn't cope; his hands were practised but considerate. His expression held the passion it used to have in the kibbutz.

I saw a difference in him. I knew that he recognised that this time we would make love and marry. We ate dinner together every night, and we chatted non-stop. I was content.

It was nearing the middle of August and my money was running out. Rita, who had already snared Noel, had collected my July and August salary at the school and sent it on to me. I had used all my savings so I would be starting from scratch when I got home.

In the last few days, we often didn't know what to say to each other. I had taken this for sexual tension and was glad of it. Often in the last weeks, I had been afraid that David regarded me as more of a friend than a prospective lover. Ironic. Usually, that was what I wanted.

As the time to leave drew near, I became irritable, wondering when he was going to make a real advance. I wanted to get all that messy stuff over.

Our last evening came. I was flying to Shannon the next day; David had his friends, his job and his parents in Boston.

At dinner, I drank a bottle of wine and three margueritas afterwards. As usual, he walked me to my hotel where I pulled him into a clinch in the foyer and bundled him into the elevator. His lips were eager as I fumbled with the key card.

He was more hesitant when, after entering the room, I let my hands rove over his body. Sensing this, I began to feel less relaxed. My tongue felt awkward and there was an uncomfortable dryness in my throat. "I need a drink." I went to the fridge where a half-finished bottle of wine was still chilling.

He said, "Tess, are you sure you want this? You're going home in a few days and I will still be here. I think what I said to you nine years ago still stands." He cupped my chin with his hand to soften the impact of his words. "Kiddo, you expect sex and marriage to go together. I'm not ready for the commitment."

I nearly died. For the first time I understood that cliché. My breath came in gasps. I could smell a faint body odour from his skin and the humanity of the scent brought me, Lazarus-like, back to life.

"*Libling*, making love for us must be special. Like our miraculous meeting. When I come to Ireland ..."

He didn't speak the words I most wanted to hear. Permanence was what I craved, the assurance that the ordeal I was prepared to go through was the threshold to a shared life. I was in no doubt about his sexual expectation. There was no way he would marry me without lying with me (as they say in Hebrew).

So, without his having led me astray with false promises, I endured having sexual intercourse for the first time. I lay under him striving to want him, striving to feel even a vestige of the sensations so graphically described in women's magazines.

He was a considerate lover; I listened to his soothing words, felt his hands on my body and forced myself to respond as they recommended in *Cosmo*. The recollection still blemished my mind like a cyst.

It got better or I got better at pretending. David seemed happy enough and I was more content than I had ever been. Afterwards, David was cuddly and I was thoughtful. Jews loved children – "Be fruitful and multiply." It was nearing the middle of my menstrual cycle.

I took out a calendar and plotted. When I cancelled my flight, he was surprised but delighted.

I squirmed mentally. My contemplation had led me far enough. There were some things best forgotten. My last thought before I engaged with reality was that David and I had grown in love after, on my part, a dishonest beginning.

A pain jabbed at my head as I dragged myself out of bed.

Two weeks had passed since I had reminisced about my meeting with David. Now I was slumped on the bed again, trying to read but failing to concentrate. I had been here long enough to know that it would be foolhardy to get into an argument with the carers but when Patricia came in to ask me how I was, I couldn't resist getting rid of some of the anger I'd been hoarding. It would hinder my chances of getting away if I let the enemy know what I was contemplating, but I was unable to resist baiting her.

I had a plan. Not a plan exactly, but a determination to get out of this hellhole. Patricia, the woman with whom I was disputing, was auburn-haired, smelling of a strong perfume.

"I want out of here."

"You're having a bad day. That's all." Patricia's voice was soothing, assured. "You cannot really be serious about leaving."

"I'm serious." I had decided that, though I was being imprudent, the direct approach was the only one.

"You'll have to share your reasons for leaving with the group."

"*You* can't be serious."

"I'm serious."

My mind was racing. It struck me that this conversation was becoming an echo. Feeling a perverted pleasure in trying to shock the amiable face in front of me, I donned my best teacher's voice. "Have to. What do you mean *have to go back to the group*?" I let the silence hang. I had read a lot about these tactics. The idea was to get me back to the group and it would persuade me to stay. They must think I'm a dumb ass.

David and Granny Goldstein would be horrified if I left. To hell with them. I would go on Antabuse. That should please them. You would be as sick as a pig if you drank alcohol on the stuff.

Because my musings had silenced me, Patricia thought she had averted a crisis. She said, patting me on the back of my hand, "It'll be soon time for tea and you can have one of your tablets. You'll feel better then." She sailed from the room on a sea of righteousness.

I suppressed a triumphant smile. Stupid woman. She may have won this round but next time I would be the victor. My knees were cracked and painful, the return of the psoriasis I'd suffered intermittently from when I was a child. My fingers, beginning to flare on the day Roamy was killed, were now scaled in silver-white and were stiff and sore.

It was a long time since I felt like throwing up without having excess alcohol to blame. Now I was sick with alcohol and sick without it; there was no escape. Of course, there *was* an escape and I was going to take it. Out the door.

I thought of Esther and Rachael. Their absence was like a presence. Damn them. Why were my daughters laying siege to me now when, for the last couple of weeks, they had abandoned me? And what about David? My step on the stair faltered and then became more sure. I needed alcohol. I had to have it. It was that simple.

I was a slut, a harlot, a whore. The accusations took me by surprise. Hey, steady on, I thought. I might drink too much but there was no crime in that. No need to flagellate myself. Despite my protestations, my tension mounted. Lurching down the stairs into the hall, I heard the counsellors in their office, conferring in the jargon of their craft. I was convinced they were talking about me.

My wrestling with the knob of the outside door was so vigorous it irritated the tips of my fingers. I relaxed, the lock turned. Where would I go? Come on, Teresa. I thought you were playing the truth game. You're heading for the local hostelry for a little sustenance.

Outside, the sun was warm on my face, the breeze gentle on

my skin. Normally I appreciated spring, but the awfulness of my situation made the brightness a mockery.

The heavy smell of stale alcohol guided me like a lodestone to the nearest pub. I stumbled around a rubbish bin dumped in the middle of the road. Where there was beer there was gin and whiskey and ... The vision, held out by the tantalising smells, failed to dissolve my anxiety. Instead, I experienced misgivings so strong I contemplated, for a brief minute, retracing my steps. I had a strange sense of inevitability when, as I hesitated by the window looking in, who should stand beside me but Kieran Crawley.

His smile looked like it had been soaked in sugar.

"Teresa." Surprise and something I was unable to fathom registered on his face. "Nice to see you." He gave no sign that he remembered that I had recently banged the phone down on him. It struck me that it would be easier to go into a pub with an escort.

A voice nagged at the back of my subconscious. *Don't do it Teresa. Don't go anywhere with him. You dislike him.* I shut up the negative automatic voice. My smile was as large as I could make it. "What are *you* doing here?"

Colour flooded his face and he rearranged his feet.

"I have to run., I said. "I'm meeting someone in a couple of minutes. No time to talk. Sorry." I had to tear him away from me, not finish the conversation but break loose of it and flee.

His benign expression slipped. "You'll have time for one surely."

I thought of Pamela Crawley hauling me to my feet at my mother's funeral. My determination strengthened. I would seek out my own pub, buy my own alcohol. I stuck my hands into my pockets; I had a premonition that he was about to grasp one of them. It was then I realised that I had left in such a hurry I had forgotten to grab my coat or bring a purse. "I'd love to join you for a jar," I said, "just one."

"Sure. Isn't it always just one?"

Was he mocking me? I'd always thought him a little weird. To me, there was something strange about someone who pinned the radiant wings of a butterfly onto a board, in a display case, for fun. A repetitive message from my brain said that Kieran Crawley was bad news. *Go now*. My mouth felt dry.

In the pub, gloom blocked out the bright daylight. Many times this kind of atmosphere, warm and dark, had worked its magic.

Kieran Crawley bought me a double gin. He raised his glass of non-alcoholic beer. "*Sláinte.*"

A bleary-faced television flickered over the bar.

"Atmospherics," the barman threw at me as I looked in its direction.

There was a snooker table on a lower level, two steps led down to it. Two cues leaned against it; balls were lined up as if somebody had left a game mid-shot. At that moment, I was distressingly sober so I noticed everything. Kieran Crawley slid his tongue over his top lip. My stomach churned. His affectations grated but I relished the double gin he ordered. The glass was cheap and none too clean but, oh God, it was alcohol. I tossed it back.

It felt familiar when I lowered my eyelids and batted them in his direction. I drank another. Having imbibed a third, I eulogised on the beauty of butterflies. My head felt woozy. I knew that my face was flushed. I'd been off the booze for three weeks; I was getting drunk faster.

He fidgeted when my legs began to go from under me.

A couple who were sitting at a table having lunch looked at us. I knew the man from somewhere, but the gin was more interesting than a friendly face. "What's he staring at?" Kieran Crawley muttered.

"Don't know," I slurred.

"Let's get out of here."

The bartender soaked up the gin that had splashed from my glass onto the counter. "Good idea, mate." He then turned his attention to a stack of dirty ashtrays. "Just so you know. We serve soup and sandwiches here."

"We'll get something back at my place."

If the words weren't so corny, I would have laughed. Kieran Crawley sounded like an ambitious Casanova rather than a middle-aged butterfly collector.

"Right so."

I had nothing to lose. Destiny House would have contacted David and he would be soon on my trail. I was harming nobody but myself. My family had adjusted to life without me. The lies worked.

Kieran Crawley's car felt familiar as he sped through the town's free-flowing traffic, negotiated a housing estate and emerged onto a winding side road ... what I was doing felt as inevitable and as wrong as my dash from Destiny House.

He swung the car onto an even narrower road, overhung with trees where we seldom caught a glimpse of *that little tent of blue that prisoners call the sky*. I couldn't banish the bloody words from my mind.

To vex me further Kieran Crawley reminded me of the last time I was in his car. He pointed to a container resembling an aeroplane sick bag. "It took a week to get rid of the stink of your vomit the last time."

Was I imagining it or was he changing his manner towards me? Becoming less respectful. I was framing my words for a rebuke when he slowed down, put his hand in his pocket and produced a hip flask. It was old and tarnished but it was full of gin. I grabbed at the further dollop of anaesthesia. A bit more of the hard stuff and I might even get to like the greaseball giving it to me. The isolation and oppressiveness of the countryside became less noticeable as I tippled.

Kieran Crawley was looking straight ahead when his left hand absently caressed my knee. The further down I got into the flask, the more pleasant I found his touch. When I breathed a sigh of contentment, he slithered his hand under the hem of my skirt.

His pale face was ruddy. I could see his chest falling and rising rapidly. I reached my hand over and pressed his swollen penis.

He gritted his teeth and hissed, "We'll soon be there. Can't you wait?"

Gin submerged stirrings of anger. To hell with him. I was going to enjoy myself. When we reached the one-storey house at the bottom of a hill, I looked instinctively to see if the name were still on the door. It was. 'Caterpillar Cottage – Welcome.'

Kieran Crawley's brow beetled as he looked for my reaction. His adolescent chin seemed suddenly very pronounced.

"Named because of its sprawl." His mouth hung wet and loose in an imitation grin.

To arrive here we had twisted through *boreens*, swerved stunted tree trunks and lunged through a continuity of evergreens whose leaves shaded the car one minute and exposed it to light the next. Now nothing surrounded the house but three lonely sycamores and a line of dilapidated sheds. The 'caterpillar' of buildings freaked me out. I was here seeking more booze, but this low-lying house, small-eyed and cold, weakened my resolve to resist what was to follow.

When Kieran Crawley opened the door, I rushed in. I needed to go to the loo badly. The bathroom was down the hall to the left and I knew where the bedrooms were. There was a big and a small one. I understood why the house looked so sightless when I saw its tiny diamond-paned windows.

"See, you recognise the place." His tone was smug. He slicked back his hair. "Sure you've been here a few times now." He saw my confusion and chuckled. "Or are you going to tell me the same as you did on the phone. That you don't remember. Want food, do you?"

"No, I want to pee and then I'll have another gin." My voice sounded as if it belonged to someone else. "Oh God, please take me off this roundabout." God didn't hear. I sat on the loo and gulped vodka; he had run out of gin, he said.

I heard him shout, "In here." I staggered from the bathroom into the bedroom. Feeling groggy, I sprawled on the bed. The acrylic stars on the ceiling made me think I was hallucinating.

"*The Stars Look Down*," he said, "That is one of Pamela's favourite books."

The mention of his wife sank into my psyche for a second, and then drowned.

He sat on the bed beside me, expansive and tactile.

My head was spinning as he unbuttoned my blouse, unhooked my bra, failed to unzip my skirt and pulled off my panties and tights. Dignified Teresa Goldstein, respected teacher and writer, lay there like a rag doll zonked by alcohol.

He took off his clothes quickly and discarded them in a heap at the bottom of the bed, then hopped in beside me.

'The wind in the willows' I sang as he lifted my skirt and blew on my pubic hair. I felt spaced out and horny. His prick was hard and sticky on my belly. We did things I didn't know I knew how to do. I certainly never did them with David. Poor David. Pity he didn't ply me with alcohol like Creepy Crawley, then I would have done anything he wanted. Didn't he know that I was frigid? That this was the only way I could perform. The obtrusive thought began to ruin my enjoyment. I lay there, miserable and exhausted, while he thumped and slammed against my body, finally spurting into me.

Rolling off me, he lay facing the ceiling, his eyes closed.

My limbs felt like lead. I scrunched my eyes for a few seconds and tried to wipe away thought. I needed to dull the memory of what I had done.

Extreme thirst prompted me to sit up and reach for the jug of water on the locker.

Beside the jug lay an envelope, butterfly stickers protruding from it. The significance of what I was seeing didn't dawn on me immediately. I drank some water. I looked again and realised that the stickers were similar to those on the envelopes containing the mysterious calendars I'd been receiving.

"You bastard."

He sat up, rested against the headboard and stared at the stickers and envelope in my hand. "Bout time you found out," he said.

I started.

"You really did forget. All the times we've fucked and you just put it out of your mind. Even when I put the dates on the calendars I sent you, you were too stupid to catch on."

"Why did you send them? It was sadistic." I felt curiously calm.

"Because you were as hoity toity the day after our assignations as the day before. I could do anything with you when you were drunk, then you sober up and the standoffish Teresa re-emerges."

"But why me? Why did we get together? We don't even like each other."

"David loved talking to Pamela. He pretended he was her client. That he was worried about you."

"But it was true. He did go to her out of concern for me."

"All he wanted to do was get into her knickers."

"You're as deluded as I am."

"Difference is, I'm not a piss merchant."

I was filled with shame. I must have had sex with him several times. What kind of a debauched woman was I?

I had no clear idea what I had in mind when I lay back on the bed and widened my eyes flirtatiously. "Come here, you freak," I purred. "Let's have some fun. Come on, settle in here beside me and I'll show you what I can do for you."

He pushed himself down on the bed again, lay on his back for a second, then turned onto his side, supporting himself with his elbow. He stared into my eyes. "I think you're like Helen of Troy. A destroyer."

A destroyer. I couldn't disappoint him. I shoved him onto his back, towered over him, grasped his face and pushed his head down onto the pillow. Using my other hand, I grabbed the short end of his tie and yanked hard.

He grasped his throat.

Flexing my fingers to get the maximum strength from them, I tightened the tie round his neck. Absently, I noted the veins in his temple swell, his face tinge with purple.

"Teresa." The word came involuntarily.

The inane smile on his face became lopsided as I tightened even more. Power surged through me accompanied by a strange satisfaction. His spindly legs lifted off the bed. Spittle spilled down his chin. His eyes bulged. An elation I hadn't experienced since my relationship with David had begun to go wrong assailed me.

Because of his gyrations, a drawing of a man and a woman, with a childish scrawl beneath it, fell off the headboard and flew over his still florid face.

I was reminded of Esther and Rachael. They used to draw cartoons like this. He had children also. They needed their father. I had loosened the hold when there was a knock at the door.

Kieran Crawley was gasping for breath. A child's sketch lay on the bed beside us. The ringing got more insistent, then stopped. The sound of someone kicking in the door was just another pounding in my head until I saw David.

He seemed to me to alight in the room's gloom like Beelzebub. His dark eyes were lit by an emotion I was afraid to name. There were red blotches at the centre of his cheeks.

"That crazy bitch tried to throttle me," Kieran Crawley shouted as he hauled himself off the bed, snatched his clothes and stumbled towards the door, looking dazed.

David's eyes became cold. He growled and snarled and pointed a single quivering finger at me.

The fist that bashed into my shoulder took me by surprise. A second wallop landed on my legs. I hoped he would continue. I deserved any punishment he chose to inflict. I *was* a crazy bitch.

He pulled viciously at the buckle of his trouser belt.

Do not make him a murderer, Teresa. You have done enough. The order, harsh and compelling, forced me out of the bed. I was exhausted from my fracas with Kieran Crawley. My knees buckled and I fell winded to the floor.

I hugged the side of the bed; I had some daft idea that I would be able to slide under it and break the rhythm of his violence.

He bent low so as not to miss me. The leather scourge seemed to take on a life of its own as he whisked it through the air. I squeezed my eyes shut, waiting for the blow to drop. It never came.

Instead, he hit the edge of the bed above me. "Get fucking dressed."

The bedroom was freezing. I was aware of the cold now, which meant that I was sober or at least getting there. That should've been a good thing but it wasn't. I was beginning to feel my shoulder throb from the weight of David's punch.

A door banged. Someone left. I allowed several minutes elapse. Then I skulked from the bedroom, still partially undressed, through to the front of the house. It was madness. David or Kieran Crawley could still have been there, lurking in the shadows, preparing to pounce. What then?

Thank God, my timing was perfect. Through the glass-panelled hall door, I was just in time to see Creepy Crawley hurtling down the drive at speed and David ensconced in his car, engine revving, waiting for me to surface.

Shivering, I sidled back to the bedroom. It took a while to hook my bra. There was blinding pain in my shoulder, which the effort had aggravated. Slowly, I buttoned my blouse, pulled on my panties, tights and shoes and straightened my skirt.

Thump, thump, thump. My heart pounded. I let out a long shaky breath and sat on the bed.

My thoughts ran riot. If I didn't accept help, I'd be a 'dypso' for the rest of my life. Esther and Rachael would tire of their drunken mother. Granny Goldstein was already losing patience with me. My colleagues hadn't voiced their objections to my behaviour yet but I sensed their disappointment. In the last few months David looked harassed and sad, even a little bedraggled, unlike the dapper I married. It was all so hopeless.

Returning to rehab was, I imagined, as difficult as making the decision to undergo major surgery, from which you might not recover. I didn't even know if there was anything wrong with me, for Godsakes.

Teresa, my internal voice said, *You managed to separate yourself so completely from your debauched behaviour with Kieran Crawley that you forgot everything about it. Of course there's*

268

something wrong with you.

But all this self-knowledge sounded great in theory. The truth was, I was neither ready nor able to return to Destiny House. The prospect of going back to all that 'understanding' was too grim. Being driven there by a censorious David, having him apologise for me and me apologise for myself, was too bleak. I knew it was imperative that I return but, worn out, dog-tired, agitated, I decided to go home first.

The day after David discovered me with Kieran Crawley, I threw a wobbly and changed my mind about returning to Destiny House. I found refuge in the usual mantra, "I'll beat this myself." Alone in my bed in the middle of the night, restless, disturbed by guilt and unable to contemplate a life without alcohol, I could no longer resist the gin at the back of the wardrobe.

When Rachael came to say 'good morning', I was shaking so violently I had to hold the bottle with both hands as I poured the last drop. "Want a drink?" Unfortunately, my saying such a thing to my daughter was not what made me agree to return. David, seeing how 'smashed' I was, issued an ultimatum. Either I sought help or they would leave.

Granny Goldstein drove me back. She struggled to mask her pity as she looked at my bloated face and mottled skin. "David will visit you, hon. He wanted to stay with the kids." She leant forward, anxious, almost crying in her desire to make me feel better. "Got your stuff?"

I winced as I lifted my bag from the floor of the car. Quick as a flash she said, "There's something wrong with that shoulder."

"It's alright." My voice was lame. I didn't want to embarrass David any more than I had already. I'd been trying to pretend there was nothing amiss, but no matter how much I wished it, no matter how much I tried to ignore it, my shoulder hurt.

"You can pretend that you are not in pain but it won't go away. Hon, you will have to accept that my son can be violent."

As I'll have to admit that I've a problem with alcohol. The words pounded in my head. I was so confused I began to see Granny Goldstein through a fog. "I'm not an alcoholic," I asserted, desperate, wishing only to break the silence.

She didn't acknowledge my denial until she'd parked the car. Then with an impassive expression she said, "Listen, Tess, you can sit around from now 'till these thirty days are up and fool yourself with fancy theories about your right to drink as much as you like. But take it from me, that isn't cleverness; it's just bullshit, deception."

The difference this time about my stay in Destiny House was that I decided to make the best of it, tried to get something out of it. Consequently, the days went by quickly. The routine was a constructive amalgam of workshops, talks, mental exercises and much soul probing.

Towards the end of my stay, the counsellors 'summoned' David and the children in to tell me how my drinking had affected their lives. I had dreaded the prospect for days, had nightmares about what they would say.

On the day, it seemed to me that the counsellors treated David, Esther and Rachael obsequiously. It was as if they felt the need to apologise for subjecting a man of his stature and two beautiful children to such an ordeal.

The room, reserved for these kinds of 'non-confrontational' meetings, was comfortable, the dark tongue and groove flooring softened by a scatter rug similar to the one in our sitting room at home. A beige speckled sofa with a shape that reminded me of a duck's egg stood by the outer wall. Over the couch was a large bevelled mirror reflecting the ivory-coloured door. Do these details matter? I'm not sure that they do but ...

David looked lean and fit in a rust-coloured suit. A colour consultant told him he looked well in rustic colours like browns and greens, that they matched his skin tone and complemented his hair. I was irrationally proud of the personal details I knew about him. He had three fillings, two on the top and one on the bottom, the type of underpants and cotton socks he preferred, the ... but not any longer what he felt about me.

What I recall is David refusing to sit, his lips a straight line, the tell-tale colour suffusing his neck, beneath his open shirt. My counsellor, in a formal navy suit that belied her touchy-feely personality, sitting on a high-backed chair beside mine saying, "It's not an option," while she gestured to a chair beside her.

Though initially none of us spoke, the room was not silent. The ticking of the watch the girls had given me for my last birthday magnified. There was a muted sound too from far below, the rushing water of the river.

I can still hear vaguely the accusations, wounding and bitter, David had flung at me. They play back to me like a faulty tape. But the memory of my blurted confession, "I became pregnant so that you would marry me," is clear.

His response is lucid in my head also: "We have been to hell and back and that is your main concern." Then, seeming to realise what such an admission meant to me, his tone had softened. "The baby did upset my plans. I hoped to marry in my late thirties. But after our time in Boston, I was not prepared to lose you again. I could have supported the baby and stayed single. I find it difficult to understand your paranoia about Rita, though. That seriously threw me."

"I was jealous."

"Of your best friend. Give me a break. You must have thought I was a prize jerk."

The facilitator had raised an admonishing eyebrow and David said, "No need to be jealous of Rita, *libling*."

The 'affair' with Kieran Crawley was painful for him to understand. My blank about it confused rather than helped him. 'Dissociation,' the shrinks told me was a coping mechanism, a safety valve. Too much stress, they suggested, may have accounted for the emotional detachment that resulted in my amnesia about Creepy Crawley. David would be sceptical if I told him. I kept my mouth shut.

Details of my mother's attitude to sex helped explain my hang-up about it. Also, while I was in treatment, David had been reading studies on childhood trauma, delayed reaction and repressed anger, which, he said, made it easier to understand. He also added wryly that, from his own experience of counselling, he could empathise a little with how difficult it was to change behaviour. He should be an expert on controlling his own anger but still 'lost it' sometimes.

When Esther and Rachael joined us from the room next door, they sat ramrod straight on their chairs. Esther, with her tales of my swearing while drunk, falling, burning food, leaving them totally to their own devices, had been scathing. But it was Rachael who made me cry. "Mom, I didn't wet the bed since but I did steal Mary Jordan's gloves. Dad went into school and explained. Teacher says it's alright. It's because you …"

"Were being an asshole," Esther finished for her.

"Maybe not that bad but . . ." Rachel said.

"Close," David added. We all laughed.

As I said, I'm sure I'm neglecting to mention the details that matter or hadn't noticed. In my memory, that was what stuck.

The following I remember clearly. Granny Goldstein collected me on the day they 'let me out'. She informed me that Kieran Crawley had known of my disposal in Destiny House and, suspecting I would leave, had hovered in its precincts that fateful day. The guy I recognised in the pub was a law clerk in David's office. After I had left, he phoned to tell David what he had witnessed. "Kieran Crawley has resigned from teaching and is now swarming with the other 'butterflies' in foreign parts," she related with some asperity, adding, "Pamela is heartbroken by his departure."

As she walked to the car with me, she had continued in a careful tone, her lids half lowered, watching my reaction while pretending not to. "David wanted to come but I insisted. I brought you here and I'll bring you home."

For a change Granny Goldstein was being diplomatic. I didn't believe that he'd wanted to come. His absence made me sad.

Granny Goldstein's expression told me his absence made her sad too.

I was sure that the alcoholic craving that had squatted in my blood for so long was gone at last. Not just away temporarily. Not wriggling in the shadows. Not confined, but evicted. I felt like crying, laughing, dancing. There's no way to explain that feeling to someone who has never housed an intruder, never been sabotaged by something they initially considered a friend and crutch. But I did none of these. I just sat on the edge of a chair in the kitchen and drained my cup of tea.

I thought of Esther. In a way it was her day; her multicultural breakfast idea was coming to fruition. Teacher had started a pen pal club at school and was encouraging the kids to write to children in other countries. Granny Goldstein, in her inimitable way, had said it was about time Irish people realised everyone wasn't Irish and Catholic. This comment had germinated the idea for Esther.

"Let's show Gran, before she goes, why we love being Irish. We'll have a fancy dress party for her."

I had refused to allow it for days. Truth was I was just managing to survive. Every day was an endurance test. Then I reminded myself that both my children had been through more than most kids of their age should. I decided to make an effort.

Now all the family were gathering, ostensibly to do Esther's bidding but really to wish Granny Goldstein *bon voyage* before she left for Boston. Esther and Rachael were upstairs putting on their *ensembles*. The woman I had employed to help Cora with the 'heavy work', which included everything except minding Esther and Rachael, had the house scoured, waxed and polished so that it glowed like the night stars. Stars, Caterpillar Cottage,

Butterflies. Stop it, Teresa.

I'm lying. The longing for alcohol is skulking all the time. It's now at its usual level, manageable just about. "Take a day at a time," I muttered.

In the middle of my affirmation, there was a knock at the door. I was so engrossed I hadn't heard the car but I knew from the silhouette of the mother and child through the glass that it was Jacinta and her baby. And where she was, I knew my father would follow.

Granny Goldstein had admitted the other day that she was 'pissing in the breeze' where my father was concerned. He had 'eyes for nobody but that young one.'

Cora sidled in behind them, looking pinched with the cold though she was wrapped in a sheepskin coat and shod in heavy boots. "You can pretend I'm from the North Pole," she informed us all.

I was glad that Esther, who knew that these were Cora's ordinary clothes, kept her mouth shut. Since she'd been discharged from hospital, Cora was always cold. "Tis the blood," she was fond of telling anyone interested in listening. She is unaware of my 'illness.' Maybe someday I'll explain to her about addictive personalities, and alcoholic psychosis.

Nearly all had assembled in the sitting room. At my invitation, they had filled their glasses from the bottles of white and red wine left on the table and were standing in groups chatting when Granny Goldstein, with a flamboyant blue and red dress, waltzed in.

"Mom, isn't it gross?" Esther's amused expression belied her words.

"You're not so subtle yourself young lady." I fondled Esther's green, white and gold trousers with care.

"Am I subtle?" Rachael twirled to display the green and red of the Mayo team. Rita came next with the striking Paul Walsh, our newly appointed vice principal, in tow. With her fiery red hair, and dressed in green silk, she made an arresting Caitlín Ni Houlihan. "No more home knits for Rita. I have done with scrimping, Teresa," she told me in a throaty whisper.

From the window I watched as our dusky puppy bounded out of the kennel, barking at a car as it drove slowly up the drive and pulled up at the front door. David had driven from Tuam. Esther and Rachael, because of their school being in Claremorris, were back staying with me. Legal separation was on the horizon.

He glanced up at the house and, seeing me, smiled a smile so warm that I felt like I was melting. For a second our eyes held, then waving the white tea towel in my hand and smiling like an idiot, I went out to open the door.

"Tess," he said, but it could just as easily have been *libling*. His voice was like my own blood thumping through my veins heating and assuaging me.

I felt shy, not having anticipated this rush of feeling. His skullcap moved as he bent his head to kiss the side of my face. As I led him in to meet everyone, I found it hard to conceal the ridiculous beating of my heart. Pleasantries over, we went to the dining room to eat.

We were barely inside the door when Esther grabbed David's hand and held it to her chest. She beckoned to me with her other hand, the one holding a soft drink. Her expression, as she gazed at David, was adoring and bereft. Taking a deep breath, she began, "Mom, Dad, I'm going to make a speech."

Hoping she wasn't going to beg David to stay, I forced myself to stand still.

She said, "I'm Irish, Catholic and Jewish. Rachael is Irish and Catholic and Jewish." She sloshed her lemonade around in the glass. "Mom is Irish and, um, Catholic, Dad is American and Jewish, Granny Goldstein is American and, um, Jewish, Granddad is Irish and Catholic, big-time. Jacinta ..." She looked at Jacinta uncertainly. "What are you?"

Baby Tettie howled. Jacinta said, "An effen mother."

"Go feed that child and we will have something to eat," Granny Goldstein said. She looked at Esther. "Finished?"

"You nearly forgot," Rachael interrupted her sister. She looked at David meaningfully. "Mom is a great mom."

"Okay, Rach. We get the idea." Not to be outdone, Esther raised her glass and hollered: "To Mom. *Sláinte.*"

Rachael squawked, "Essie."

Her tone implied, "Are you stupid or something?" She had seen my jaw stiffen and had reacted to it. Pouring out a glass of orange juice, I echoed Esther's toast. "*Sláinte.*" The drink tasted like liquid sugar on my tongue, awful stuff.

"Your good health," Granny Goldstein's eyes misted as they rested first on Esther still clinging to David's hand, and then moved to Rachael, surreptitiously wiping her eyes with her sleeve, then to me. "Let's eat," she said, "I'll soon be leaving for Shannon."

My father started on the sautéed onions, rashers and sausages.

Rita, who had been trying to show me her engagement ring that morning at the level crossing, shared a helping of scrambled eggs with her fiancée, our colleague.

Esther and Rachael devoured hash browns.

David had his plate poised for fish when Granny Goldstein beckoned us into a corner. She let her ring-bedecked fingers rest lightly on her son's arm and said, "Before I go, I must tell you this. You know how I like to shoot my mouth off." After inhaling, she continued, "I know you're going to a kibbutz on some kind of fitness trainer lark, but I hope you and Tess are not planning to part permanently." There was moistness in her eyes. "I doubt if you should." Her voice was soft but clear. "That doubt is my parting gift to you."

I stared, breathing quickly, coughing a little, and downed the nauseating orange juice.

Dragging myself away from the party, I made my way to the makeshift office in the corner of my bedroom.

It was easier to stay off the booze when surrounded by supportive professionals skilled in the field of treating addiction. Now that I was 'out', there were all my usual haunts to resist. A longing for alcohol tormented me and caused me to shake like the pineapple jelly made for the farewell party. "Oh for a beaker full of the warm south." I put my head down on the coolness of the desk, enduring the longing.

Counsellors, wise and experienced, had warned me this would happen, that I'd experience confidence, self-doubt, mood swings, memories and irritability. "Find a way to ease the agony," the words of a shrink echoed.

I had discovered that, when I was tempted to go back on the booze, it helped to record my thoughts. "Find your own personal stress reliever," the physiatrist had advised.

Before I turned on the typewriter, I stopped to flex my fingers. Since my 'recovery', I had been trying to make sense of what had happened. Perhaps create a record to share with Esther and Rachael when they are older. I haven't thought it out completely yet.

My thoughts went backwards. I typed, 'I heard my voice crackle as it mentioned sex ...'

Lightning Source UK Ltd.
Milton Keynes UK
UKOW042244300413

210009UK00002B/4/P